BACK STABBERS

A Novel By
NYEMA

This is a work of fiction. Names, characters, places, and incidents either are the product of the author's imagination or are used fictitiously. Any resemblance to actual events or locales or persons, living or dead, is entirely coincidental.

Edited by Sonja Brown
Interior design by Brian Holscher
Second A New Quality Publishing L.L.C.
trade paperback printing 2008
For more information about author or to purchase copies, visit or email correspondence to:

A New Quality Publishing
P.O.Box 589
Plainfield New, Jersey 07061

anewqualitypublishing@yahoo.com
www.anewqualitypublishing.com
facebook/nyemataylor

ISBN: 0-9817756-2-4
ISBN-13: 978-0-9817756-2-3

10 9 8 7 6 5 4 3
Second Paperback Edition
Printed in United States Of America

This book is dedicated to Two of the Worlds most Greatest

Donell T. Murphy
"Nell"
&
Duane T. Smith
"Rell"
Never Will You Be Forgotten!

ACKNOWLEDGEMENTS

To J.M. Benjamin & A New Quailty Publishing Family
Thanks for Believing in *M*e, Ain't No Stopping Us Now,
Let's get this Money!
And To All My Family, Friends, Supporters, Bookstores
and Vendors
Thank You All For Your *L*ove, *T*ime and *D*evotion
Through You I Survive!

-NYEMA

"They smile in your face when all the time they want to take your place."

-Back Stabbers

Introduction

The dangerous streets of Philadelphia have bred many hustlers. Some rob, steal, deal or kill in pursuit of their next dollar. Others handle their business in a more subtle manner by using what they've got to get what they want. One female in particular happened to have this kind of paper-chasing mentality, using her assets to get to the top of her game.

Azia Elliston wasn't your typical gold digger. She just happened to be sleeping her way through college. Tired of struggling to make ends meet, she was always on the hunt for sponsors, also known as men who could take good care of a sistah financially. Armed with the sexual attitude of a nigga, her motto was: Use what you got to get what you want. Hailing from South Philly, Azia dealt with her share of dope boys. She was known in the hood as a gutter bitch, but she was good at what she did and strutted hard doing it. Living the life of a schoolgirl by day and a freak by night, getting paid was her motivation—by any means necessary.

Azia had no problem swapping sex for money. She would take any form of compensation for her services, as long as it was of monetary value. In her mind, one hand washed the other so if you couldn't be used you were useless. Having a model-like figure and being half Black, half Asian made it easy for her to be successful at her craft. Azia was 21 years old with black, chinky eyes; fair skin; long, curly black hair; and she stood five feet seven inches tall. Presently a junior residing on campus at Temple University, she was hated by most women and craved by all men. Assuming she knew it all, she was about to learn the most valuable lesson of her life: Like every dog, every bitch has her day.

BACK STABBERS

A Novel By NYEMA

CHAPTER 1
What Feels Good Ain't Always Good For You
"It's hard to turn a ho into a housewife."
-Mike

Azia was skimming through some shirts on a rack in Neiman Marcus down at the King of Prussia mall when, out of nowhere, walked in one of the finest niggas she'd ever seen. She got momentarily sidetracked giving this stranger her undivided attention. He was tall, dark and handsome. Even with the oversized white t-shirt on, Azia could still make out his rock-hard body. He sported freshly done braids, a beautiful yet intricate design made popular by NBA players. As a matter of fact, he looked like an athlete—a baller or thug straight off the pages of *XXL* magazine. She just had to have him. In the back of her mind, she wondered if he could fuck as good as he looked. Azia was definitely willing to find out.

This was one opportunity Azia couldn't let pass by. Normally, she was the object of a man's desire, but today the tables had turned. Azia didn't know if the guy had noticed her staring at him, but she was determined to attract his attention one way or another. Thinking fast, she put the shirt in her hand back on the rack and watched as he stood in line at the cashier. The skintight miniskirt she had on would surely attract his attention. Timing it perfectly, she slowly made her way to the exit just as he was about to leave the store. They met up at the doorway at the same time, and he generously held it open for her to exit first.

Azia watched his eyes rove up and down her flawless body, undressing her. She knew he was feeling her.

"Thank you," smiled Azia. "You're a real gentleman."

He smiled back. "Ya welcome, Ms… "

She extended her hand. "Azia. And you are?"

"Mike. What a pretty girl like you doing out here alone?"

"You were busy," she flirted.

Right then Mike knew what it was hitting for. Not one to turn down a possible shot at some new pussy, he stepped his game up.

"Well, I won't be busy too much longer. We can exchange numbers and get up a little later if you ain't doing nothing."

"Yeah, we can do that."

Mike produced a cell phone from his hip, which was hidden by his shirt. Flipping it open, he careful punched her digits into his phone. He double-checked with her to make sure the number was correct. In the past, he had lost a chance with a bad broad by not putting in the right numbers. He was not about to let that happen again. He had a good feeling about this chick in front of him. He thought maybe, just maybe, he could hit it today.

"You gonna call me tonight?" she asked.

"Am I?" Mike sighed. "Is that a question I need to answer?"

Azia smiled. "You better if you know what's good for you."

They both fell silent as Azia's statement hung in the air. It seemed to have a sexual overtone to it. Still smiling and batting her eyes, Azia was in no rush to clean it up either. She let Mike draw his own conclusions.

Mike picked up on her sexual insinuation immediately. Now that the ball was in his court, he had to try his hand. He had to see how far and how fast this could go. Was Azia merely talking the talk or would she walk the walk? Mike didn't know how she got down but he didn't hesitate to find out.

"Where you headed? Are you driving?"

"Nah, I ain't driving," came her reply. "Hopefully I'm headed to the car wit' you."

"That's wassup!" He quickly responded. "That's what I'm talking 'bout! Follow me."

Azia's eyes lit up at the sight of Mike's blue, 2007, BMW 750i. There definitely had to be more money where that came from. But at the present moment, there was only one thing on her mind, and that was getting some.

Mike hit the automatic unlock button on his keychain making the yellow lights flash. Azia walked to the passenger side and climbed in. Lyfe Jennings was playing when the engine came to life. His song *S.E.X.* escaped softly through the speakers. She leaned across to the driver's side once Mike was seated and said, "I hope the first stop isn't my house."

That was all Mike needed to hear. He knew it was destined that he got a taste of her sweetness before she exited his car. "If you ain't in a rush, I got a spot we can chill at for a minute."

"I'm in a rush. But not to get home."

That was all she wrote. The sun had already set and Mike had the perfect place in mind. They ended up at Lover's Lane, a well-known park by the Schuylkill River where people usually went to get a quick nut or two.

Mike turned to her with a condom in hand. Azia took the condom and put it to the side. She began to unzip his jeans, anxious to wrap her lips around every inch of his pure thickness. Intensely doing the job she was sent down to do, she felt Mike explode in the back of her throat. She swallowed every bit, rose back up into an upright position, and cocked one leg up on the dash, revealing all her goods. After licking two fingers, she placed them inside of her and went to work. Mike listened as her moans and juices made their own music. She dried all the pussy juice that ran down her hand with her tongue. The look on Mike's face read, *I'm gonna tear that ass up.*

It didn't take long for Mike to rise back to attention. Azia asked, "You ready to give me this?" gently enveloping him in her soft hands. "Fuck me on the hood."

Before he could respond, she was stepping out of the car and walking to the front. Mike slid the condom on and obeyed her command. Azia welcomed him by spreading herself over the hood with her ass in the air. They were in plain sight of the other cars that were around, slightly hidden by surrounding trees. This excited her more. "You better fuck me good."

Her aggression wasn't something Mike was used to, but there was a first time for everything. "Damn, baby! Harder!" she continuously growled.

"THISPUSSYSOFUCKINGOOD," he couldn't help but admit it. He hadn't had this good of a time in a while. All the chicks he'd been dealing with lately were dead fucks, just flat out lame all around the board. Azia was someone he could get used to.

"Say it's the best. Tell me you love this pussy and you'll do anything for this pussy."

"Whatever you want, you got it," he whimpered, drilling his manhood inside, at every angle possible.

Minutes later, Azia climaxed all over him and abruptly fell flat on the hood. Mike took that as his cue to get his nut and call it quits. He jammed every inch inside of her, doggy style, before filling the Magnum that was tightly gripping his dick. Between breaths, he suggested, "We gotta do this more often."

Azia responded with her signature smile. Mike swiftly pulled his pants and boxers up from the dirt as Azia slid her tiny jean skirt back into place and re-entered the car with a smile. Love for him would be more costly in the long run. But for now, all she saw were dollar signs.

Back on campus, Azia's final thought before leaving Mike's side was that he would definitely be back for more. The show she put on wasn't for nothing. But the next time he decided to get at her, he had better be ready to spend some change.

Azia skated through the door of the three-bedroom apartment that she shared with two other females. One was Tonya, and she, too, was naughty by nature. The saying: The darker the berry, the sweeter the juice fit her to the T. The other female was Mal. She was the more settled type, and she didn't care for Azia and Tonya. Mal knew what they were about and didn't want any parts of it. Overwhelmed with jealousy, it was just a matter of time before she acted on her malicious intent to exploit them.

Tonya came out of the bathroom wrapped in a towel to greet Azia who was wearing a big grin. "What's up, heffa? What you grinning so hard for? I know you ain't wearing that raggedy-ass smile for nothing, ho."

"You so damn nosy," smiled Azia, keeping her friend in suspense.

"Stop holding out on me, 'cause I know ya ass been up to no good."

Just as Azia began to spill the beans, in walked Mal. Azia and Tonya began to speak in hushed tones. They always tried to keep their business on the down low from Mal because she didn't approve of their whorish ways. Mal slammed the front door and walked past both girls as if they were statues.

Tonya turned her nose up at Mal and asked, "Do you have to make it known when you come in?"

"Don't fuck wit' me right now, I got too much shit on my mind," Mal warned. She rolled her eyes and went into her room, again slamming the door behind her.

"That chick is crazy," mumbled Azia, heading to her room to get undressed and give Tonya the details of her latest sexual conquest.

"Ya freak-ass is crazy," exclaimed Tonya.

Azia smacked Tonya gently. "Shut the hell up wit' ya loud ass."

"Fuck that ho," Tonya flagged in the direction of Mal's room. "Oh, listen to this shit. That nigga Rashaud is crazy. I don't know why you still messing wit' that fool. He came by here twice looking for you. He got offended when I answered the door the second time calling him a stalker," she chuckled.

"I don't know why you enjoy clowning him, but you know he's a few cans short of a six pack, so you better leave him alone before he hurt you." Azia finished undressing and walked across the hall to the bathroom. Tonya followed. Azia went straight for the bathtub to set the water temperature to her liking and stepped into the shower. Tonya was still blabbing on about how she disliked Rashaud.

Rashaud was another one of Azia's men. She had been dealing with him for close to four months. What turned Azia off about Rashaud were his possessive ways. He wanted to know where she was, what she was doing, and who she was doing it with at all times. Azia was a bad bitch; the kind Rashaud had never had. He made sure he kept up his hustle so he could continue to lavish her with all the nice things money could buy, and his always being in the streets on the grind gave Azia time to maneuver with other guys. Aside from his threats and the ass-whippings he laid upon her every so often, the money was good. That was the main reason Azia hadn't given him the boot.

"Dayum! Can I take a shower in peace? You sound like a damn robot, talking my head off."

"You never wanna hear what I got to say when it comes to him. But I don't care 'cause I'm still gonna say it anyway. He needs to stop putting his hands on you. I don't know why you be taking that bullshit."

"Tonya!" Azia yelled from behind the colorful shower curtain. That was the last word she had to say about it, letting her friend know it was none of her business.

"Alright, dayum! I'm just tryna look out for you." Tonya sighed. "I'm 'bout to go get something to eat before we head out to Fiso's. I'll bring you something back."

Once Tonya closed the door, Azia closed her eyes and allowed the soapy bubbles and hot water travel down her backside. Thoughts of her on Mike's hood giving him her all ran through her mind and brought a smile to her face. Minutes later, she was out of the shower trying to locate her ringing phone through the steam circling in the small room. Her disposition changed after she saw who was calling. "What you want?"

The voice on the other end was heavy and aggressive. "You need to find a better way to answer when I call. Do you need me to hang up and call back so you can try again?"

"I'm not tryna hear that shit, Mudda," Azia sneered. "When you bringing me my money?"

"That's all you ever think about. You eat, sleep and shit money don't you?" He snickered then continued. "Ya ass need to stop being all saditty and get a real job instead of counting on me."

Mudda was what Azia defined as a sponsor—nothing more, nothing less. She released a soft sigh, letting what he said go in one ear and out the other. She was tired of his ass and how stingy he'd become. She cut off the shower and headed across the hall, back to her room. Finally she spoke, "Mudda, it's been a week now. You know I had to pay off the balance for this semester," she lied. Rashaud had already taken care of the payment weeks ago.

Tired of him stringing her along, Azia spazzed out on him. "I'm tired of you thinking I'm your fucking trophy! You just wanna walk around wit' me on ya hip to make ya ugly ass look good!"

She wasn't lying and he knew it. Mudda looked like the King of mouse-men. Azia wasn't physically attracted to him but, just like a lot of other females, she put up with it for the money. He arrogantly replied, "You tryna stunt on a nigga?"

"Fuck stuntin'! I'm not the one to put up wit' the bullshit. Let me tell you this—You're gonna wish you ain't never fuck wit' a bitch like me." He snickered. "Laugh now, 'cause ya ass will be crying later."

"You call yourself threatening me, ho?"

"I got your ho alright. Make this your last time dialing my number or your wife will find out exactly what you do wit' your spare time."

Azia ended the call, making sure she got in the last word. She knew cutting Mudda loose was a drastic move but she was his loss. It was time to find another bank. A chick like her never had problems finding a money maker that was willing to spend, and Mike was surely looking like a good candidate. After dropping her towel, she stretched across the bed, clicked on her 27-inch television, and fell asleep to MTV Jams.

A couple hours later, loud music blasted through the air as Azia and Tonya bumped to Jay-Z's *The Black Album*. They were getting ready to head out to Fiso's Bar/Club where many went to lounge and fall back. It was located on South Street, so the strip was always popping. At this particular establishment, you were bound to find whatever it was you were looking for: a baller, pimp, hustler, fling, good or bad boy or girl. This was definitely the spot to be at on a Wednesday night.

"Hurry up, Azia! It's going on midnight!" yelled Tonya from her bedroom door, which was located diagonally from Azia's.

Azia turned the stereo down a notch and yelled back, "Them niggas ain't going no where! Chill the fuck out!"

The doorbell rang, bringing Azia to a halt. Knowing it could be Rashaud made her paranoid because she had been ducking his calls all day. She peeked only her head into the hallway just as Tonya went to answer it. "If it's Rashaud, tell him I'm not here," she whispered before ducking back into her room. Tonya rolled her eyes and kept walking.

Tonya reappeared in the hallway after conversing for a few minutes at the front door. "That wasn't him. Hurry ya scary ass up so I can go get my drink on."

When they arrived at Fiso's, the crowd was already thick. Every part of the city was there representing: South Philly, North Philly, West Philly, Germantown, Darby and even some Jersey and New Yorkers. The line to get in was halfway to Broad Street and the surrounding parking lots were filled to capacity. Azia, always at the top of her game, flirted her way in past the security guard ahead everyone else.

The club was divided into three different levels. The bottom floor was more of a social setting with padded seating down one wall and a bar stretching down the opposite wall. The second floor had a dance floor, large VIP booths in the back, and two bars—one on the side of the dance floor and the other in the back for VIP guests. The third floor, also known as the Roof Top, had another VIP section and more booths around all the walls. The bar was located left of the stairs and there was plenty of room to dance if that's what you came to do. That level was most popular in the summertime because the roof would usually be removed so the crowd could enjoy the breeze.

Still trying to make their way from the first floor to the second, Azia and Tonya slid through the narrow walkway between any slight openings in the mix. They hugged people they knew and eyed ones they didn't. Azia became unnoticeably furious after seeing Mudda posted in the corner, sitting at the circular-shaped booth with two other females, popping Cristal like it was nothing. She assumed that the heavier female stuck to him like a magnet was his wife. *I got something for that nigga,* she smirked while making her way up to the second level.

After seeing that it was uncomfortably crowded on the second level, Tonya yelled over the *Shake Ya Money Maker* beat that blasted from the speakers. "It's too crowded on this floor. Let's go upstairs to the roof."

Azia agreed, but just as she went to follow her friend, a familiar voice and firm grip stopped her dead in her tracks. She jerked back. "Damn, Rashaud, let me go."

He gripped her tighter and spoke directly in her ear. "Where you been, and why you haven't been answering my calls?"

"I was in class all day," she lied. "Why are you on my head all the time? Let a bitch breathe."

"I'm gonna let you breathe alright." He let her go and nodded his head. "I should fuck ya dumb ass up in here, but I'ma go ahead and let you have ya fun. I'll catch up wit' you later to finish this."

With her nose up in the air, Azia pushed through the airtight crowd to get away from him. Tonya watched from the stairs with a look of disgust on her face. Rashaud noticed and winked his eye at her. Disgusted, she continued up the steps, hoping Azia wasn't too far behind.

"Excuse me … excuse me," Azia pushed. "Damn, bitch!" she barked, as a drunken female wobbled over Azia's two-hundred dollar shoes. "Excuse me," she continued, and made her way up to the last level.

By the time she got to the top, it was just as packed as the first and second floors. "Fuck this shit!" she snapped.

"That's no way for a lady to talk. You 'pose to have more class than that," an unidentified male stated. He looked and smelled sweaty.

Azia twisted her lips and replied, "You gonna find out a lot more about me if you don't get your stinking ass out my face. Move!" She pushed past him and went to meet Tonya over at the bar.

"You stuck-up bitch," he shot angrily at her back.

She threw up her middle finger and moseyed on, saying nothing in response. Tonya had already ordered their first round and was waiting on the bartender to bring them over. She turned to face her friend. "Rashaud be on that dumb shit. What he say to you?"

"Nothing. Just give me my drink, please."

They got their drinks and stood around the bar for a while, checking out the scenery. Tonya noticed one of her old male friends opposite them at the other end of the bar with some of his homies. "Dayum, he looks good. I should'na left his fine ass alone."

"Who?" asked Azia, following the direction of Tonya's eyes. "Oh shit, that's the nigga I was wit' earlier."

"Who? Juan?" Tonya questioned with a puzzled look.

"I don't know which one is Juan, but I'm talking 'bout the one in the middle wit' the braids. He told me his name was Mike."

Tonya damn near choked on her drink. She set it down in disbelief. "Are you serious? You got to be joking." She waited for an answer, which puzzled Azia who was waiting on an explanation herself. "That's the guy Mike from South Philly that I was tryna hook you up wit' months ago. You was all twisted over Rashaud and shit, so you wasn't paying me any mind. I can't believe you're from South Philly and don't know who that dude is."

"Am I supposed to? I mean, after today, what I do know is he got some good-ass dick and a nice-ass ride."

"I'm telling you, Azia. You get him, you hit the jackpot, girl! The dude is paid! Listen when I tell you he's bringing in major paper--"

Azia stepped away from the bar and headed in Mike's direction. There was nothing more she needed to hear or another second to be wasted. With Tonya on her heels, she mumbled, "Time to work my magic."

Juan noticed Tonya heading his way and smiled. Mike, never noticing Azia, continued his conversation until he was interrupted by Juan nudging him. But before Juan could give the full forewarning, Azia took the Corona bottle from Mike's hand and swallowed the remainder of it. Caught off guard, he couldn't do anything but smile. "You always drink after people you don't know?"

Azia grinned in return. "I wouldn't say I don't know you after meeting you earlier. But you learn something new about a person every day."

Mike gently clutched her chin, moving it from side to side. "You got a lot more to learn about me."

"Name the place and time and I'll be there, willing to let you teach me."

"The way you left me smiling earlier, it will definitely be sooner than later." Azia couldn't help but blush.

Juan, still surprised that Azia was the fling Mike had told him about, suggested that the four of them go grab a bite to eat. It was almost two in the morning, so the only spot nearby that would be open was the South Street Diner.

"Sound good to me," said Mike, clutching Azia's hand.

"Well, then. Let's roll out," advised Juan.

The thought of Rashaud lingering inside or outside of Fiso's dawned on Azia. She tapped Tonya and turned to face the guys. "We'll meet ya'll outside. I have to use the restroom."

The two girls went to the restroom while the guys headed out. Azia pulled her cell phone from her pocketbook and placed three calls to Rashaud hoping he was already gone. There was no answer. "Watch him decide to call me back as soon as I sit down in the diner," she said to Tonya. Giving up on any more attempts, both girls headed toward the exit.

Just as fast as their feet hit the cement out front, Tonya spotted Mudda's wife double-parked directly in front of the entrance. She elbowed Azia to get her attention. They headed in that direction, checking for any signs of Mudda as their heels clicked away.

Azia approached the car, making sure to keep herself at a short distance. The window was already rolled down, so she wasted no time. "You're Mudda's wife, right?"

The heavy, light-skinned female responded with her brows raised, "Yeah! Who are you?"

"You can say I'm an old friend of your husband's." Azia smiled when she saw the same exact bracelet he had bought for her wrapped around the woman's thick wrist. "I see he likes to treat all his girls the same." Azia took the identical diamond tennis bracelet from her arm. "I'm sure we have the same inscription, too."

Mudda's wife flicked the interior lights on, turned Azia's bracelet over, and melted in her seat when she read the words: Mudda loves Azia 2006. Gritting her teeth and trying her best to keep things humble, she asked, "And ya reason for giving me this?"

"Because I see you have the same one on your arm and I'm exclusive. I ain't got time to sport the same shit another chick is rocking if I can help it." Azia spoke as if she was genuinely concerned. "I ain't tryna cause no confusion, but you look like a woman that deserves a lot better." Azia noticed Mudda trying his best to make it over to his wife's car. Satisfied with getting that off her chest, she walked away before he made it all the way over and blew him a kiss. *Take that, wit' your cheating ass*, she smirked.

Azia and Tonya walked away laughing. Just as they figured, Mudda started blowing up Azia's phone, but again, Tonya, being on top of all game, spotted Rashaud leaning up against a tree. He was boldly exchanging phone numbers with another female. "That's why he didn't answer your call," Tonya said.

Azia's first instinct was to cut up, but she didn't want to draw any attention to herself. So she strolled by, making sure Rashaud knew she had seen him. "The pussy better be worth it," she spat, and then disappeared into the crowd. Rashaud thought about following her, but opted to deal with it later. He wasn't about to pass up the opportunity to complete a mission he'd been on for way too long. Strong-arming people—also known as sticking them up—was what he was good at. If you had money and you flaunted it like you were Mr. Untouchable, Rashaud would make sure he touched you. But his latest game plan had more to do with pride than money. Although Azia thought she was good at hiding her extracurricular activities from him, she had another thing coming. He focused his attention back on the female standing in front of him. "Make sure you give that address to your brother tonight. It's important that you do that for me."

The freckled faced female looked up at him and smirked. "What you gonna do for me in return?"

"Come on, Peaches. You know I can't even mess wit' you like that. Busta is my man and he ain't having it."

"Don't blame it on my brother. The real reason is because you all stuck on her gold-digging ass," she pointed in the direction Azia was last seen.

"Don't be like that. I watched you grow up; we like family."

She sucked her teeth and pushed him away. "We like family, but we ain't blood."

Rashaud chuckled to himself as she walked away with her lips tooted up. Peaches was fine, but she was off-limits. Busta, his right-hand man, would never approve of their relationship, so the even thought wasn't an option. Rashaud mingled with a few acquaintances a little while longer before heading back to his car to return Azia's call. On the way to the parking lot, he glanced over at a small group of people gathered around Mudda and his red Range Rover, chitchatting. Rashaud nodded his head, anxiously anticipating the day when Mudda would get what he had in store for him. He climbed into his car and aggressively yanked his cell from the case on his hip. When Azia didn't answer the three back-to-back calls, he became even more infuriated. He sped out of the lot, drawing attention to his car, and headed for Temple University's campus.

When the girls pulled away from the scene, Tonya called Juan and told him there had been a change of plans. Instead of the diner, the group would meet up at IHOP on City Line Avenue to avoid a big crowd. Azia was enjoying every minute with Mike, and for some apparent reason he felt the same way. Weakness had never been a part of his motto, and his heart had never skipped a beat over any female until that very night. He had been with a lot of pretty chicks before, but he was connecting with the beautiful creature seated beside him. Azia had his full attention. Mike came to know that she had more to offer than just beauty. She had book and street smarts. She knew when to be classy and when to reverse to nasty. But even still, the fact remained that she was a ho, which made Mike self-conscious because he was well aware that it was hard to turn a ho into a housewife.

CHAPTER 2
Easier Said Than Done
"All I want to do is love you."
-Rashaud

Just after the sun rose, Azia was awakened by the beeping of her cell phone. She opened her eyes just slightly, catching a glimpse of the sun peeping through the crack between a pair of black drapes. The unfamiliar setting quickly brought her to an upright position. Her head was throbbing as a result of all the liquor she'd drank the night before. She turned to her left and saw Mike sleeping beside her. She took a moment to recall how the night had played out.

After leaving IHOP, the four of them headed to Mike's house for some more drinks and fun. Azia smiled remembering how good a job she'd done to have him sleeping like a baby. She scanned the room, amazed at how clean and cozy his bachelor pad was. Everything was intact. The comfortable pillow-top, king mattress with its red silk sheets made her wish it was her own. The beautiful custom-made lamps on the cherry wood nightstands showed that he had good taste. There were mirrors throughout the entire room, and a minibar filled with different liquors beneath a 42-inch flat screen television that was mounted to the wall. There was one tall dresser and chest set in the same cherry wood design as the headboard, sitting opposite one another in each available corner.

Azia's smile vanished when, again, she heard the soft beeping from her pocketbook. She eased out of bed and picked up her bag from what looked like a Persian carpet. Her cell phone displayed thirteen missed calls from Rashaud and several unheard messages. *What am I gonna tell this dude*, she wondered, hoping he wasn't parked outside her apartment. Azia began to get dressed, still scoping out every angle of Mike's room. *I could get used to this*, she thought. Then she crept out the bedroom and down the hall to locate her friend.

Both Tonya and Juan were spread across the bed, buck-naked. She eased into the room and shook Tonya gently to keep from waking Juan. "C'mon, girl," Azia whispered. "Get up!" Tonya drifted from the bed and began to get dressed. On their way out, Mike met them both in the hallway. He pinned Azia to the wall and began to kiss her neck with his soft, tender lips. She was ready to strip and go another round, but Rashaud's angry face played in her mind like an ongoing alarm clock.

"I have to go but we'll get together later," she advised. She gave him one last intimate kiss and headed out.

The downstairs was just as immaculate as the upstairs. The only difference was the larger bar area, the 60-inch plasma television and stereo system with surround sound, the decked out dining area, and the Italian leather furniture. The Dock Side luxury apartment was a place Azia would surely love to call home.

The whole ride home, Azia rehearsed excuse after excuse. She knew Rashaud would pick her brain until she slipped and told the truth. When she pulled her '96 Honda Accord into the small parking lot across from her apartment, she scanned the area for any signs of Rashaud, but his car was parked out of sight, so neither girl had a clue he was watching from afar. They hopped out of the car, never noticing him chucking toward them on foot. Before Azia had the chance to make it up one step, Rashaud gripped her neck with one hand from behind. Her instincts made her elbow him and spin in his direction. "Get off me, boy!"

"Bring ya ass on," he demanded, dragging her with him.

"Why don't you let her go, Rashaud," yelled Tonya.

Rashaud released Azia and gave Tonya an evil glare. "Mind your business before I make you swallow your crooked-ass teeth," he warned.

Tonya weighed her options. She was used to all their breakups to make up. Knowing that, a couple hours later, everything would be back to normal, Tonya didn't intervene further. But she hated seeing her friend go through so much drama, and hoped that one day Azia would open her eyes and realize that no man—or what he carried down below—was worth the headache. *Fuck it*, she thought, before storming into the apartment.

Rashaud badgered Azia with questions all the way to his car. She refused to get in and go with him until he started smacking her around, causing a scene. Embarrassed because there were bystanders looking on, Azia leaped in the car and slammed the door. Like the madman he was, Rashaud sped off like a contestant in a NASCAR event, wasting no time interrogating her.

"You got some nerve to be slamming doors and shit! Where you been all night, Azia?!" he asked. "I see me killing your ass if you keep taking me for a sucker!"

Azia flagged him like her night was innocent. "Please, Rashaud. That's your conscience eating at you." She tried using reverse psychology. "You probably left wit' that bitch you had all up in your face."

Without looking, he backhanded her from the driver's seat. The right side of her head knocked against the glass. She put two fingers up to her mouth. Hoping that God was on her side, she sat quietly with the taste of blood in her mouth as Rashaud drove to a more secluded area.

"You're staying out all night now?! 'Fuck you think this is?! You think I'm having that shit?! I'll beat your ass down to a pulp if you ever try me like that again!"

Rashaud's voice made her cringe. She began to reason with him, but the look in his eyes said not to bother. Instead, she did what she had to do to ease his mind. She started by rubbing the side of his face and caressing the back of his neck. She tried her best to sound as sincere as possible when she told him how much she loved him.

"There will never be anyone worth giving your goodies away." She tongued him down, caressing his manhood at the same time. Rashaud was stuck. Her touch was like no other. He closed his eyes, placed his right hand on top of her head, and guided it down steadily. Azia sucked every inch of him dry. She licked and sucked until she couldn't suck anymore. She cupped his balls and deep-throated all of him without gagging. Before she could finish, Rashaud was screaming out her name and speaking in tongues.

Azia, going in for the kill, stopped so she could give him another reason to forgive her. She straddled him, reached behind her back to grab hold of the steering wheel, and rode him like a professional bull rider. She twirled her hips like a hula-hoop in that small, tight space, whispering sweet nothings in his ear.

"Oh, Azia, I love you," he whimpered, about to discharge all he had built up inside. "You better not ever give my shit away." Although he knew for a fact that she'd given herself to others besides him in the past, he was too caught up at the moment to remember. That's the power of the P-U-S-S-Y …

■ ■ ■

The next three days flew by and Saturday night came. Rashaud had everything mapped out, hoping things would go as planned. He met up with Busta outside the Wilson Projects alongside the 25th street bridge, ready to meet his mark. They had been planning a hit on this cat for a couple weeks now. Finding out the information they needed was a piece of cake, including his hangout spots, where he liked to eat, sleep, shit, and who he was fucking.

Rashaud sat patiently behind the tinted windows of a burgundy '94 Impala. His eyes were glued on Mudda's shadow walking from room to room inside his stash house. Korman Suites on Lindbergh Blvd. was where the majority of his product and profit was kept. After doing his homework, Rashaud had his daily schedule down pat like it was his own. There were no bodyguards, lookouts, cameras, or anything to keep him away from this hit.

Maskless, Rashaud and Busta retrieved their heat and headed for their target. Rashaud stood guard on the left side of the front door while Busta took the right. Both men stood silently, anticipating their next move. Seconds later, on cue, the upstairs light was shut off. After another two minutes, the downstairs light went out. Then the front door lock clicked and the doorknob turned, all in one motion. As soon as the door had the tiniest crack in it, they wrestled their way inside with their guns raised to their chests.

"Get the fuck on the floor! Get the fuck down now!"

Mudda was stunned. He got caught slipping. He was smart enough not to let anyone know where his stash was, but dumb in thinking his ass couldn't be followed. Caught up in all the pretty girls and living the life of a high roller, he lost sight of the greed in niggas. Anybody getting money on the streets in the City of Brotherly Love was either hustling or getting hustled. And at that moment, Mudda just happened to be on the wrong side. He knew he was sucking in what would be his last breaths.

Using what little light was shining in from the street light outside, Busta shoved Mudda down and kneeled on top of him. "Pass that shit over or I'll take ya fuckin' dome off," he threatened. "And where the fuck is the money?"

Mudda said nothing. He passed over the bag in his hand, which contained over fifty-thousand dollars worth of cocaine and marijuana. He knew either way he was dead, so why give up the money, too?

With hard eyes, Rashaud repeated the question. "You heard 'im. Where the fuck is the money?" The thought of Azia fucking Mudda's ugly ass made him chuckle. "Yo, how the hell you be getting these bitches to love you? What the fuck you be doing to them? 'Cause you ugly as shit, dawg." He chuckled again. "Get ya ass up." Rashaud gripped Mudda from the floor as if he were racing the speed of light.

"Fuck ya'll niggas. Kill me now, 'cause I ain't telling you shit." Mudda hawked and spit in the face of the man closest to him, which was Busta. The butt of Busta's gun slammed against Mudda's two front teeth and knocked him back to the floor. Blood oozed from Mudda's lip. Even in pain, he wouldn't back down. "Fuck you! Either take that shit and roll out, or kill me now, muthafuckas!"

Busta, wiping the saliva from his face with his shirt, said, "It'll be ma pleasure—"

But Rashaud held up one hand, gesturing for Busta to stop. As bad as Busta wanted to send him to meet his maker, he had to follow Rashaud's lead. Still calm and cool Rashaud spoke.

"This is your last chance to tell me where the fucking money is." His gun shifted from side to side as he spoke each word.

Mudda wanted to keep playing the tough guy, but he was in no position to do so. He continued to spit blood on the floor every time it accumulated in his jaws. "Ya'll niggas gonna kill my ass either way. You expect me to—"

Rashaud cut him short. "Do yourself a favor and have a fucking seat." He grabbed Mudda up from the floor and tossed him aside. Mudda landed crooked on the sectional; one leg across the arm of the sofa, the other foot on the floor, and his head between the oversized pillows. Rashaud pulled Mudda's cell phone out of his pocket and started calling out the names of his most recent flings. "Desiree … Shaniya … Kesha … I'ma kill every last one of these bitches if you don't stop fucking around wit' me."

"I don't give a fuck about them hos."

Rashaud jammed the barrel of his gun down Mudda's throat. "But you give a fuck about this one!" Rashaud turned the phone around so Mudda could see his wife's name on the small screen. "I'ma get her to tell me where ya momma live so I can kill her. Then I'ma make her watch me kill ya daughter before I blow her fucking brains out! Keep testing me, muthafucka!"

Mudda's eyes watered instantly. He hadn't always been committed to his wife but was always loyal to his family. He hoped that, maybe—just maybe—if he gave up what they were asking for, no harm would come to his loved ones. "A'ight…a'ight…I'll tell you where the money is. Just please don't hurt my family."

"So you do know how to be a good boy," smiled Rashaud. "Give that fucking money up, pussy!" Rashaud gripped Mudda by the back of his head, palming it like a basketball, and forced him back to the floor.

Mudda led them to a medium-sized safe he had planted in the floor. He pulled back the artistic rug and punched in the seven digits to the combination. The door slowly opened. Jackpot! The safe revealed over two-hundred thousand dollars, more to add to what they already had. Under the safe was a hidden compartment in the floor that had more coke and weed in it. Both Rashaud's and Busta's eyes lit up. They knew Mudda was loaded but not to that extent.

"Now I see why they be giving the pussy up," teased Rashaud. Busta began to scoop out everything in the safe into a duffle bag. Rashaud let him handle that so he could jump to a more personal level. He stood in front of Mudda who was slumped over on his knees. "Before I let you go, I just need you to know one thing." He dropped a wallet-sized photo that landed at his feet and slid it over with his foot for Mudda to pick up. Mudda looked at the face in the photo like he'd seen ghost. It was Azia. "You took some pussy that didn't belong to you. And for that it's time to die, my nigga."

In the blink of an eye, Busta came out of nowhere with a hunter's knife and slit Mudda's throat from ear to ear. The sight of the blood gushing out sickened them both. Busta completed the job he had started while Rashaud made sure there was no more money or drugs laying around.

Busta wondered why his friend had held back that sensitive information. If the hit was all about Azia, then there was a strong possibility that Rashaud was getting too caught up. Him mixing business with pleasure could one day be the downfall for them both. "Why you ain't tell me he was fucking your girl?"

Rashaud stood there, expressionless. "We were on a need to know basis. Everything you needed to know I told you. That, you didn't need to know."

Busta looked disgusted. "I don't like that trick. I don't like nothing about her gold-digging ass. You need to leave her alone before she ends up being the death of you."

This dude better be glad I got love for him, thought Rashaud shaking his head. Anyone else coming at him like that would have been feeling the next round from his gun.

When Azia and Rashaud first met, Busta had tried to convince him to cut her off. He knew a lot more about Azia and how she was living. She was supposed to have been a "hit it and quit it," but Rashaud kept going back for more and his feelings began to magnify. Busta continued, "I'm just telling you to be careful. You don't need to get caught up in no dumb shit over no pussy. It can't be that good. Shit, if it is, you need to let your boy over here get a little taste of that, 'cause I ain't never had no snapper like that before!"

The tension in the room eased up as both guys shared a laugh. They swept the house one last time before leaving. Busta exited first. He powered up the Impala and waited for Rashaud to join him. And just like that their mission was complete, leaving nothing behind except for Mudda's headless body.

■ ■ ■

Tonya and Azia were speeding up North Broad Street dodging potholes and rocking to Beyonce's *B-Day* CD. It was only spring but you would have sworn it was a summer day. Drifting through one light after the other, they flew past gas stations, fast-food joints, and abandoned homes that young hustlers used to distribute crack. Tonya stared out the window feeling sorry for the homeless people scattered around using newspaper and pissy concrete as their beds.

Both girls were eagerly trying to reach their destination. All four windows were down on the Honda. The wind blew through their hair as they sang the words to "Freakum Dress" like it had been written by no one other than them. They were heading to the Eagle's Bar to meet up with a couple guys they'd met at Fiso's last week. It was just after eight and already a crowd was forming around Broad and Erie. The Eagle's Bar was best known for its drink specials so this was to be expected. There were no parking spots in sight. After contemplating the situation, they wound up parking a couple blocks down. Walking distances in stilettos was not one of Azia's special talents, so when she got in the bar and saw there weren't any seats available, she was pissed.

"Fuck that. I ain't standing in here all night. Where these niggas at, Tonya?"

Tonya got out her cell to make the call. "Yo, where ya'll at?" She paused. "Make a run where?" Azia rolled her eyes and made a quick u-turn toward the door. "We ain't waiting here. I'll catch up wit' you next time." Tonya ended the call and went to find her friend. "You wanna stay here or what?"

Azia didn't have the patience for a stuffy, crowded, smoky atmosphere. Her eyes were locked on a guy standing beside the bar pissing on the wall. "I ain't staying over here wit' these ghetto-ass people." If it wasn't for all her expenses, her time would be well-spent snuggled up with one man, popping some popcorn, and making it a BlockBuster night.

The girls were heading back to their ride when a familiar voice yelled out Azia's name. She looked in every direction trying to place where the voice had come from. A car backing down the block, weaving in and out of oncoming traffic, captured her attention.

"Who the hell could this be?"

When the tinted window came down on the Dodge Charger, a familiar face appeared. His name was Brian. He was an acquaintance of hers from a couple classes they shared together. It was surprising to see him out that late, especially in that neighborhood. He was cute but weird; someone she could never see herself with, or so she thought. Every time they'd conversed in the past, it had been about schoolwork, nothing more. He didn't seem like the roughneck type at all, that's why she had never propositioned him. But tonight she would get a chance to see just how much looks could be deceiving. He dragged on the end of his blunt before crushing it in the ashtray. "Where ya'll ladies headed?" he asked, slowly releasing the smoke. The girls shrugged their shoulders and walked over to the car in unison. "C'mon and chill out with us."

That was music to Azia's ears. She was happy to get off her feet and hop in the car with him. Both girls climbed in, got introduced to his friend, and they were off.

"It's jam-packed up in the Eagles's bar. I hope that's not where ya'll going," Azia said.

"Nah," Brian responded, "we going to Dream's to get some crabs and a few drinks."

Dream's Lounge was a hangout a little further down. The crowd was usually older and more mature. As long as there was somewhere to sit down, Azia was all for it. She intended to learn a lot more about Brian. Maybe he was worth pulling up under her wing.

With a smirk etched across his face, Brian stared Azia down as they sat at the horseshoe-shaped bar tearing up some Dungeness crabs. He was amazed by her beauty. Aside from the outside, her inner beauty and conversation was a grabber. After sitting and listening longer, he knew why men fell on their faces for her. Afraid he would become a statistic, he tried his best to keep things civil. "What are you getting into when you leave here?"

Azia smiled. Not knowing whether to come at him strong or bite the bullet, she went with her gut. "I'ma hang out wit' ma girl for a little while longer, then probably call it a night." *Please ask me to come with you*, she thought. After hearing about his plans to start his own company once he graduated in June, Azia wanted the chance to sink her claws deep into him and make sure he never forgot her name.

"Well, I'll catch you next time. You know school is almost over; I hope I can see you again outside of class."

Shit! Fuck my gut! I should have come at him full throttle. A minute after thinking that, Azia was wishing she hadn't run into Brian at all. She felt herself get yanked from the barstool she was sitting on and dragged out of the bar backwards by her shirt collar. Unable to see who had strong-armed her, the annoyed look on Tonya's face spoke a thousand words. Since her friend didn't get up to say or do anything, it was safe to assume it could only be one person: Rashaud.

Tonya drank the rest of her watermelon martini and slid the glass back onto the bar top. "I can't believe he just embarrassed her like that. I can't believe she let him. It never ceases to amaze me." She took her time heading outside.

Brian opted to mind his business. He asked no questions, just shook his head in disbelief. Of course, he and his friend would have plenty to say once Tonya wasn't around, but he chose to stay quiet for the moment. Tonya apologized for them being so rudely interrupted and said her good-byes to the guys. She grabbed Azia's purse, which she'd left behind on the bar, and chucked for the exit. Neither Azia nor Rashaud were in sight. Now, even more upset that she had to walk all the way back to the car alone, she cursed them both all the way.

Rashaud was flying through the streets of North Philly, running red lights and stop signs like he was a city official. Azia was panicking. She had seen him act crazy in the past, but never really considered that it was true. She tried to plead her case but he couldn't care less. That night, she was going to find out that when you play with fire, someone's bound to get burned.

"Rashaud!" She repeated his name over and over, trying to get his attention. His body was there but his mind was elsewhere. Azia stared at him from the passenger seat to see if he was blinking and he wasn't. He was completely zoned out. Although he hadn't wanted to hear what Busta was saying, it was the truth. He got a whole, twenty-minute lecture after they left Mudda's stash house about all the negative things about being involved with Azia. Quick to come to her defense, Rashaud would only let him say so much. With every negative Busta came out with, he came back with a positive. Then, to make matters worse, he received a phone call about her sitting up in a spot having drinks with some other niggas, after he just finished killing one over her.

"I got a present for you," he finally spoke.

Aww man, please don't let this fool kill me, she silently prayed, too afraid to respond.

Taking her silence as disrespect, Rashaud whipped the car over to the side of the road down by the Schuylkill River, hopped out, and walked around to the passenger side. Azia tried to hit the lock but was too slow. He yanked her door open and jerked her out by the hair. "Why do ya ass gotta play me for a pussy all the time? Why you gotta act like a fucking whore? I would do anything for you! I should throw your ass in that fucking river right now! You keep trying me and trying me." He stared at her with an evil look in his eyes. "You know what? I can show you better than I can tell you."

Azia looked to the left and the right, trying to find an escape. Rashaud sensed it and became offended. He grabbed her by her shirt so tightly it ripped, revealing both breasts.

"This is how the fuck you come out dressed?" He struck her in the side and knocked the wind out of her. Slowly, she slid down the car onto the ground. "You better tell me something good, baby. And you better tell me now, Azia. I swear I'm 'bout to kill your narrow ass out here."

She couldn't utter a word. Seeing that she couldn't move, he took the opportunity to bend over into the car from the passenger side and pop the trunk open. He walked to the back of the car to grab the duffle bag out the trunk. Gasping the slightest bit of air, she tried crawling away on her knees. Rashaud saw this but wasn't worried, knowing she wouldn't get far as hard as he'd hit her. He dropped the bag in front of her. Still on her hands and knees she looked up at him, her eyes questioning what was in the bag.

"Open it and find out," he ordered.

Azia slowly unzipped the bag. She stared down into it but couldn't see anything. Again, she looked up at him, and again, he urged her on. Putting one hand into the bag, she was horrified to touch what felt like a human nose. Finding some strength, she jumped to her feet and tried to run away. Rashaud stopped her. "What is in that bag?!" she screamed, crying uncontrollably now. "Let me go, you sick fuck!"

Rashaud gripped her wrist tightly and reached into the bag with his free hand, pulling out Mudda's head by his hair. Azia was hysterical. She tried punching Rashaud to get away from him but wasn't strong enough to do any damage. "You like fucking around on me wit' niggas like this?! I will do you the same way I did him! Do you believe me now?! Huh?! Is a nigga like this worth losing your mutherfuckin' life over?!" Azia didn't say anything. "Answer me!!"

"NO!" she yelled, drenched in tears. "I wanna go home! Please let me go home!"

He released her wrist and backed up toward the river. As if Mudda's head was a football, Rashaud took a three step drop-back and launched it like he was Eli Manning throwing his Super Bowl winning touchdown. It landed a ways out into the water. Azia couldn't run, scream, yell, kick or anything else for that matter. She felt like her feet were pinned to the ground. She didn't want to be moved or touched. She froze, scared to think, speak or breathe. If she made the wrong move, *her* head could be the next to go.

Rashaud came back over to where she was standing and wrapped his arms around her frail body. "All I wanna do is love you. That's all I want to do. Is that asking for too much?"

A fit of crying overwhelmed her. She allowed Rashaud to take her into his arms, afraid to turn away from him. She saw the bloody remains of Mudda every time she blinked. This frightened her even more. She was willing to accept and say anything that would get her out of the predicament she was currently in. "I'm sorry. I love you. I need you," were just a few of those things. This was a lesson for them both. Her heart was beating like she had just finished a sixty-minute aerobic workout. "Your secret is safe wit' me, Rashaud. I promise I won't say anything." She meant every word. Her imagination was running wild with visions of his crazy ass with *her* head in his hand, dribbling it down the street like a basketball. It didn't matter who tried to convince her to rat him out, her lips were sealed.

Rashaud was sinking back in, slowly but surely. Everything he and Busta had spoken about was dead and out the window. He was deeply in love and didn't want to lose the feeling. He wanted to be the Will to Azia's Jada, the Clyde to her Bonnie. It was time to turn the loose, little schoolgirl into the real ride or die chick he'd been looking for. Tonight was the first step into a whole new world for them. He just had to find out if she was a soldier or a weak link. They would both know soon enough.

CHAPTER 3
Mixing The Bitter With The Sweet
"A closed mouth won't get fed."
-Mustafa

The second semester was coming to an end and summer was just around the corner. Azia and Rashaud had grown a lot closer after that terrifying night. At least it had been frightening to her. For Rashaud, it had just been another day's work in the hood.

Rashaud and Busta made out heavy with the profits. Everything was split down the middle. With it being only the two of them, there was nothing for either of them to be mad at. But the way Rashaud started inching Azia into what they had going on really started to bother Busta. It was bad enough that he didn't trust her with Rashaud to begin with, now she was in their circle and he had to watch his own back. It started with her being the getaway driver for a couple jobs. Then she started throwing in her own thoughts about who they should hit up next and how it should be done. She came up with the bright idea that it would be easy for her to lure the niggas in, and then let them come in for the kill.

"I don't think that's a good idea, baby. I don't want you in the mix like that," stated Rashaud.

"Yeah," snarled Busta. "I think it's a very bad idea. Who knows which nigga you'll end up falling for? That'll be our own death sentence," he blurted out, not caring whose feelings got hurt by his comment.

Azia sucked her teeth, aggravated with him and his attitude. "Fuck you, Busta," she spat.

Why did he have to go there with her? Rashaud asked himself. "Don't start wit' ya slick-ass tongue, Busta," he warned.

Azia tried to keep herself occupied with the money she was counting to avoid a confrontation. She and Busta had been beefing ever since she had started hanging around more frequently. Their eyes met briefly. Both could feel the heat. *I can't stand his monkey ass*, she silently said to herself. There was no love between them and, if it was left up to them, there would never be. Azia gave Busta a very strange vibe. She was a bad girl with a bad attitude and he didn't like anything she had to offer.

Azia put up with Busta's mouth because she had to. If he had been anyone other than Rashaud's best friend, Azia would have shut him down a long time ago. "Nine hundred ninety-seven, nine hundred ninety-eight, nine hundred ninety-nine, thirty-five." She exhaled after all that counting and tossed a rubber band around the last thousand-dollar stack of money. "This is thirty-five thousand right here. I'll count the rest later."

Money was flowing in left and right like water. Azia was glad she had chosen to stick by Rashaud's side. He had paid off all her debt, upgraded her '96 Accord to a '06 Solara, rented a one-bedroom apartment for the two of them at the Presidential City Suites on City Line Avenue, and filled her closet with a whole new wardrobe. Hanging up under Rashaud left Azia little time to spend with Tonya or anyone else. As the days went by their friendship weakened. Azia could smell the tension and animosity in the air. Jealousy is a bitch, and because Tonya wished she were walking in Azia's shoes, the heat was on.

"**Mal...Mal...the** door!" Azia yelled, upset at being rudely awakened by the annoying sound of the doorbell early in the morning. She marched down the hall to Mal's bedroom and banged on the door until she got an answer.

The door swung open. "I heard your ass the first time," said Mal, brushing swiftly past her.

Azia rolled her eyes and went back into her room, slamming the door behind her. She was glad the school year was almost over. She couldn't wait to pack up all her things and move into the apartment with Rashaud. The only reason she hadn't done it already was because staying at the campus apartment was more convenient when it came to making it to class on time, especially now that it was time to take finals.

Tonya was still acting real stank at times, but Azia tried her best to pay it no mind. When she would spend the night with Rashaud, Tonya barely wanted to speak the next day. But when she stuck around to spend time with her it was all love.

Azia stretched across her bed, clutching a pillow tightly to her chest. For some reason, Mike had been on her mind a lot lately. They hadn't talked but once or twice since the last time they'd seen each other. When Rashaud demanded that she get her cell phone number changed, she didn't bother calling to give it to him, scared to death what might happen if Rashaud found out. She tried to block Mike out of her mind, but couldn't win the battle against temptation. She began to reminisce about their last night together and how good it felt. The thriving sensation between her thighs yearned for attention. Azia spread her legs apart and let her hand find its way down to that warm, familiar place. Two fingers did a dance around her clitoris, making her crave more. She stopped for a moment and leaned across the bed to grab The Great American Challenge from inside her nightstand. She rolled back over onto her back and replaced her hand to finish the job it had started. With her other hand, she slid the ten-inch dildo between her inner walls. Soft moans escaped her throat as she fought to reach her climax. Images of Mike's muscle-bound body dripping wet flashed through her mind as she lay with her eyes closed and her hips up in the air. The vibrator attached to the dildo is what helped bring Azia to ecstasy. Her body trembled as she slowly lowered her hips back down onto the bed. After showering, she dialed Tonya to see where she was. "Where you at?"

"Why? You ain't boo-loving today?" she asked sarcastically.

"No, bitch," Azia said angrily. "Let's go do something. We ain't been out together in a while." Azia continued before Tonya could get a word in. "Before you say anything else smart, just hurry ya ass home. I'll see you when you get here." Azia ended the call, making sure she got the final word.

"Your hair is cute. Did Sabrina do that?" was the first thing out of Azia's mouth when Tonya walked through her bedroom door.

Knowing she looked good, she couldn't help but flaunt it. "Yup!" She pranced around the room, letting her natural hair swing. "You better call and set your appointment 'cause they 'bout to be booked up for a while."

Azia hopped on the phone right away to make that call. Then she and Tonya freshened up and changed into their newly purchased outfits, courtesy of Rashaud. From time to time, when she would be out shopping for herself, she would pick up something for Tonya to let her know she was thinking about her.

Azia was looking flawless in her hot pink, BeBe, fitted sweatsuit. The soft material traced every curve perfectly. She threw on some pink, BeBe, thong sandals and grabbed her Gucci clutch. Knowing how the crowd got in the Star Track, she wanted to be comfortable. "I'm starving!" she told Tonya. "You better hurry up before I leave your ass here."

Tonya put on the last of her makeup, smoothing it over her naturally high cheekbones, and then followed Azia out the door.

They arrived down in Center City in less than ten minutes. Tonya could tell something was weighing heavily on her friend's mind, but when she asked her about it, Azia brushed the question off. Traffic was hectic on Broad Street, so they made a quick right down Vine Street to hop on the expressway to head down to 22nd and Ellsworth in South Philly.

Star Track Lounge was packed when they arrived. It was doing the damn thing! This was the hang out spot for all the locals around the area. On that particular night, motorcycles, high-priced cars, hating-ass females, and good looking guys were in force, outside and in. It seemed as if the nice weather had brought the whole city out. The corner boys were out serving the scrambling fiends; mothers were walking their children; kids were scattered about, playing jump rope and hopscotch, while others ran around playing freeze tag. It always felt good to hang out around her old neighborhood, but it wasn't the same. Most of the people she'd grown up with were either away at college, on drugs, dead or in jail. *Damn, I miss the ol' days*, she thought. Seeing an old friend quickly approaching snapped her out of it.

"Hey, Kia! C'mere, girl! Where the hell you been?" Azia was glad to see her. After checking her out on the sly from head to toe, Azia knew things had changed a lot. What used to be one of the flyest females around the way now looked like one of the corniest.

"Muthafuckin' Azia!" Kia said, coming close enough for a hug. "What the fuck's been up wit' you?"

"Same shit, different day. I heard about Peanut. That shit was wrong how they did that boy," Azia said, sounding apologetic about the girl's dead ex-boyfriend. "Did you go to the funeral?"

"Yeah, I went. All the gutter-ass bitches that swore he belonged to them were tripping out on some bawling-their-eyes-out type shit. But you know I took it for what it was worth and moved on. I ain't about to be fighting over no dead dick. You feel me? What ya ass doing down here in this neck of the woods? You act like you from North Philly just because you go to school up there."

"It's not like that. I've just been chilling out on campus, that's all. Have you seen my cousin lately?"

"I saw her not too long ago. I think she's in Atlantic City getting it in wit' some new cat she met a little while back. She told me ya'll had a big fallout. What was that about?"

"Over a fucking lame-ass nigga. Can you believe that shit?"

"Dick is a muthafucka. 'Specially when it's good," she giggled.

"Yeah, well, fuck that. I've had a lot of good dick, but ain't none of it ever going to make me cut my family off for it. That shit is just flat-out crazy. When you see her simple ass, tell her to answer my damn calls, please. Matter fact, give her my new number." The female stored the number in her phone. Azia brought the conversation to an end noticing that Tonya was becoming impatient.

"They're having a fish fry up in there tonight. That's why it's so crowded," Kia informed before entering the lounge ahead of them.

Azia and Tonya had only been inside for twenty minutes before all the dudes surrounded them trying to buy drinks. They found a couple of seats in the cut and got busy on their fish platters. The vibration of Azia's phone drew her attention away from the wanna-be gangsta that was up in her face. She looked down at the caller ID and read Rashaud's number.

"Hey, baby, wassup?" she answered.

"Walk outside or something. I can barely hear you over the music." Azia did as she was told. Once the music was out of his ear, he spoke again. "Where you at?"

"Down South Philly at the Star Track, eating a fish platter. Why? Wassup?"

"Order me one. I'll be down there to get it." Azia let out an undetectable sigh. "I'll call you when I get outside 'cause you know I'm not coming in."

"Alright, I'll make sure I look out for the call."

At first she was upset, thinking Rashaud was coming to rain on her parade. But after hearing that he wasn't coming inside, she felt a lot better. That meant she wouldn't have to hear Tonya's whining because he wouldn't be sticking around too long. Azia headed back inside to place the order for another platter to go. When she turned around, she bumped into a very familiar face. Standing speechless, she didn't know what to say.

"Hey, stranger." Mike greeted her with a hug. "Tonya told me you were back here. Why you been hiding from me? What I do to deserve that?" he asked.

His smile was mesmerizing, he smelled so good she could taste him, and his body was cut just right. She wanted to jump up in his arms and wrap both legs around his waist.

"Hello?" He grabbed hold of her hand. "Are you gonna tell me why you went missing in action? You got your number changed on a nigga and everything."

"I was just going through some things," was the best answer she could come up with.

"Well, if you're finished going through some things," he mocked, "I would like to pick up where we left off. If that's okay wit' you."

Thinking fast, she gave him Tonya's number as if it were her own. Not sure whether Rashaud would call first like he said he would, or try to sneak up on her, she cut their conversation short. "Call me later. Maybe we can get together."

"I'll do that."

Ooooh, I could just swallow him up right now, she thought, walking back to sit with Tonya, who was being entertained by one of the locals. She must have had one drink too many because the guy she was allowing in her space looked like a creature from the closest swamp. And his breath was humming 'cause Azia could smell it from where she was standing.

"Hey, Azia," he greeted as if he knew her." She gave him a riddled look. "I know you remember me. It hasn't been that long." Azia shook her head no. "Tyrone from 18th Street. You used to mess wit' my cousin Reggie, back in the day."

"Oh, okay. I remember you," she lied, trying her best to dismiss the trashy smell coming from his mouth.

"I was just telling your friend that we're giving a party on the Spirit of Philadelphia next week. Ya'll need to come through and have some fun."

Saved by the bell, she pressed the button to stop her phone from vibrating, never responding to his suggestion. "That's Rashaud, Tonya. I'll be back in a minute." Tonya flagged her on.

Azia tried to squeeze her way through the crowd toward the door. She felt her phone vibrating again but ignored it. When she finally made it out, she scanned the area looking for Rashaud's car. Noticing it parked down the block on the corner of 22nd and Federal, she headed for him with his platter in hand. Once she reached the car, she tapped on the passenger-side window suggesting he roll it down.

"Get in," he commanded.

Damn, what the hell he want now? Azia climbed into the passenger's seat and handed him his plate.

"Ain't you forgetting something?" he asked.

She leaned over and blessed him with a kiss.

"Don't get out here and start acting like you ain't got no sense. I'm tryna give you some breathing room."

"Ain't nobody acting crazy," she mumbled. "Where you on your way to?"

"Back up top." His nose caught a whiff of the fish and his stomach sang a tune. He uncovered the platter and had a taste. "Damn! Whoever seasoned this did a hell of a job!" he said as it melted in his mouth. "This some good shit."

"Yeah, I know. I love Shelly's cooking. I ain't come down this end to get one of her platters in a while." Thinking about how good her own plate of food tasted, she was ready to get back to it. "Let me get back to mine before Tonya finds her way into it." Then she asked, "You coming in or what?"

"Nah, you know I don't fuck wit' these kind of places."

"C'mon, baby," she whined like she really wanted him to stay. "Stop being so paranoid all the damn time."

"Naw. I got some shit to handle. But I do have a question for you." He continued to stuff his face with fish and potato salad. "How serious were you the other day when you said you were down wit' luring niggas in for us?"

Azia began to fidget in her seat. "I was dead serious."

"I got a proposition for you. If you do it right, we can all be set for life."

Azia knew it was a risky suggestion when she threw it out there, and now being asked to follow through on it made her a little uncomfortable. "What kind of proposition you got, and what it consist of?"

Rashaud didn't answer right away. He continued to chew and stare out of the windshield of his car in the direction of the Star Track. After swallowing he spoke, "I been on this nigga for a while now. He thinks he's untouchable, but I'm gonna be the one to show his ass ain't nothing in this world untouchable if you're hungry enough to take it."

Still clueless about what he was getting at, Azia asked, "Who thinks they're untouchable?" with her brows raised.

"Him!" Rashaud pointed in the direction of the bar. "His ass gonna get touched real soon." He sounded like he was spitting fire from his tongue.

When Azia saw who Rashaud had it out for, she almost shit her pants. She felt like she had swallowed an orange watching Mike get into his BMW. She was breathing but felt as if the world had stopped moving. Her head began to spin and she got an instant headache. "Who is that?" she asked, hoping and praying he was talking about somebody else.

"Supposed to be the King of the Streets. That's what they call him."

"If that's what they call him then I'm sure it's true. Why would you wanna put yourself out there and mess wit' a nigga like that?"

"Because," he said, starting his engine. "That title belongs to me."

Azia was trembling inside. She desperately wanted to tell Rashaud to back off. At the same time, she wanted to go to Mike and tell him to watch his back. Her man was an animal, and when he got started there was no stopping him. What was a girl to do in a situation like this? "Rashaud, you throwing me out to the big dogs. How can you expect me to get close to a nigga like that?" she spat with attitude.

"You talking about him like you know him or something. What the fuck you getting all upset for?"

Regaining her composure, she played it off. "I'm not getting upset. I just don't want to put us in a situation we can't get out of. I don't know him, but just by the way you talking— he's a boss and bosses carry weight. Again, I'ma ask you, do you wanna put me out on a limb like that?"

"We'll talk about it later. I got somewhere to be."

She didn't want to get out of the car until she knew for sure she had changed his mind. Knowing that continuing to debate the issue would raise his suspicions, Azia made a mental note to raise more hell about it later. "Alright, boo. I'll see you later." She gave Rashaud another peck on his lips and exited the car.

"Hey, Azia. Don't get your head split messing wit' those cowards in there. If you're playing the game right, I might be getting a phone call later from you telling me you got one for me," he smiled, referring to a set up. "You can use one of those wankstas for practice. That way you'll be prepared when the time comes for you to step to the king."

Rashaud's laugh sickened her. It had been all her idea from the beginning, but she'd had no plan on Mike becoming the prey. Giving a fake smile in return, she closed the door and watched Rashaud pull off. *What the fuck did I get myself into?* Many thoughts ran through her mind as she jogged back to the bar to find Tonya.

Unable to get the conversation out of her head, she stormed through the enterance with her lips poked out. The proposition she had been presented with really troubled her. *I am not working my way through this thick-ass crowd again. Tonya better bring her ass up here.* She reached for her cell phone with one hand while flagging down the bartender with the other. "Hey, Bug. Can I get a Butt-naked?" she requested, referring to one of his specialty drinks. When he came back over, he slid the drink in front of her and told her it was already paid for. Azia gave him the *by who* look. Just then someone tapped her shoulder. She mentally prepared herself for it to be one of the fake-ass tough guys that had been on her head all night, but it wasn't. This guy she had never seen before, she could sense that he was definitely an out-of-towner.

He confirmed her assumption when he spoke in his heavy southern accent, "You want to talk to me or my chain." He grinned.

She could tell by his appearance and the scent of his Kenneth Cole cologne that he was a thoroughbred indeed. He was iced down and they weren't cubic zirconiums. His hair was freshly cut, each edge meeting the other with the same degree of sharpness. Azia couldn't take her eyes off his chain. All she could say to herself was *Jackpot!* After he smiled, Azia was blown away. He had the palms of her hands and the tip of her nose sweating. It took everything she had to stay grounded and not lure him outside to fuck his brains out. When she realized how star struck she was acting, she knew it was time to bounce back on her square and let the game begin.

"Thanks for the drink." She raised her glass head high before taking her first sip.

"That's all I get?" he asked, throwing his hands up to the air.

"What did you expect to get for a drink? You got to come a little better than that if you looking for more of my time."

He nodded his head in agreement as she walked away, disappearing into the crowd.

The let out was ridiculous. Everybody hung around to see who was talking to who, who was riding with who, and who was taking who home. When Azia stepped foot out the door, she spotted the guy who had bought her the drink sitting on top of the hood of an Umbrian red Bentley Coupe gulping down a Heineken. There were females posted up all around him and his friends, trying their hardest to get noticed, but his attention was elsewhere.

Azia and Tonya had to play the role and roll out like they had better things to do. As they strutted across the street to Azia's car, he spoke as if on cue. "Shawdy, can I holla at you for a minute?"

Both girls looked at each other like they didn't know who he was talking to. Azia smiled and flagged him to come over. He flagged her back suggesting that she come to him, but that wasn't happening. Azia always did the welcoming, she never did the go-getting. "Maybe next time," she said. It slid off her tongue smoothly as she proceeded to the car.

The guy slid off the hood and walked over to Azia. "How you gonna play me out like that?" he quizzed.

"I don't do the groupie love thing. You could have taken my 'maybe next time' and ran wit' it. You know Philly ain't but so big; we woulda bumped into each other again."

"Well, if it's so small, why am I just finding ya sexy ass?"

"Good things come wit' time," she blushed.

With a smirk etched across his face, he responded, "Well this must be my time. What you getting into tonight?"

Azia smiled. "How about catching my name first?"

"Azia, right?" he shrugged.

Who the hell been telling him my damn business? she wondered, nodding her head. "Too bad I didn't do my homework or I would have had your name by now."

"You'll learn to keep up," he joked. "Mustafa's the name." He paused. "So you tryna ride out wit' me or what?"

All of a sudden it was like an electric current had hit her. Invisibly, Rashaud's name was written all over Mustafa's body. *Rashaud told me to start practicing. This can be my first victim. I wanna fuck his sexy ass anyway.* "Somebody must have told you I was a fast one considering you tryna take me wit' you and all I know is your name."

"I wouldn't say all that. But they did tell me you about that money, so if I ain't stepping correct then don't step at all." He laid five hundred-dollar bills on the hood of her car. "I'm not one to beat around the bush, so you either wit' me or you not." He stuffed the rest of his loose ends back into his pocket, awaiting her response. "I'm heading out in the morning. I was only here on business. So either we find a way to make this happen or you gonna be on your way and miss out on a chance to hang out wit' a real nigga like myself."

Azia thought about it for a moment. Then she grabbed the crisp bills from her hood and pulled Tonya to the side. They began to speak in hushed tones. "This dude think he the shit for real. Why you ain't put his ass in check? What the fuck he think five-hundred dollars gonna do for you? He gonna toss that shit on your hood like he doing something. That Bentley probably ain't his any damn way—" Tonya went on and on, knowing that if it were her he was trying to ride out with, she would've been jumped in his car by now. But because it wasn't, she wasn't being anything more than a hater.

"Tonya, slow the hell down. I know what I'm doing. Just take my car and go ahead. I'll get it from you tomorrow."

"If Rashaud find out, he gonna whip ya ass. You might as well leave the nigga alone if you gonna keep fucking all these other niggas," she retorted.

Now Azia was heated. "Mind ya fucking business and stop worrying about what I need to be doing! You really been crossing the line lately. If you got some kind of gripe, spit that shit out or shut the fuck up!"

"That's on you," warned Tonya, snatching the keys from her friend's hand. "Don't come crying to me if ya ass get all caught up in some bullshit."

Azia rolled her eyes and took a step back from the curb allowing Tonya to pull off. She made a quick phone call to

Rashaud before heading to the corner where Mustafa had drifted. He must have been discussing something personal with the three guys standing around him because when she got close, they got quiet. She walked up on the group like she was the one in charge. "Don't get quiet on account of me."

One guy snickered while the other two looked irritated by her words. "Alright, Mustafa," they said in unison. "On that note, we out of here." They all gave each other dap and headed in different directions.

Once they were alone, Mustafa spoke, "What? You had to get mommy's or daddy's permission to stay out?"

Asshole, you don't even dig what I got in store for you, is what she wanted to say but instead replied, "I'm a grown-ass woman. Whatever I want to do, I'll do. Whoever I want to fuck, I'll fuck. You just so happen to be on my list for tonight, so stop rapping and let's be out."

Mustafa was taken aback by her aggressiveness. He wanted to see if she had what she needed to back up all her shit-talking. Having been told about how good she was in bed and how tight her mouth game was, he was looking forward to their one night extravaganza. "I'm right behind you."

Azia led the way to his car and climbed into the passenger side. Everything was intact, from the premium-grade leather, wood veneers, and built-in navigation system. "It's nice in here. Maybe I'll get me one someday."

"Keep fucking and bucking wit' all the right folk and I'm sure you'll have one of these in no time. Shit, this is a lot of chicks' hustle. You got to pay to play. Ain't that the saying? You need to let a nigga know up front what the deal is, especially a nigga like me. 'Cause a closed mouth won't get fed."

It wasn't clear if his comment was meant to flatter or offend her. She decided to exercise her patience and withstand all his outspoken statements as best she could. She caressed his leg as they headed for a hotel down the waterfront. "You sure you ready for a chick like me?"

"I've never had a problem handling a chick like you before. But I'll let you tell me, after the night comes to an end, whether or not I can uphold that claim."

Azia nodded her head in agreement thinking that would be a good idea. She would certainly love to be the one to get the final word. When the time came, she was ready to teach Mustafa a valuable lesson in life that he would wish he had learned a long time ago: When living in this cold, cold world, never say never.

■ ■ ■

On the other side of town, Tonya was driving back toward campus contemplating whether or not she wanted to call it a night or go chill with one of her male friends. She pulled her cell phone from her bag trying to catch the call before the voicemail answered. "Hello? Hello?" There was nothing but dead air and the call was marked private. A few seconds later it rang again. "Hello? Stop playing on my goddamn phone," she yelled, furious. Already feeling vexed because Azia had bailed out on her, the prank calls weren't making her mood any better. She turned the radio up, rocking to Power 99 when the phone rang again. She had already made up her mind not to answer it if it was marked private, but it wasn't. She turned the music down to a more conversational level. "Hey, baby. Where you been all day?"

"They had me working like a slave today. I didn't have a chance to check my messages until now," the guy on the other end replied.

"I miss you. Can I see you tonight so I can rub you down and make you feel better?" she tempted.

"Tonight is not a good night, baby girl. My wife has been on my back all day, so I gotta go straight home. I'll make some time for you tomorrow."

Her demeanor changed dramatically. "Tomorrow ain't good enough. I can't ever see you when I wanna see you."

"Why you gotta take it there? You knew the circumstances before we started fucking around. Look, I said I can't do it tonight. I'll try to make something happen tomorrow."

"Just a minute ago, you said you would make it happen. Now you saying you'll try to make it happen. Which one is it?"

"I'm tired, Tonya. I'm not up for the ramping and raging in my ear right now. I'll holla at you tomorrow or—"

She cut him short. "Don't bother. Lose my number, and if you see me in the streets, keep walking." She ended the call abruptly. *I'm so fed up with all these niggas. They all can kick rocks.* Tonya tossed her phone onto the passenger's seat and turned the music back up. "This my song!" she said, swaying back and forth to "Teach Me" by Musiq Soulchild, paying no attention to the green Denali that pulled up beside her at the red light: *I was told the true definition of a man was to never cry, work 'til you die, got to provide. Always be the rock for my fam, protect them by all means...*

In the midst of all her singing and all her emotions, the window of the SUV slowly came down. Mike had been beeping his horn the whole time, trying to get the driver's attention, assuming Azia was behind the wheel. Tonya was so caught up singing her heart out that she didn't realize this. The light turned green. Mike continued to follow. He dialed the number Azia had given him back at the bar earlier in the evening. But the music was blasting so loud that Tonya didn't hear the first couple of calls. Finally she snatched the phone from the passenger seat, scanned the caller ID, and answered.

When Mike heard Tonya's voice instead of Azia's on the other end of the line, he was confused. "Hey, Tonya, I was looking for Azia."

Tonya caught Mike's voice right away and snickered. "I guess you can say she's tied up at the moment."

"Are ya'll in the car together?"

"No! Didn't I say she was tied up?" she spat.

"Well, I'm following her right now. Who she in the car wit'?"

"You're following the wrong person." Tonya pulled to the corner at the next light and waited for Mike to pull over next to her. She rolled down the tinted window, revealing her dark skin. "How long have you been following me?"

"For a few blocks. I thought you were your girlfriend. Where she at?"

"She ain't here talking to you, is she?"

"Why you always got to get smart all the time? Act like a lady sometimes," he shot back.

"I'm grown. I can talk however I want, and you ain't gonna be the one to stop me."

"If I wanted to, I would, trust me. I'll make sure Juan handles that."

"What if I don't want Juan to handle it? What if I want you to handle it for him?"

Mike was caught off guard. He decided to play along to see where their conversation would go. "I can definitely handle it. I got something big enough to calm down all that lip action you got going on."

"Well, this is your chance to find out. I'm sure a grown-ass woman like me can handle all you got to give and more. I know you been wanting some of this sweet berry juice anyway," she smiled.

"What would ya girl have to say about this?"

"What Azia don't know won't hurt her." Tonya cut the lights, killed the ignition, climbed out of Azia's car, and hopped into Mike's without thinking twice. She was desperate to get a piece of the pie. This was a chance for her to sink her claws into something of Azia's. She wasn't about to let the opportunity pass her by.

Mike wondered if this was a test. Azia could have been trying to set him up, but he didn't care. Games are for children. Tricks are for kids. He was very much a grown man. "So where are we going?" he asked, waiting for a suggestion.

Tonya began to unbuckle his pants. "I don't know where we're going, but I know where I'm about to go." She placed her head in his lap and went to work.

It took Mike a moment to get focused. Tonya was working out full-time, swallowing every inch of him without gagging. It made him wonder if he'd been chasing after the wrong one. The traffic light had turned red, then green, twice before he pulled off. It took everything he had not to lose control of the wheel as he drove down the street to nowhere in particular. Fifteen minutes later, he exploded all over her face and down her throat.

"You taste good, baby," Tonya said, not missing a drop. She realized that the SUV wasn't moving. She looked around and saw that they were back where they started. "Why are we back here?"

"I told you I could shut you up. It was only for a little while, but I guess it gotta do for now," he smirked.

Tonya sat there looking confused, embarrassed, and insulted. She felt like a pice of bubble gum on the bottom of a shoe. And she was horny as hell. "What?!" Mike sat quietly, waiting for her to catch the hint and exit his ride. "You a sheisty-ass nigga. Fuck you!" She hopped out and slammed the door. Just before climbing back into Azia's car, she turned back to get her final words in. "I wonder what Juan and Azia are gonna have to say 'bout this, you no-good-ass nigga."

Mike noticed that she'd left her panties behind. She had taken them off to fondle herself while pleasing him. "They're gonna have a lot to say about your trifling ass." He flung her panties out the window of his Denali onto the ground. "Shut up and go rinse ya mouth out." He pulled off, leaving her behind. He was satisfied with what had just transpired. He figured if it was a test, he hadn't failed. All he had done was make it known that Tonya was just as phony as they came. He planned to play her cards and let Azia, as well as Juan, know what had gone down. If Azia couldn't handle it, that was on her. But he was sure that once Juan found out, it wouldn't be taken personally.

Tonya stormed to Azia's car. If she had slammed the door any harder, the window would have shattered. She hit the steering wheel repeatedly in a rage. "Why?! Why?! Why?!" she repeated. Tears streamed one after the other down her face. Jealousy had taken over leaving her in a place she didn't want to be in. Things had been so much different when both girls were playing men together. Now that Azia had found someone to take care of her the way they both had been wishing, it brought on envy. She had no true intentions of telling Azia or Juan about her rendezvous with Mike, and silently prayed that Mike didn't either.

She sped up Erie Avenue toward Broad, heading back to campus. As the minutes ticked by, she battled her inner thoughts. By the time she got from 23rd to 18th Street, her demeanor had changed. *Fuck it* was her new attitude. If anyone found out what she did to Mike, oh well. If she had to lose Azia as a friend, she would go find a new friend. If Juan cut her loose, it was nothing for her to go find some new dick. After thinking about it some more, she began to giggle to herself, not realizing she was no longer alone at the red light. Suddenly, a blast of gunfire filled the midnight air, making those feelings the last she would ever feel.

CHAPTER 4
Two's A Couple And Three's A Crowd
"Wrong place wrong time."
-Busta

Before the light could change to green, Busta unloaded his clip through the driver's side window of Azia's car. Once the tinted glass shattered, he caught a glimpse of the dark-skinned female behind the wheel. "Shit!" he exclaimed, hopping out of the car before anyone could arrive on the gruesome scene. *That ain't Azia*, he examined, inching in closer.

Busta was on his way to meet up with Rashaud to discuss another job when the familiar car crossed his path. He couldn't help but follow, thinking his luck couldn't have been any better. He knew it was Azia's Solara because of the custom-made license plate: My wish is your command. He followed the car for blocks, waiting for the right time to cut in and handle his business. He'd had it out for Azia for some time now and was tired of losing sleep over it. He deemed her a sheisty, no-good, gold-digging ho, out to get whatever she could get her hands on, no matter the stakes. It was time to lay her to rest so he and Rashaud could move on and let bygones be bygones. Unfortunately for him, it wasn't Azia's time. But from the looks of it, it was the time for her best friend.

Tonya was hunched over the steering wheel fighting for her life. Blood and glass filled the inside of the car and surrounding area. The sound of sirens coming closer and closer could be heard from afar. Although her death reflexes didn't force her foot on the accelerator, the car was slowly rolling toward the intersection.

Busta cursed himself over and over again after seeing he'd shot the wrong girl. Tonya's eyes were closed and he wasn't sure if she was still breathing. He panicked. "I thought you were Azia, baby girl. I can't let you live now. You're in the wrong place at the wrong time."

POW! He ended her life with a bullet to the head. He ran back to his car and sped away in the opposite direction of the sirens. The sound of screeching tires was all you heard.

■ ■ ■

Rashaud was sitting around a square-shaped table at Biggs' detail shop, also known as the chop block, a place to bring stolen cars. Biggs' establishment was growing by the day. There was always one hustler after the other bringing in hot cars to swap parts for some fast cash. They were discussing Rashaud's latest quest and the one he was trying to put together. Although Biggs was totally against his job ethics, he supported anything when it came to Rashaud. After Rashaud's father died and left Biggs in charge to look after his young son, he took him in as his own.

Rashaud arrogantly spoke his mind. "I'm me and you know I do whatever I got my heart set on doing, Biggs. I'm gonna hit that nigga Mike and that's that. Ain't no nigga untouchable, Biggs. You just gotta know how to maneuver around their position."

The heavyset, salt 'n' pepper-haired man took a seat in the chair beside Rashaud and crushed his cigar in the ashtray. "No offense. But you try to dip on a high roller like Mike, you better send him six feet under or ya ass better be prepared for whatever you got coming to you. It's all a part of the game. You live by the gun, best believe you gonna die by the gun." Biggs swore he saw fire in Rashaud's eyes. He was tired of trying to talk sense into the hard-headed street soldier. "Alright," he sighed. "I tried to talk you out of it, but I see this ain't going nowhere." He lit another cigar. "So what's up wit' this job you got going on tonight?"

"I'm waiting on my girl to call to give me the info. I wish that nigga Busta would come on. He ain't answering his phone." Rashaud snatched his cell from his waist to attempt to call Busta for the seventh time.

"Hold up! Back up a minute! You waiting on who to call? I know you ain't talking about that little schoolgirl. Are you crazy? Tell me how in the world you think she fits in wit' ya'll two crazy-ass niggas? Please tell me you got more sense than that."

Jumping to her defense, Rashaud leaped out his seat. "It was her idea! She know what she doing, I ain't worried about that. She's gonna be good at it too." With confidence, he slammed his fist into his chest and said, "I'ma teach her all she needs to know."

"You might be right, but where does that leave you? You got your woman out there whispering up in other niggas' ears and God knows what else so you can step in and rob 'em? That's not no grown man shit, Rashaud!" Biggs put two and two together. "Oh, I see. I guess she's the one that's gonna help you get close to Mike."

"Exactly!" confirmed Rashaud.

Biggs laughed. "Well, you know she ain't getting too close to him without giving up the pussy. Are you willing to let another man have a piece of your cake for a few extra dollars?"

Rashaud thought about it for a minute before shaking his head no. "She ain't giving it up to none of these fools." Thinking about her alone with their latest target became nerve-wracking. He called Busta's phone again but still got no answer. As soon as he hit the end button on his phone, a text came through from Azia.

DEL AVE-HYATT-O.M.W

Rashaud looked closely at the text, catching on quickly to the abbreviations. Azia and Mustafa were on their way down Delaware Avenue to the Hyatt hotel. He tried calling Busta one last time but got his voicemail. While gearing up, he said to Biggs, briefly, "If Busta come here, tell him to sit tight."

"Be careful out there, Rashaud. I hope you know what you're doing. Remember, these streets have mercy on no one."

"I hear that, old-timer. I gotta go, but I'll give you a call as soon as I get a chance."

■ ■ ■

Azia already had her game plan together. She was just hoping that when Rashaud and Busta came they'd be on point. Pulling into the parking lot, she scanned the area to see if, by any chance, Rashaud had beaten them there. Realizing that he hadn't, she thought quickly on her feet. When Mustafa hit the lock to the door, she discreetly unlocked the doors without his knowledge. With him being deeply involved on a business call left her a window of opportunity to do so. As soon as they arrived in the room she got comfortable and started to undress.

Mustafa ended his first call and was dialing another number to begin a new one. "I need something to drink. You want something from the machines?" Azia shook her head no. "Have that ass ready for me when I get back." He pushed the security lock out so the door wouldn't close all the way and stepped in the direction of the vending area.

Azia used that time to call Rashaud with some information. "Hey, where are you?" she asked in a panicky voice. "I'm at the Hyatt."

"I know. I'm about to pull up in a minute. Where that nigga at?"

"He stepped out for a minute. Hurry up, Rashaud. How you planning to do this?"

"Azia, just chill out and let me handle it. Get off the phone before that nigga come back and catch you."

She walked to the door to peep in the hall. "He ain't coming yet. Look, he drive a red Bentley, it got Florida tags. I left the doors open for you."

"Bet!" he exclaimed, glad she was making things a little easier for him. Rashaud planned to do a stake out in his car until Azia and Mustafa headed out, but this latest bit of information changed that plan. "You cool? You sure you wanna do this?"

"I'm here, ain't I? You just worry about—" She heard Mustafa's voice. "He's coming. See you soon." Azia tossed her Blackberry back into her Gucci bag and hopped in the bed like she'd been there the whole time.

Mustafa entered the room and locked the door. "Alright, I'll get witchu when I get back down in the dirty. One." He placed his phone on the nightstand beside the king-sized bed and looked over Azia's voluptuous body. His second head rose to attention immediately. "Damn, girl. Wit' a body like that, a nigga fin'a put a ring on your finger."

Mustafa was laying his thing down full force, showing Azia what a southern boy had to offer. They'd been getting it in for the last half hour, kissing, flipping, sweating, moaning, groaning, and everything else. Although he was making her kitty cat purr, she was sure to back up all the shit talking she'd done on the way to the hotel.

Damn—Uhh—Umm—could be heard clearly on the other side of the door and through the thin walls. She was sure she had never been in that many positions before. It felt so good she was ready to change her mind, just so she could have another dose of him when she needed it. Too bad Rashaud was already in play. "Cum for me baby," she purred like a kitten. Hearing her sweet, delicate voice and feeling the nibbling around his ear brought him to an orgasm he didn't know was possible. His eyes squeezed shut, each toe curled in a different direction, and his heart raced. Seconds later, he collapsed onto Azia's stomach, taking her sweaty breast into his mouth.

Minutes later, he was on his feet heading to the bathroom to wash off. With her back turned to the bathroom door, she grabbed her purse and sent Rashaud a text.

BE READY

She glanced over at the clock and realized it had been almost an hour and a half. *Shit. I hope he ain't mad. His ass probably crunched up in the back seat of that car cursing me out. Oh well. Ain't my fault the dick was too good to quit.*

Mustafa caught the smile on her face as he came from the bathroom. "What you grinning for?"

Azia smiled harder. "Maybe you were right. I got to give it to you. Maybe you do know how to handle a chick like me."

"For the most part. But I know there's more to you." He came in closer and gripped her ass cheeks in his palms. "You're gonna be my permanent Philly chick, the one that comes before all the others."

I can't believe this fool. He really got me twisted. "Ya Philly chick, huh? I guess you the type of nigga that got many hos in different area codes."

"None of that matters as long as you're taken care of. Just be glad I'm letting you get added to the list."

No mutherfucka, I'm adding you to my list. She perked her lips up like she was happy to be one of Mustafa's Angels. "I guess I can deal wit' that."

Azia was right. Rashaud was jammed up in the back seat of the car sweating like fien trying to kick the habbit. Thoughts of her upstairs having sex with Mustafa filled his mind the entire time. This aggravated him even more. He was ready to slump them both as soon as they got in. Hearing the sound of high heels clicking in his direction snapped him out of his daze. He clutched his gun with his sweaty palms waiting for the right time to move.

Mustafa hit the button to unlock the car door a few feet away from the car. When he didn't hear the usual *churp churp*, he tried hitting the button again. Nothing happened. Azia's heart raced a thousand miles a minute. Getting to the passenger's side before he got to the driver's side, she opened the door and said, "See, you were so tied up on that phone call, you forgot to lock the doors. Or was I the one that had you slipping?" she grinned.

Mustafa lost his focus. Azia made sure she deterred any suspicions. They climbed in together and Azia played with his ear to keep his attention away from the back seat. As soon as he turned the key in the ignition, he got the shock of his life.

"Don't move another fucking muscle," Rashaud ordered. Although Azia knew he was in the back, he still startled her. She almost jumped out of her seat. She held her hand across her heart and turned around.

"Damn, did you have to scare me like that?"

Mustafa turned and looked at her in total disbelief. Rashaud used the barrel of his gun to gently turn Mustafa's face back toward the front. "Didn't I say don't move?" Hearing the authority in his voice sent a rush of adrenaline through Azia's body. She had been scared at first, but now she was ready for whatever. "Drive out the parking lot and make a left. If you turn your head again to look at me or her, I'ma blow ya brains out."

Mustafa did as he was told. They took Delaware Avenue heading in the direction of the shipyard where Biggs' spot was located. The car was silent. The longer they drove, the more Azia had mixed thoughts about the whole thing. Rashaud, on the other hand, was furious. If the scene had been animated, steam would have been shooting from his ears. He mugged Mustafa with the gun and asked, "Was the pussy good? Was it worth losing your life?"

He shook his head no in response. Ignoring what Rashaud had previously told him, he looked over at Azia. "Fuck this trick-ass bitch. Her pussy ain't worth shit.' He gathered up a mouthful of saliva and spit on her.

Feeling disgusted and violated, Azia backhanded him with all of her might. She wiped the spit from the side of her face and rubbed it in his. "I can't wait to see you die."

Rashaud was enjoying the entertainment. Mustafa spitting on her was nothing compared to what he wanted to do to her for having sex with him. He pulled his cell out with his free hand and dialed Biggs' number. "We pulling up," he said before placing it back into his pocket. "Turn here." He directed Mustafa to a dirt-filled road. There were a lot of abandoned cars, car parts and junk scattered through the dimly lit lot. Azia's attention was focused on the sound coming from the garage door opening a little ways back. She had never been there before. There was a black, heavy, Biggie Smalls look-alike standing behind the garage door. He seemed very strange to her, but she dared not ask any questions at that moment. Azia hopped out of the car first.

"Alright, my man. Kill the engine and get out. Make sure you keep your hands where I can see them. Please don't make me use this. I really don't feel like getting no blood on me right now." Biggs stood on the outside of the driver's side door with his own heat at his hip. He stared the stranger down, waiting for him to make any sudden moves. Mustafa climbed out, eyeing Azia, then Biggs, then Rashaud as he climbed from the back seat. Rashaud led the way to the back of the garage into another room. It was dark, cold, and smelled like motor oil. Mustafa sat down in a wooden chair, awaiting the countdown to the end of his life.

"What you gonna do wit' him?" asked Azia.

Biggs looked over at her. "Baby girl, you did your job. Leave the rest of this to us." He didn't want to get her more involved than she had to be. Biggs was still mad at Rashaud for involving her in the first place, but didn't let it show. "Go ahead back up there into my office."

Azia cut her eye at Rashaud who was making her feel real awkward. "We made a stop on the way to the hotel. I'm sure whatever he put in his trunk will make you happy," she advised. Then she headed toward the office as Biggs had instructed, but she was stopped dead in her tracks by Rashaud.

"Don't go anywhere." He threw Biggs the keys to Mustafa's car. "Go find out what's in the trunk and let me know." Biggs had a bad feeling about what was about to go down. He curiously looked at Rashaud for answers but got none. Rashaud grabbed Azia by the waist and slid her over to his side. "Go handle that, Biggs." He aimed his weapon at Mustafa. "I'm tired of being in suspense. What's in the trunk?"

He answered without hesitation. "It's four kilos of coke and close to sixty thousand." Mustafa decided to use whatever breath he had left to proposition himself out of the predicament. "If you play this out right you can walk away wit' a lot more. All I ask is that you spare my life. I got over six—"

WOP! Rashaud cut him off with a blow to the face. Blood filled his nose and mouth splattering onto his white Armani shirt. "I'm asking all the questions here, and I'm making all the rules. I'm not in it for the long run, I'm in it for the moment. I ain't got time to try to pursue somebody to dish out some ransom for your ass. It's a one-shot deal wit' me, so you can kiss your life good-bye. Ain't that right, Azia?" He pushed Azia to the floor just inches away from Mustafa's feet.

Using that moment to his advantage, Mustafa gathered all the strength he could while sitting and sent a powerful kick to Azia's head. "That's for setting me up, you sheisty-ass whore." He followed the kick with a mouthful of bloody saliva.

That hadn't been part of Rashaud's plan. He watched Azia let out an agonizing scream. Biggs ran back to find out what could've possibly happened that fast. By the time he returned to room, the chair had been flipped over and Mustafa was flat on his back. Rashaud was over him, beating him half to death. Biggs helped Azia from the floor. Then he yelled for Rashaud to stop. Rashaud was on fire as he landed each blow. Then he grabbed Mustafa from the floor and said, "That's no way to treat a lady," as if he was a respectable white-collar gentleman. He smacked Mustafa upside the head like he was his child, then threw him back into the chair and badgered him with questions.

"Who's your connect out here?" Mustafa answered with silence. "Oh, you don't want to answer me, huh?" Rashaud grabbed Mustafa's hand and placed it firmly on the arm of the chair. Between breaths, he pointed to a hammer that was lying on the floor. "Pass me that shit." Biggs picked it up and tossed it to him. He flagged Azia over. "C'mere."

Her equilibrium was still off from the kick. She got herself together and staggered to Rashaud's side.

"Was this nigga better than me? Did he fuck you better than I do?" Azia shook her head no. "Ay! Stay wit' me," he said, smacking Mustafa's face to keep him focused. He was going in and out of consciousness. Rashaud grabbed his hand, holding it steady. He looked at Azia and asked, "Was this the hand he was grabbing ya ass wit'?"

Azia was baffled. She didn't know whether to say yes or no. *Is this a goddamn trick question?* she wondered.

"Is this the hand or what, Azia?" She nodded yes, praying the hammer in Rashaud's hand didn't connect with the side of her head. *BAM!* The hammer came down on Mustafa's fingers, breaking two of them. Mustafa bit down on his lip trying to take it like a soldier. "Now, I'ma ask you one more time. Who's your connect down here?"

"Fuck—you—mutherfucka," he slurred.

The hammer came down again, this time on his other hand. Mustafa yelled out in pain. "Who the fuck's the connect?" he asked again pulling his heat from his waist. Mustafa didn't give Mike up. If there was one thing he wasn't, it was a snitch.

Rashaud put his gun in Azia's hand and asked if she would do anything for him. She looked him in his eyes and replied, "You know I would."

Biggs stood in the corner about to witness a point of no return. This is what he didn't want to see happen. Azia was about to be stained with the mark of blood. "Don't make her do it," begged Biggs. "C'mon man, think about this." The wise man knew that once Azia pulled that trigger, it would drain all the purity left in her soul.

Rashaud ignored him. "If you riding wit' me like you say you is, go ahead and lay this nigga to rest."

Azia took one look at Mustafa. All the bruises and blood had her shaken. She thought back to Rashaud holding Mudda's head in his hand. Then she recalled the kick from Mustafa, which sent her into a rage. Without ever having any target practice, she let one shot loose. It landed smack into the side of his neck. Seeing the blood gush out made her sick to her stomach. Mustafa didn't go down right away. He grabbed the side of his neck and gasped for air. Azia panicked. She released her grip on the gun and it fell to the floor. Biggs silently shook his head, wishing she had never been involved. Rashaud picked the gun up from the floor and put two shots in Mustafa's face, taking him out his misery.

Showing no emotion at all about everything that had just happened, Rashaud ordered, "C'mon. Call the cleanup team so we can get this faggot out of here."

CHAPTER 5
Like The Saying Goes: Life Must Go On
"One day you'll realize it pays to be more smart than careful."
-Biggs

The sound of a jackhammer out in the street awakened Azia the following morning. Her stomach was in knots. She was sure it was because of last night's tragic event. She attempted to climb out of bed, but fell back down onto it in an uncontrollable crying spell. A few minutes later, she scrambled to her feet and found the strength to drag herself out of the room.

Rashaud was sitting in the living with his eyes focused on the television. He was so into the latest news on Channel 10 that he didn't realize he was no longer alone. Azia called out his name three times before getting an answer. "Go lay back down. I'll be in there in a minute." He clicked the TV off and headed for the kitchen.

His behavior was strange. Seeing that he was watching the news, she assumed the police had found Mustafa's body. "What's the news talking bout?"

"Nothing! Go wait for me in the room, I said."

Azia sucked her teeth and stomped off like a third-grader.

Rashaud had been on the phone all morning trying to find out what the hell had happened to Tonya the night before. When the call came in from Biggs, he was floored. He was trying to get as much information as possible so that when he relayed the news to Azia, he could be ready for whatever questions she had.

He was a little too late. Rashaud dropped his chin to his chest when he heard Azia screaming his name from the bedroom. She ran to the kitchen where he was. Wings couldn't have gotten her there any quicker. "Rashaud! Oh my God! Tonya! They shot her! Oh my God! Somebody killed Tonya!" She lost all feeling in her legs and hit the floor.

Rashaud pulled her up and secured her in his arms. "I told you to wait for me, Azia. Why did you have to go and cut the TV on?"

"Who would do this to her? Who would want to kill her?" she cried.

"Somebody shot your car up. I don't know who, but I'll find out. Don't worry about it. Go get yourself together." Azia ran off into the bathroom and slammed the door. *Damn, who the fuck would kill that girl?* Rashaud questioned himself. He got back on his cell and called one of his sources. "Ay, Stutter-man. You got anything on that shooting last night?"

"Rashaud, wa—was—ss—up? I—I—can—can't believe th—they ki—ki—"

Rashaud cut in. "C'mon, Stutter-man, spit that shit out."

"—killed that girl." He forced the words out. "I heard it wa—wa—was a hit."

Rashaud was at a loss for words. "A hit? Who the hell would have a hit out on her? I know she ain't fuck nobody over that deep to risk her life."

"I do—don't know. I'll ke—keep my ears open for you."

"Alright, make sure you call me as soon as you get any more information." Rashaud slid his phone onto the countertop and went to make sure Azia was okay. "Open the door," he demanded. He knocked several times but got no answer in return. The water from the shower could be heard. "Azia!" he continued to bang. "Let me in!" When no response came he got worried. He went to grab a knife from the kitchen drawer and picked through the unsteady lock on the bathroom door. Rashaud couldn't believe his eyes when he opened the door.

Azia was slouched over the tub in her panties and bra. Beside her was an empty bottle of Tylenol she had washed down before falling out. He quickly checked for a pulse. *Good, she's still breathing.* He examined her body briefly and scooped her up from the floor. "Azia, talk to me," he said, smacking her cheeks. She was fading in and out of consciousness but never said a word. Swiftly, he slid the closest piece of clothing, which was a long, silk nightgown, over her head, grabbed the keys to his car, and rushed out the door. There were plenty of people begging to help as he ran through the lobby with Azia in his arms. "Did you call an ambulance? Is she still alive? Is she breathing?" bystanders were yelling.

"Just open the fucking door for me," he snapped. Waiting for an ambulance wasn't an option. By the time one arrived, they'd be hitting the emergency room doors.

Lankenau Hospital was a few blocks away from their apartment. As soon as Rashaud pulled into the lot like a madman, he captured the attention of a paramedic team that was outside the emergency entrance. They rushed over, placed Azia on a stretcher, and hurried her inside, checking her vitals on the way. Rashaud ran beside them until one of the nurses stopped him and said, "This is the farthest you can go, sir."

Unnerved about what would happen next he advised, "She took a whole bottle of pills. Go pump that shit out of her."

The nurse looked offended. "They'll do whatever they can, sir. You can have a seat in the waiting area." She ran into the room to inform the doctors.

Two hours later, Rashaud still hadn't heard anything. He'd been sitting around blaming himself. If Azia died on that hospital table, it would be partly his fault. She had already been stressed out about what he'd made her do to Mustafa. She tossed and turned the entire night because of it. Tonya's murder was the thing that sent her over the edge. He pulled his cell from his waist to see who was calling. Seeing that it was Busta, he got up from his seat and took a walk out front to keep the rest of the waiting room out of his business. "Where the fuck you been? I been calling you since last night," he answered, livid.

"I had some shit I had to handle," replied Busta.

"You coulda answered my calls, Dawg. What if I had been in some shit?"

"My bad, Rashaud. I said I had some shit to handle. Now what the fuck is up?"

He brought his tone down a notch. "Ain't shit up. I'm up at Lankenau. Azia threw back some pills and passed the fuck out. They should be in there tryna pump it out of her or something."

Hearing that gave Busta a little bit of hope. If she died on the table, that would be one less headache for him. "Damn, she tried to off herself? What the doctors saying?"

"I don't know. I'm 'bout to head back in there now. Did you hear anything about her girlfriend getting laid out last night?"

Like he was a nun in a convent, he responded without blinking. "I heard what happened, but I ain't heard nothing extra. That was some foul shit that happened to her. You ain't heard no rumors yet?" Busta was trying to get any information possible. Although he had scanned the area for witnesses before he left the scene, being in the rush he was in left a possibility for anything.

"Last I heard it was a hit. I'm waiting on Stutter-man to get back at me. We'll link up later so I can give you the latest on last night."

"What I miss?"

"Ya ass went MIA on a nigga. Whether you wanna hear it or not, my girl was there to ride wit' me. You already know I ain't saying too much over these lines, so I'll get with you later. Let me go check on my folk."

When the nurse realized Rashaud had returned, she flagged him over to the nurse's station. "I just wanted to let you know she pulled through. What's your relation?"

Seeing where the nurse was going with this, Rashaud became annoyed. "She's a friend."

"I'm going to need any information you can give: name, address, social security number, and any insurance information, if you have that."

"Is she talking?"

"No, not yet. They pumped all they could from her stomach. She was dehydrated, so she's hooked up to a couple of IVs to get her up and running again. Do you have any of the information I named?"

"I'm asking questions about her health and you're worried about getting paid. What type a shit you on?"

"It's policy, sir. There's no need for you to get out-of-pocket with me."

"Whatever," he flagged. "Just let me know when I can see her."

As he walked away, the nurse blurted out, "Can I at least have her name?"

Rashaud turned back and said sarcastically, "Jane Doe."

After waiting another half hour, he climbed to his feet to go grab a snack from the vending machine. Coincidentally, he ran into an old friend from around the way. When they got to talking, the female nurse volunteered to escort him to the room where Azia was being held. He planted his feet beside her bed and caressed her hand. "Baby girl, are you okay?"

Azia's head was pounding. She recalled the pain from the doctors pumping her stomach. "I gotta throw up," she slurred. Rashaud grabbed the small, pink tray from the table and held it close to her. She coughed up all that was left in her stomach. "I can't believe I did that to myself. What was I thinking?" she huffed.

"I don't know what the hell you were thinking. You better come up wit' an alias, 'cause if you give them your real information, not only are they gonna bill ya ass up, you might get some people knocking at your door thinking you all suicidal and shit."

She saw the truth in what he was saying. "I wanna go home."

"Well, let's get out of here then. I hate the smell of hospitals."

Against doctor's orders, Rashaud helped her climb out of bed and get dressed. One of the nurses ran in after noticing that the heart monitor had stopped beeping. "Maam, I don't think it's a good idea for you to leave right now."

"I want to go lay in my own bed," she whined.

"I understand that, but—"

Rashaud butted in. "Well, it ain't up to you is it?"

The nurse focused her attention on him. "If you were any kind of friend you would be advising her of the same. She needs to get some rest."

Trying to avoid a confrontation between the two, Azia pleaded, "Just let me know what you need so I can leave, please."

After speaking with the doctor, the nurse came back with some papers and told Azia they couldn't keep her against her will. "I know you can't," said Rashaud, arrogantly. "I can't stand these damn hospitals."

"Rashaud, please be quiet." Azia took the papers from the nurse's hand and looked them over. She filled in all the blanks with incorrect information. Taking Rashaud's advice, she gave a phony last name, address, social security number, and anything else she had to give. "Is this all you need?" she asked, handing the papers back over. Then the nurse gave her some discharge papers, which advised her on what to eat and drink, and how much rest she was going to need until she was back to normal.

A few hours after they arrived back at the apartment, Rashaud was tired of sitting in the house. He grabbed the Pier 21 seafood menu from off the refrigerator and went into the bedroom where Azia was resting. He shook her gently. "I'm 'bout to go grab a bite to eat. You want something?"

"Just grab me whatever." She rolled back over in bed where she stayed for the rest of the night. "Bring me back some painkillers, too. 'Cause we out, and my body is killing me."

"Whose fault is that?" he asked, before leaving the room.

Rashaud graced the streets of Philly in his Cadillac, a car he drove very seldom. He politicked with a few people around the way before meeting Busta over at Biggs' detail shop. He couldn't wait to give him the latest and find out why all his calls went unanswered.

"Get the fuck out of here," said Busta, sitting back and listening to Rashaud's story.

"I'm telling you that's how it went. Ask Biggs," he said, pointing over to where Biggs was seated.

All three men were laughing, joking, and passing words back and forth. "Don't ask me nothing," warned Biggs. "I wish you had been here to talk some sense into this young whipper-snapper," he said to Busta.

"Aw, come on, old man. You know when I black out I'm liable to do anything."

"That can get you hurt in the long run. You better slow down before it's too late, boy."

"Why you always have to talk to me like I'm one of these youngens that don't know how to get the job done? No matter what I do or how I do it, the job always gets done."

"Kinfolk," Biggs began, "Sometimes it pays to listen before you talk, like you know every damn thing. I done tried to school you for years now, but you always gotta take a detour and do things your way. One day you're going to realize that it pays to be more smart than careful. Think about what I'm saying," suggested Biggs, tapping the side of his temple with his fat finger.

Busta sat quietly. He looked from one to the other as they exchanged words. His body was there, but his mind was on the other side of town. He was wondering what the latest news was about Tonya's killing. Just as he was thinking about it, Rashaud's cell began to dance across the wooden table.

"Hey Stutter-man. Hope you got some news for me," he said. He didn't care much about Tonya, but his girl was hurting inside, which was hard for him to swallow. If he could get revenge on whoever did this, he figured it would show Azia how down he was for her.

He stumbled over his words. "I—I—a—ain't heard noth—nothing yet."

"Well, what the hell you calling me for then, Stutter-man? I said call back when you find out some more info, not when you felt like it."

"I kno—know, Ra—Ra—Rashaud, but I ha—had to tell you s—s—some—thing else. I—I—I—"

Frustrated that it was taking Stutter-man so long to say what he was trying to say, Rashaud hung up in the middle of their conversation. He threw the phone back onto the table. "Shhh … it take that nigga a damn hour to tell a five-minute story."

Giggles filled the room after the comment.

"He heard anything yet?" asked Busta.

"No, he ain't heard shit. Just calling me to be calling me like I ain't got nothing better to do but listen to his stuttering ass all night." Rashaud hopped up from the table and brushed the wrinkles from his shirt. "Let me go pick up this food before Azia start blowing my phone up."

"That bitch is crazy," Busta remarked. "Ay, Biggs. Did Rashaud tell you homegirl tried to kill herself?"

Rashaud was pissed that Busta had opened his mouth. He had decided to keep that part away from Biggs to avoid any of his lectures. Sensing that Biggs was about to blame him for Azia's actions, he stepped closer toward the door with his hand up. "I'm not even tryna hear it, Biggs. That shit ain't on me. I ain't make her take them pills."

Biggs remained humble. "I ain't got to tell your sorry ass that it's on you because I'm sure you already know. That damn girl done gone wild. I hope you ain't leave no rope in the house," he joked.

"She was hit wit' a lot at once that's all. She good now; we had a long talk."

"About what? How she was fucking that nigga while you were bawled up in the back of that small-ass Bentley?" Biggs knew his comment would hit a sensitive spot but he didn't care. He wanted Rashaud to realize that all fast money ain't good money.

Rashaud never let them see him sweat. He sparked his blunt, inhaled deeply and exhaled slowly. "She was in there fucking him so her man could come up. I'm good wit' that," he lied. All that did was open up a can of worms for Azia. Because of the Tonya incident, he hadn't had the chance to deal with her yet. But he made a mental note not to forget.

"Whatever, nigga," flagged Busta. "I know you better than that. You straight up loving that ho."

"Watch ya mouth, Busta. I'm not gonna keep telling you that shit either." Rashaud exited the shop with no good-bye to either one of them. He sat in his car for a few minutes before pulling off, thinking about how he wanted to deal with the situation. *ERRRR!* He pulled off hastily, leaving a cloud of dirt in the air.

Biggs stood at the garage door shaking his head in disappointment. He turned back to Busta who had opted to stick around. "What's up wit' ya boy? Sounds like he loosing focus out there."

Busta replied, "Pussy is what happened to him."

Biggs chuckled to himself. "Keep an eye on him for me. The nigga is definitely slipping," the wise man ordered before exiting the room, leaving Busta alone.

Rashaud sped across town to pick up the seafood he ordered. Something in his gut was telling him to call Stutter-man back. Before he got the chance he was distracted by an incoming call. "Who this?" he answered, not bothering to look at the ID.

"Yo, Rashaud, where you at?" a deep voice yelled on the other end, overpowered by music blasting in the background.

"Where *you* at, nigga?"

"Over at the spot. Come through."

"I'm 'bout to head in man, I'll get at you tomorrow."

"It's some bad bitches out here—"

On his way to Pier 21, Rashaud purposely rode through the neighborhood to see if Stutter-man was around. When he spotted him, he said, "Yo, I gotta go handle something. I'll link up wit' you tomorrow." He ended the call, pulled to the side of Watkins Street, and hopped out of the car, dapping all the bystanders gathered around an ongoing crap game. "Stutter-man, let me holla at you for a minute."

He and Stutter-man walked off around the corner to talk in private.

"It sounded like you had something to tell me earlier. Wassup?"

Stutter-man hesitated before responding. "Ra—Rashaud, you tol—told me to le—let you know if I hea—heard anything else."

"And you said you didn't. So wassup?" Rashaud stood with his eyes glued on Stutter-man's.

"I—I didn't kno—know who was arou—around you," he spat.

"What the fuck you got to say? Spit that shit out and stop beating around the bush! You making a nigga impatient right now!"

Stutter-man took a step back. "I heard Bus—Busta mighta ha—had some—something to do wi—wit' that girl get—getting kil—killed."

"What, nigga? Is you tripping? Busta?"

Seeing that Rashaud's hands had become fists, Stutter-man raised his hands in defense. "Yo—you sa—said wha—whatever I hea—heard. I—I'm just the mess-messenger."

In the blink of an eye, Rashaud's hands were around Stutter-man's neck. "You about to be a dead messenger. Are you fucking wit' me, Stutter-man?"

Stutter-man was terrified. Gasping for air, he found a breath to speak. "No, man. I—I woul—wouldn't do that. I was just try—tryna help you fig—figure this shit out."

Rashaud pulled his gun from his waist and put it directly on Stutter-man's temple. The pressure of the barrel forced his head to the side. "Who told you that?" Stutter-man was scared to reply. "Nigga, I asked you who told you that?"

Stutter-man answered when he heard the loud click of the gun being cocked. "TOMMYTOLDMEITWASBUSTA." That was the first time Rashaud had heard Stutter-man speak an entire sentence without stuttering.

Rashaud released Stutter-man and put his weapon away. He knew exactly who Tommy was and couldn't stand him one bit. The only reason he was still breathing was because he was Busta's cousin. "Don't repeat that shit to nobody. Do you understand me?" Rashaud threatened.

Stutter-man raised his hand to the sky. "You got my word, Rashaud."

Rashaud couldn't help but giggle, realizing he had scared the stutter out of him. "I would've been scared your punk ass if I knew it would make you talk better."

Stutter-man stood expressionless, not finding the situation funny at all.

"Aww, you know I wasn't gonna kill you. Straighten your face," he said, patting him on the back.

The stutter was back. "Yo—you had a nig—nigga scared Ra—Rashaud. Damn!"

"Man up!" Rashaud said as they headed back around the corner. Then he hopped into his car and glanced back at Stutter-man who was making his way back to the crap game. "Nobody!" Stutter-man agreed by nodding his head.

■ ■ ■

Azia tossed and turned in bed, dreaming flashes of Tonya. She popped up in a cold sweat, realizing she'd napped longer than she'd meant to. Just as she attempted to climb from the bed, her cell phone rang. The name on the ID was shocking. It was her cousin Keemah who she hadn't spoken to for almost three months. "Hello," she answered humbly.

"Hey, Azia," Keemah said. Hearing her cousin's voice made her realize how much she had missed her.

Azia was fighting to hold back the tears. Hearing Keemah's voice had her choked up along with everything else going wrong in her life. "Keemah, I'm so glad you called. I was just asking Kia about you."

"I know, she gave me your number. I wanted to check on you. I heard what happened to your friend."

Knowing Keemah didn't care too much for Tonya she appreciated the call. The fight was over. She cried out to her cousin. "I can't believe somebody would do that to her. What if it had been me in that car, Keemah? I would be the one dead right now."

"Don't think like that. It wasn't you. It's sad that it had to happen to her, but I don't know what I would've done if it had been you," Keemah cried along with her.

"I miss you so much. Why did you have to let a nut-ass nigga come between us? It's so much going on right now you know nothing about. My life would be so much different if you were around."

"Don't start pointing fingers, Azia. Why don't you come out wit' me and have a drink. I know all you've been doing is staring at the walls. They gotta be closing in on ya ass," she joked.

"I'm not coming out. Them streets is rugged right now. Ain't nobody playing fair no more. I tried to kill myself. I don't want to be here anymore. I'm ready to call it quits."

Cutting her off, Keemah commanded, "Slow up, Azia, dayum! What the hell you mean you tried to kill yourself? Please tell me you're fooling wit' me." Azia continued to cry. "Come on now! I know that was your girl, but you gotta charge it to the game until we find out what happened. You know the drill." Quickly changing the subject, Keemah continued. "Wassup wit' the dude you been dealing wit'? I know he's looking out for you, right?"

"I guess so," Azia whined. She climbed from the bed and cut the light on. She rummaged around the room looking for some painkillers to relieve the headache that had her head thumping. She accidentally pushed some papers off the dresser. They floated to the floor and slid up under the dresser. She dropped down on all fours to retrieve them and noticed a piece of wood separated from the wall. *What the hell?* "Hold on, Keemah," Azia said, placing the phone down.

She jumped to her feet and used all of her might to push the dresser out from the wall. Her eyes widened and her mood lightened when she saw all the money hidden in what was supposed to have been a secret hiding place. Without touching or counting it, her eyes estimated that there had to be a half-million, if not more. Her spirits lifted. *So this is where that nigga keeps it at. Now I know.* She put the piece of wood back into place so Rashaud wouldn't suspect she'd found it. She slid the dresser back into place and put the phone back to her ear.

Azia never had the chance to go into detail about all the changes she'd been through in the months they'd been apart. When she heard the front door shut, she ended the call recommending that they get together the following day to discuss it more.

Rashaud was in the living room on his cell phone wrapping up a call. She flopped down on the sofa next to him and grabbed the bag from the table. "I'm getting tired of seafood."

Rashaud responded without looking her way. "You hungry, right?" She shot him a disappointed look. He snatched the bag from her hand. "Give it here, I'll eat it."

She snatched the bag back and dug in. "Whose house you talking 'bout buying?"

"You listening in on my calls now?"

"No! When I walked up, I heard you." She rolled her eyes. "You really have been tripping lately."

Rashaud's vibrating cell phone stopped him from saying what was on the tip of his tongue. After he answered the call, his demeanor changed and he started fidgeting in his seat. Azia could hear a female's voice raving on the other end. Baffled by his unusual behavior, she sucked it all in, acting as if she couldn't hear. *That's exactly why I be fucking around on ya ass.*

Rashaud angrily closed his phone and jumped to his feet. "I gotta go. I might be back tonight, I might not."

This nigga is really tripping. "What the hell you mean you might be back and you might not?"

"Exactly what I said." He tossed her a bottle of painkillers. "As long as you got them you'll be cool." He went into the bedroom to grab something out of the closet, and then walked back into the living room. Azia was still seated in the same position. "What are you staring at me like that for? You need to be glad I'm stepping off instead of breaking ya face for fucking that nigga. If you want me to do that instead, I can." He approached her quickly. Azia flinched. "I'm starting to believe you like it when I whip your ass."

"Just go ahead, Rashaud. All of a sudden you want to act crazy. You ain't mad because I fucked that nigga. You tryna make a way out for you to go tie up some loose ends wit' whoever that bitch was on the phone. I'm not stupid."

He laughed. "Try to make it through the night, Azia." He turned and headed out the door.

She flagged him on his way thinking, *to hell with him.* She didn't have the strength to chase him down. She wasn't even concerned with who he was going to see. There were a lot more important things on her mind. She went to take a hot shower and called it a night. She couldn't have guessed what the next few days would bring.

■ ■ ■

The turnout for Tonya's funeral was small, but it was beautiful. A lot of her classmates from school came, as well as distant family members and friends. Azia made her way to the podium to give her dearest friend a good-bye speech. She'd beaten herself up for the argument they'd had the night Tonya died. Tonya's life being taken away from her before they had the chance to settle their differences was eating Azia up inside.

There wasn't one dry eye left in the room by the time Azia finished. Tonya would truly be missed. Just as Azia was hugging Tonya's parents and giving them her condolences, Mike walked up.

He greeted her with a hug. "Hey, precious," he smiled. "How are you feeling?"

"I'm doing better as the days go by. I'ma miss my girl. You know she was my partner in crime." They laughed in unison. "Did you come alone?"

He pointed behind him. "Naw. Juan in the back waiting on me. I just wanted to make sure you were cool before I stepped off."

A smile spread across her face. "I'm glad to know I still cross your mind."

"You cross my mind a lot, no doubt. It would've been nice if you had given me your number instead of Tonya's the last time I seen you."

Busted, Azia was speechless. "Well—"

Mike cut her short. "Before you hit me wit' all the lame-ass excuses, don't worry about it. I'm cool. Ain't no hard feelings." Mike chuckled. "But I was cursing ya ass out when I heard Tonya's voice instead of yours."

"You know what? Since I no longer have Tonya to answer for me, I guess I gotta give you the correct information this time."

"That's only if you want me to have it."

Mike was so smooth it made her melt. She reached for his phone, added her number to his contacts, and told him she'd be waiting on his call. "I'll talk to you sooner than later, hopefully."

"I got you, sweetie. Take care of yourself." He bent his tall frame down and laid a kiss on her forehead.

Azia watched as he walked off, looking finer than she remembered. The family finished viewing Tonya's body for the last time, the casket was closed, and the pallbearers led the way out the door. Azia stepped aside to let them through, wishing she could hug her friend one last time. She headed to her car to join the funeral procession with all the other cars on their way to the gravesite for the burial. All the way there, thoughts of Mike crossed her mind. One came after the other. She envisioned him all over her. She imagined what life would be like with them living together and starting a family. Then she thought about Rashaud and knew it would never happen as long as he was alive.

Suddenly the images in her mind changed. Her previous visions of a happy life with Mike ended. Now she was visualizing him tied up to the same chair Mustafa was sitting in before he met his maker. Everything that had happened to him was now happening to Mike. Azia closed her eyes for a moment and shook her whole body trying to get rid of the image. The last thing she wanted to do was set Mike up for the kill. How was she going to get out of a situation like this? How was she going to convince Rashaud to leave whatever gripe he had with him alone? In her mind, there was only one way to play this whole thing out: Get close enough to Mike to gain his trust and confidence. Once she got that, she could turn the tables on Rashaud and live out her dream with the street king.

CHAPTER 6
Because I'm A Go-Gette
"Don't let nobody steal your joy."
-Mike

Azia and Keemah were sitting in Copabanana sipping on blue margaritas, eating some Spanish fries, and laughing the night away. They were catching each other up on everything they'd missed while they weren't speaking. Azia ran down everything from school to her Tylenol overdose. "I miss you so much," she said, wrapping her arms around her cousin.

"I was thinking about calling you but I didn't want to be the one to give in first," admitted Keemah. She stuffed two fries into her mouth and smirked.

"You so petty, you stinking wench. So who you go to AC wit' the other night?"

"Some fool that thought taking me down there to watch him gamble was going to be exciting for me. Shit, I wanted to gamble myself but his cheap ass ain't bother to give me any money to blow. He had the nerve to say I was bad luck because he lost all his money at the Blackjack table."

Azia laughed. "Better be glad he ain't leave you down there to find your own way home. You would've been a walking ass." Both girls laughed in unison. Then Azia said, "I can't believe Tonya's gone. What if I had been driving? What if we had been in the car together?"

"I gotta ask, Azia. Have you pissed anyone off bad enough to make them come after you?"

"No! Listen. You know how I do. A nigga throw me a little bit of money and I throw him a little bit of pussy in return. No strings attached."

"You and Mudda got awfully close. He was more than just a sponsor to you. You caught feelings for him."

Azia disagreed. "I did not. I played him closer than the others because he was doing more for me than they were. No more, no less."

"Did you cry when you found out he was dead?"

"What kind of question is that?"

"He was taking care of you. You had to be mad he wasn't gonna be slinging that money your way anymore. I'm sure his wife's not going to pick up where he left off."

Thinking back to the night she approached Mudda's wife made her chuckle. "Girl, let me tell you," she began, telling Keemah the story.

Keemah sat with her hand up to her mouth in disbelief. "Are you serious? You crazy for that one." She took down the rest of her drink. "If she would've got her big ass out the car to fight, you would've pissed in your pants."

"You know I ain't never been no punk," advised Azia.

After pausing their conversation to check out some nice-looking guys entering the building, Keemah came forth with the question she'd been dying to ask. "I heard you left Star Track wit' Mustafa the other night."

Azia was glad she had already guzzled her drink down before hearing Mustafa's name. If she hadn't it would've been all over her and Keemah. "Damn, who was stalking me?" she asked jokingly.

Thinking quick on her toes, Keemah came up with a lie. "You know Kia don't miss nothing. She said you hopped into his Bentley after he tossed some money up on the hood of your car."

"That bitch is nosy. What she come telling you for?"

Keemah shrugged. "I don't know. We got to talking about how the turnout was and who left wit' who." The lies slid off her tongue like they were rehearsed.

"Yeah, we went to the hotel and got it in." Azia tried her best to remain casual. "I gotta say, them southern boys know how to lay the pipe."

Keemah gave a phony smile. She wanted to dig for more details but didn't want to push for too much information at once. Her real reason for coming back into Azia's life wasn't because she missed her, it was for two reasons and two reasons only. The first reason was that she needed information on Mustafa's disappearance. The guy she had been in AC wit' wasn't really the fool she was making him out to be. He was actually her latest lover and Mustafa's twin brother. After finding out that Azia was the last person to see him alive, he was determined to find out what had happened and if she had been involved in any way. He didn't plan on returning to the South until he did. Keemah's second reason was payback. Azia had gone behind her back and stolen the first man she'd ever truly loved, and then she threw him away like it was nothing. Although she was acting as if the whole ordeal had been forgiven, she hadn't forgotten. Satisfaction would be hers by the time she was finished with Azia.

"Come on, Azia. Ride over wit' me to Annette's house. They got a Spades game going on over there tonight. I feel like busting some ass."

Azia frowned. The last time they went over there together they almost got into it with a couple North Philly girls. "Hell no, I ain't going over there wit' them ghetto-ass people. I know the damn house is filled wit' smoke and drunk-ass niggas that don't know how to hold their liquor."

"Come on, Azia," Keemah whined. I feel like hanging out tonight. I know you ain't ready to go in the house no way. I know them blue margaritas got you feeling nice right now." Azia smirked. "Am I lying, ho?"

Azia sucked her teeth. "Let me run down to Unica and grab a sweatsuit. I need to be in something more comfortable in case I gotta whip a bitch ass."

The girls headed out of Copabanana. As usual, the sidewalks on South Street were filled with people walking, chit-chatting, flirting, sightseeing and shopping in all the surrounding stores. Anything you wanted or needed was available all around that area, from cheesesteaks to Gucci shoes. It was a well-known hot spot for tourists.

On their way to the store, Keemah had an idea. "You ain't got to buy nothing new. We can stop by your house on the way over there if you want to."

Azia thought for a moment. The No. 1 rule Rashaud made clear before moving her in was not to allow anyone to know where they lay their heads at night. Family or no family, she wasn't about to disregard his wishes. "Why would we drive all the way up City Line Avenue and then turn around and come all the way back down to North Philly? What the hell are you thinking?"

She wasn't thinking. Her intentions were to find out where Azia and Rashaud were shacking up at. "It was just a thought. Shit, I was tryna save you a couple dollars."

"Don't worry about me saving nothing 'cause I got it to spend."

I bet you do, bitch. One of these days you gonna reap what you sow, you conceited trick. Keemah was careful not to let her true feeling slip out. She rolled her eyes discreetly as they jogged across the street. "Just get what you gonna get and come on. I'm ready to ride out."

The small brick house on 33rd and Susquehanna Avenue looked exactly as Azia had visualized it. The loud music could be heard a block away, before they even got to the front door. There were people hanging around outside, sparking blunts and popping bottles. The scent of liquor mixed with marijuana smoke and sweat was in the air. A couple guys looked up from the dice game they had going on the front porch. "Bring ya fine ass over here to daddy," one said, while another hollered, "Fuck ya'll niggas! Give me my money! I'm going inside wit' their fine asses!"

Keemah recognized one of them. She replied, "Come on in. Let's see how well Sarah handle you chasing after some new pussy," referring to his girlfriend.

The guy suddenly changed his mind. "You ain't got to put a nigga on blast like that! I was just fucking wit' ya'll!"

"Yeah, I bet you were."

Finally entering the house, the girls were not surprised to see three different card games going on. They approached the table where Annette was seated to greet the host. She wasn't hard to find at all. She was the loudest one in the whole house. The more she drank, the louder she became. "Let me find out you got another diamond in your hand and I'm taking three books!" she yelled across the table to her opponent. She looked at her hand and then at her partner before throwing out the big joker to win the next book. Her opponent won the next two hands. Then Annette and her partner won the last two books. She jumped from her seat so fast her chair flipped over. "I told ya'll niggas ya'll can't fuck wit' us! That's right, partner!" she said, giving her homegirl a high-five while dancing in place. "Next!" she taunted, grabbing the money pot.

Azia and Keemah stood back against the wall, giggling at their friend. "Annette!" Keemah shouted. "Bring ya excited ass over here!"

"What ya'll bitches doing here?" She gave them both hugs and passed over two bottles of a Bacardi Silver blend. "Ya'll missed all the action. Mookie got his ass kicked earlier by some dudes from the bottom. They came out here deep as hell looking for him." The girls' eyes widened in anticipation. "He thought I was supposed to let him hide out in my house. I told him to get the hell out, 'cause if they would have busted down my damn door, I would have been added to his list of problems."

"Why were they after him?"

"He flaunting around here like he king of the castle and these streets is his. They showed him just how much of a king he really was." Annette noticed someone about to sit in the seat where she had just won the game. "Get ya ass up 'cause I won, nigga. You better tell one of them to get up." She walked away before she could finish the story, not wanting to lose her spot in the next game.

Keemah stepped away for a minute to take a call while Azia took a seat at one of the open tables. "How much is in the pot?" she asked, staring at the other three that were already seated."

The female sitting directly across from her turned her nose up to the ceiling. "I got a partner already."

"I ain't ask you that. What I asked was how much was in the pot." Azia scanned the area to see if there was anyone waiting for her to get out their seat but there wasn't. "As far as I can see, your partner ain't nowhere to be found."

An angry, fat man at the table butted in. "Just play the damn game and stop acting like a snob," he told the girl, mad that he had just lost five hundred dollars in the last game they played. "The pot is up to twelve hundred. You got your three?" he huffed.

Azia pulled out five twenties and two hundred-dollar bills. "Throw in your money if you playing. If not, raise the fuck up from the table." She and the girl eyed one another briefly. That was the way you had to talk in a game like that. If you came into a place like that without the right mentality, you were destined to get played. "Are you gonna help me win this money or what?"

Hesitant, the girl took half of her winnings and threw it into the pot. The deal was on Azia and the game began. "First hand bids itself, right?" she asked. The fat man nodded his head yes.

Clubs led. Azia took the first book with an ace. Then hearts led with her partner taking the next book with a king. They won the next three books after that. The fat man became annoyed with his partner who was making stupid plays. There was a lot of shit-talking being yelled across the table by all four players. When Azia realized that she and her partner had collected eight books, and she was still holding on to both the big and little joker with only three cards left to be played, she knew the pot was theirs.

"What you got, big man? Study long, study wrong." Azia said, taunting the other team. "Partner, you know we got this right?" *WHAM!* She slammed the little joker on the table with all her might. *And you didn't wanna play with me. I bet ya ass is happy now,* she thought, smiling over at her partner who'd had a total attitude adjustment after seeing that she had skills.

"That's right, partner! Give it to 'em raw!" she demanded.

Azia threw out the five of spades. The fat man followed with the queen, praying that his partner had the last joker. Azia's partner threw down the jack. When the other guy threw down a deuce, the fat man knew it was all over. Azia and her partner had collected ten books in the first round making it an automatic win for them. The fat man cursed himself for partnering with a jackass. Azia removed her six hundred from the pot and gave the other half to her partner.

"We need to be partners more often," the girl winked.

Bitch, get your phony ass out of here, is what Azia wanted to say, but she just returned a phony smile instead. She went to find Keemah who had disappeared for almost an hour. When she grabbed her phone from her bag to call her, she saw there were two missed calls. The number looked very familiar but she couldn't place who it belonged to. She stepped outside and pressed the Send button. *Who the hell is this?* she thought with the phone ringing on the other end.

"Are you screening my calls?" asked Mike, smiling from ear to ear. He stopped what he was doing when Azia's number appeared across his screen.

She was smiling just as hard as he was. "No, I didn't hear my phone ring. I was in the middle of whipping some butt in Spades."

"Let me find out you know how to put it down on the tables. Do I need to take you down to Atlantic City wit' me? I'm always down for a chick that can make me some money."

"It depends on how I'm making the money. One thing I don't do is get pimped."

Mike chuckled. "I'm glad to know that." Talking to her made Mike want to see her. "Why don't you come and meet me so I can see that pretty face."

"I rode up here wit' my cousin," she blushed. "I left my car parked at her house."

"Tell her to drop you off and I can take care of you from there."

"I like the sound of that but I don't even know where she wandered off to. I was just about to call her butt when I seen your missed calls, you became more important."

"You got a lot of game," he laughed.

"I got a lot more than that if you give me a chance to show you."

North Philly was a part of the city that Mike tried his best to avoid. There was something about North Philly that made his skin crawl. But being that where Azia was wasn't too deep in, he went against his better judgment. "I'll come scoop you. Give me, like, a half hour and I'll be outside waiting on you."

Azia dashed back into the house to find Keemah. She spotted her at the other card table getting beat by Annette and one of the locals. Azia glanced down at the score, which revealed they were behind by over a hundred points. "Damn, how much you losing?" Keemah rolled her eyes, trying to stay focused. "One more setback and that's it. But your ass swore you were the champ."

"Shut the fuck up!" Keemah spat, cutting her eyes at Azia.

"Don't get mad at her 'cause I'm tapping that ass," teased Annette.

"I'm leaving!"

Keemah turned and looked at Azia, "Where you going?"

"A friend of mine is coming to get me. I'll get my car later on."

"Whatever." She turned back around and played her hand.

Keemah's shitty attitude wasn't something Azia was trying to entertain. Assuming it had something to do with the phone call Keemah received when she walked off, Azia brushed it off and went about her business. On her way out the door, she was approached from behind. The last thing she remembered hearing before being punched in the back was, "I knew I knew your trick ass from somewhere."

It was the female who had been Azia's partner in the Spades game. She had crept up from behind and started laying punches on Azia before she could turn around and defend herself. "That's for fucking my man, you bitch," she screamed, punches and kicks flying in all directions.

It took a minute for Azia to realize what was going on. She had tripped over someone's foot and fallen to the floor. She shielded her face with both hands. A circle of drunken spectators had formed around them, cheering the girl on. Azia used the shirt of a bystander to pull herself up from the floor, and when she did, it was on. She was now on top of the girl putting her thing down. The crowd that had once been cheering for the other girl immediately switched sides. They were all for whoever was winning.

"Get her the hell off me!" Azia shouted from the floor. Their positions had reversed again, putting Azia back on the bottom. After seeing enough, some guy pulled Azia into the kitchen while another guy carried the other girl outside to get some fresh air.

Keemah appeared after everything was over saying she didn't know Azia was involved. "What the hell happened that fast? I thought you were leaving."

"She snuck up on me. I'ma beat that bitch ass." Azia could feel her face stinging. She rubbed two fingers against the right side of her face. There were about four or five welts. "Oh, she play dirty. She tried to scratch my face all up. Who the fuck is that bitch?" Her adrenaline got to pumping again and she was ready to finish what the other girl had started.

Keemah examined her cousin's face. "You don't remember Helena? She used to live down the next block from Grandma."

"Hell, no, I don't remember that bitch!" The music had been shut off and the other girl could be heard from outside ranting about not being finished and how bad she was going to whip Azia's ass again. "Let me and her have it out. I don't back down from nothing." Azia tried to force her way to the door but a few people held her back. "My ride is outside. Damn! Let me go!" she ordered.

"Let her the fuck go," demanded Keemah, following her out the door.

Mike was parked outside waiting impatiently. Seeing how pumped and rowdy the crowd was made him realize even more clearly why he stayed away from that end. He dialed Azia's number a couple more times and got no answer. Of course the last thing she was concerned about was answering the phone. Just as he was about to pull off, Azia stormed out the front door with a trail of people behind her. He looked on in disbelief.

"Yeah? You want some more?" the female threatened.

Noticing Mike parked on the other side of the street brought her classy act back. She knew she would have to explain what went down but she dared not let him see her acting like an animal. "You got your ass beat already so go ahead on home and suck whoever dick it is you say I was fucking. I got better things to do than play wit' your simple ass."

Keemah trailed her cousin like she was her bodyguard. The female continued to shout every curse word and bad name she had ever learned, but nothing was going to make Azia detour from where she was headed. When she walked up to Mike's car, all eyes were on them. Keemah thought silently herself, *How the fuck she grip up Mike's ass. I can't stand this ho.*

Mike took Azia's chin in his hand and examined her bruised face. "You out here letting these ghetto-ass hoodlums mess up my pretty face. Get in so we can go handle that." Azia walked around to the passenger's side of his BMW and climbed in. He looked at Keemah, who he knew he'd seen somewhere before but couldn't remember where. "Do you need a ride?"

"No, my car is parked right there." Azia leaned forward and instructed her cousin not to stick around. "I'm heading home. Call me tomorrow or something."

Mike made his way around the city, tying up some loose ends before calling it a night. Azia sat quietly with her seat leaned back, enjoying the cool breeze. She was in her own little world thinking about everything that was going on in her life. In between stops, Mike took the opportunity to learn more about her. Azia told half of her story. She shared things she rarely told anyone, like how her mom had been killed by her father when she was six years old, and how her father was serving a life sentence. She told him how she and the rest of her family had never been close and that graduating from college was something she was determined to accomplish.

"I know you're only telling me what you want me to know and not everything, but it seems like there's something more going on wit' you. It sounds like you got a void in your heart. I know you been through a lot, and not having a mother around has put a strain on you, but look how far you've come on your own."

Azia gave a weak smile before saying, "It's all about the hustle."

"You sound like you got a head on your shoulders and I'm feeling that. I hear your name ringing in the streets but I'm not one to judge. You made it through the best way you knew how and that's real. Some people give up but you didn't, and that tells me a lot about you. If you're serious about getting into the fashion industry I'll work something out for you. Just make sure you do your job and make your mom proud."

It had been a long time since a guy had spoken to Azia in such a concerned way. Money was almost always the main topic of her discussions with anyone. Mike, on the other hand, made her realize how important school was. There was something about him that had her wanting to change the game. The soft ringtone from her phone inside her purse captured both their attentions. Rashaud's name and number appeared across the screen. She hadn't heard from him all day so that was the perfect excuse for her to start an argument and stay out all night. She excused herself before answering.

"What you want, Rashaud?"

"Before you jump the gun and say some shit that's gonna make me want to whip your ass, just know that I got caught up in some bullshit. That's why you haven't heard from me. Where you at?"

"I'm out getting some air."

"Getting some air where?"

"Somewhere you ain't."

Rashaud wasn't interested in the head games. "A'ight...Go finish doing you and having your little tantrum party, pity party, or whatever it is you're having wit' whoever it is you're having it wit'. But you better beat me home."

"Muthafucka, I ain't heard—"

She was cut short. "Azia, watch your tone and remember who you talking to. I said I got caught up, and that's all I need to say."

"Nigga, fuck you!" She hung up, furious, and threw herself back in her seat. She closed her eyes, holding back the tears that were desperately trying to escape. Being that close to Mike again and getting to know him a little better made her want to kill Rashaud herself.

Mike gently took her chin and turned her face to his. "Don't let nobody steal your joy, precious. Life is too short for that and tomorrow's not promised to any of us." It was just a matter of time before his point would definitely be made.

CHAPTER 7
Sometimes All I Need Is

"Don't be impressed. Be as fortunate as the rest."
-Gisele

"What?! Tommy said what?!" Busta put on the perfect performance for Rashaud. "What reason would I have to kill that girl? I didn't even know her like that."

"What the fuck your cousin gonna make up some bullshit like that for?! I told you that nigga was jealous of you! He wanna see you go down so he can take over and be head of the family! You shoulda been let me lay that nigga down after that last stunt he pulled! Ain't no telling who else he said some shit like that to! What you gonna do about it?!"

Busta dialed Tommy's number and left him a voicemail when he didn't answer. "Yo, Tommy, hit me back when you get this message. As soon as you get this, call me. It's important."

Rashaud chuckled. He knew there was no way Tommy would be able to answer his phone or ever hear that message. He knew this because Tommy was stuffed in the back of his Cadillac, duck-taped and gagged. Rashaud wasted no time using the situation to his full advantage. "Busta, you ain't never kept nothing from me before so don't start now. You know you my nigga for life. Just keep it all the way real wit' me. Did you have anything to do wit' Tonya's death?"

"Rashaud, word to my mother, I ain't have nothing to do wit' it."

"Enough said." He walked around to the trunk of his car and popped it open. Tommy was laying still, as if he was in a peaceful sleep. The real reason there was no movement was because Rashaud had beaten him half to death.

"What the fuck going on? Is that nigga dead?"

"Naw, he ain't dead yet. But if you let him live, you'll be in a minute. He's going around running his mouth about nothing. You need to handle that or I will." Rashaud pulled his gun from his waist, placed it on the side of the trunk, and waited for Busta to make a move.

Busta inched closer to examine Tommy. "'Fuck you do this for? How the hell am I supposed to explain this shit to my aunt?"

"I don't know. Tell her ass she still got you. As long as you take care of her she won't miss the little sheisty-ass nigga. He ain't no good no way. He's a rat. I was doing you a favor." Rashaud spit into the trunk, disgusted by the sight of him. It landed on Tommy's unconscious body."

"Next time don't do me no favors. You shoulda let me handle the situation how I wanted to handle it. You got my blood thrown in the back of your trunk like it's one of those niggas we be out to get. That shit ain't cool, Rashaud." Busta was feeling guilty. He did tell Tommy what he had done. After leaving Tonya, he got drunk and loose at the mouth, so it was his fault for slipping. He couldn't watch his cousin go out like that. "Take him out the trunk."

Rashaud sighed deeply. "That's on you." Both of them pulled Tommy from the trunk. His eyes were fighting to open. He just knew his time was up until he heard the sound of his cousin's voice.

"Tommy—Tommy," Busta slapped on his face with force. "Wake up, man." Rashaud was in the background snickering. Busta shot him an evil grin. "Wake the hell up, fool." Busta shook him.

After some shouting, hitting, shaking, and pouring water in his face, Tommy finally came to. He knew Busta was there, but the first person he came in eye contact with was Rashaud. "You—a dead nigga," he slurred.

Rashaud jumped up in his face with his heat drawn. "What the fuck you say?"

Busta cut in. "Yo, Rashaud! Back the fuck up man!" He pushed Rashaud an arm length away. "Tommy, shut your fucking mouth before I let him put one in you! You call yourself bringing me up on false charges?! What you running your mouth about, little cousin?!"

Tommy thought before he spoke. He knew he was in the wrong. The killer glare Busta had in his eye informed him to be careful of what he said. "I was just rapping man. I was high as hell and running off at the mouth. I made the shit all up," he lied. "I just wanted people to know you a real killer so they better not fuck witchu. And they better respect me 'cause we blood."

Rashaud flung his arms in the air. "Unfuckingbelievable. That shit don't even sound right, Busta. You believe this nigga?" Busta replied with silence. "Fuck that. I'm out. I ain't listening to this nonsense. Do what you wanna do wit' him." Rashaud hopped in his ride and sped off.

Busta stood quietly, barely listening to what Tommy was saying. Everything was going in one ear and out the other. Out of nowhere, Busta backhanded Tommy in the mouth. Tommy tasted blood in his mouth but didn't react. "I should put a bullet in your head right now. I should put that shit right here," he stated, mugging Tommy with the gun.

"You siding wit' that nigga over your own blood? It's like that?" he squinted.

"Don't try to reverse the role on me. You here 'cause you had to open your big-ass mouth. What I said to you was for your ears only, and if you was a G like you say you are, you woulda known that. Your ass wouldna been stuffed in the back of a car, waiting on a bullet, you dumb mutherfucka. Keep talking slick and you gonna find out exactly how I play. If you wasn't my blood you'd be floating in the river by now. I don't do too much talking." He took a step back. "And then you ran your mouth to Stutter-man of all people, like he the damn Godfather or something. I'm gonna give you one more chance to tell me what's really good. Why you tryna put my name on blast like that? Don't I take good care of you? I make sure your pockets stay filled and your whip stay fly. Why you tryna take me under?"

Busta was debating himself in his mind the whole time he lectured Tommy. He didn't know if he wanted to let him live or die. The decision would be based on whatever his cousin's real motive was for running his mouth. If it sounded good enough for Busta, he was willing to give his cousin a second chance at life. If not, he was going to take a bullet where he stood. "Come on, Tommy. Tell big cousin why you biting his back out." He brought his gun into plain sight and began to brush it off like he was shining a shoe.

Tommy was petrified. If he had his own gun at that moment, it would have been him or his cousin. Only one would've made it out alive. But since he didn't, he tried his best to talk himself out of the jam. "Cuz, you know me. You know I wouldn't intentionally bring no harm your way. We got to drinking, smoking, and clowning, and I slipped up. He was asking me did I know the girl, and I said fuck that bitch, my cousin laid her down. It came out before I caught myself."

Busta slammed Tommy up against the car and stuck the barrel of his nine down his throat. "You scared yet, little nigga?" Tommy nodded his head. "That's good, 'cause I want you to be scared. If you had any sense at all you woulda killed that nigga before he had the chance to run his trap. Now I got to go clean up your sloppy work." He loosened his grip and shoved him to the side. Tommy used his hand to catch himself from falling all the way to the ground. "Get the fuck in the car."

They drove around for hours looking for Stutter-man, but he was nowhere to be found. He wasn't answering any calls or returning any messages. He was no fool. After Rashaud left so did he. He had no plans on sticking around and waiting on Busta to be the next one to pay him a visit. He snatched up the little money he'd won in the crap game, went to pack a few things, and headed to Baltimore to chill out until things died down.

"'Fuck this nigga at, Tommy? Call his phone again," Busta snapped. He was getting more annoyed by the minute.

Tommy did as he was told and got the voicemail again. "He ain't answering."

"Fuck this!" Busta made a quick u-turn, almost leaving skid marks in the street. He disconnected his phone from the portable charger and dialed Rashaud. "Yo, you talked to Stutter-man?"

"Not since earlier when I saw him. Why? Wassup?"

"Nothing, I just wanted to holla at him."

Rashaud, knowing his friend, knew exactly what he wanted with him. "Where ya punk ass cousin at?"

"He sitting right here wit' me."

"What you plan on doing to that nigga?"

"I'll fill you in later. You still out or what?"

"I'm in the house. I'm in for the night if you don't need me for nothing."

"Naw, I don't need you. I'll holla at you tomorrow."

Before ending the call Rashaud said, "If you gonna spare his life then you might as well give Stutter-man a free ride. He ain't gonna say nothing to nobody. He already know what it is if he even think about it. And you say you ain't do the shit, so what you looking for the nigga for anyway?"

"He talking shit, that's why."

"Whatever, nigga. Go do you then if it's like that. But the way I see it is, if Tommy said something once he gonna say it again. Don't leave a job unfinished. Ain't that what we learned?"

"I hear you. I'll call you when I get a chance." Busta ended the call and focused his gaze over at Tommy. "Boy, I swear you better be glad you my blood. 'Cause if you wasn't—" He was too upset to finish the sentence. He started breathing real heavy. Pulling over to the side of 18th and Dickinson Street, he forced the lever into park before he had the chance to fully stop. The car jerked, making Tommy's head hit the dash. "Walk ya ass back home 'cause I ain't taking you."

Tommy looked dumbfounded. "Walk?!"

"Yeah. I ain't stutter, nigga." Busta got out of the car and walked around to the passenger side. In one swift motion he pulled his nine and shot Tommy in the shin and said, "Matter fact, limp ya ass home." He walked back around to the driver's side and climbed in. "And if you part your lips to snitch, I'm gonna make sure I aim higher next time." He sped off, leaving Tommy on the ground, bloody and in pain.

■ ■ ■

Mike dropped Azia off at her car after they'd spent a couple more hours together. Both of them had sexual intentions in the beginning, but when they got to talking about other things, just being in each other's company felt good enough. They never made it past conversing in the car. He was giving her the kind of attention she needed.

After that night, she made a habbit of sneaking off with him every chance she got. It was hard to do with Rashaud breathing down her neck, but she made a way every time. If she wasn't using Keemah as an alibi, she went as far as saying she had picked up a couple summer classes to make up some low grades for the next semester. Anything she could come up with, she did.

Just to keep Rashaud happy, she maintained the hustle. Randomly, she would pick out guys that looked like they had money. Whether she was at the club, store, or just walking down the street, she was pulling them in from all angles. After a while it became fun for her. But it turned into a headache just as fast. Rashaud was well aware that sometimes she might have to go a step beyond and give up the kitty, but after the fact, he acted like he couldn't handle it. "If it's too much for you, I can stop doing the shit," is what she would tell him. But the money was too good to walk away from. He was making more money with Azia being the bait than when it was just him and Busta.

Some jobs he called Busta in on and some he didn't, out of greed. A hundred percent profit sounded a lot better than fifty in his book. Usually, Azia would run straight home to give Rashaud the low-down, like he was one of the girls. But for some reason, when she blabbed on about the latest potential victim she'd found, he wasn't interested. It seemed like there was something much heavier weighing on his mind. The game turned out to be much different that time around.

Azia had been watching this particular guy for weeks. He was laced and she knew it. She made it her business to go spend time at Keemah's house every day just so she could keep an eye on him. He didn't live in the city but his mother did; on the same block as her cousin. Around five o'clock every day, she knew his white Q45 would be turning the corner like it always did. He never paid either her or Keemah too much attention until Azia made sure to make her presence known one day. She watched as he parked his car and got out. He was darker than chocolate and sexy as hell. He walked around to the trunk to pull out a few grocery bags and headed into his mother's house to pay his daily visit.

"If he buys any more groceries for her, she's gonna be able to start her own market," Azia whispered to Keemah before making her move. Every day he came, so did about three or four brown paper bags. "Excuse me," she said, switching her plumpness across the street.

The tall African man looked at her without stopping. "How can I help you?"

"You can try by stopping for a minute if you have time."

Realizing that he was being rude, he placed the bags on his mother's steps and gave Azia his undivided attention. "I apologize for that."

"No need for an apology. I just wanted to come introduce myself. I see you every day and don't even know your name. That's not very neighborly on my behalf." She gave her signature smile, which no man she'd ever come across could resist.

"Abdul," he said, reaching for her hand. "I don't mean to come across as antisocial, but I come to see my mom to make sure she's cool, and I keep it moving."

"If possible, I would like it if you came around here to see me and your mom. How can we make that happen?"

He smiled. "You seem like a lady that knows what she wants."

"I'm more of a lady that knows what she needs. Right now, I'm thinking I would love to have a friend like you."

"How do you know that?"

"Because first things first wit' me. You taking care of your mother tell me a lot about you. That's what makes me want to get to know you better."

Abdul nodded his head. He rarely gave just any old female his attention, but Azia knew what she was doing. He was the kind of man she had to pull out the rule book for. Manipulation was the key.

A half-hour later, he was inviting her inside to meet his mother. Azia was stunned. *Damn, I'm good,* she thought. If Rashaud didn't want any parts of it, she was all for herself. She started spending as much time with Abdul as she could, and got whatever she could get out of him. And it was all done without giving up the booty. For his own reasons, he never pressured her for any sex. Abdul knew his time would come soon enough.

"Hey, Azia, hunny. I'm glad to see you again. I see you keeping my boy here happy," his mother would say in her sweet Nigerian accent.

"The truth is, your boy is keeping me happy. I can't keep taking all the credit," came her reply.

Abdul greeted his mother with a kiss and a hug. "Hey, Mami. Here are your groceries."

He placed the bag up on the counter. When one of the bags tipped over, both Abdul and his mother were too eager to catch whatever was falling out before it hit the floor. Azia had never really paid any attention to what was in the bags before, but this time she did. There wasn't one box put away or anything put into the refrigerator or freezer, which made her curious to know what was in those bags. It was one thing to grocery shop for mom, but every single day was a bit much. There was definitely more to the story. "Come on, Azia. Take a ride with me," Abdul suggested.

They departed from the house and went out to his car. It had been weeks since they'd been kicking it. She was feeling more comfortable when asking personal questions. "Tell me more about your hometown."

His smile was so perfect. "What do you want to know?"

"What made you come to America?"

"Who doesn't want to live in America? It's the home of the free, right?"

"Are you beating around the bush? If you don't feel comfortable sharing that kind of information wit' me, that's okay. I'll understand."

"It's a sensitive topic. I don't like talking about my past. I'm just over here tryna make things better for my family back at home. They're over there fighting to survive." He raised his Rolex to view the time. "The way that some of you live is nothing compared to what we go through on a daily basis. What you see on TV is how it is. It's not a game. People in my country are over there dying as we speak."

"So how are you helping? I'm sure you can't save everyone."

"I can't, but I can certainly die trying."

Azia was flabbergasted. She didn't know how to respond to what he had just said. But the real question was never answered. She didn't want to know *why* he was supporting the people in his country, she wanted to know *how* he was doing it. "What kind of job do you have that enables you to take care of you, your entire family, and others? I know it can't be a regular 9-to-5 job."

He chuckled under his breath. "Are you asking because you want to help or because you're just trying to be nosy?"

"I—I'm not tryna be nosy," she stumbled.

"I might have a job for you if you're interested."

"As long as I'm not sucking dick or selling ass, we might be able to work something out," she joked.

They laughed together. "I want you to meet someone. She's very special to me. She's like a sister, and I think you two can make a lot of money together."

Hearing Abdul say "can make a lot of money" made Azia snap to attention. "When can I meet her?"

Azia was so caught up in their conversation she hadn't realized the car was no longer in motion.

"You can meet her now."

She looked to her right and saw that they were sitting in the driveway of a beautiful single-family home. She stepped out of the car and twirled in a circle, checking out the retaining wall she didn't remember passing through. The landscaping from the front to the back was amazing. It looked like one of the celebrity homes straight off *MTV Cribs*. Abdul led the way around the back of the house, through a rock garden and up some patio stairs. To their left was a two-car garage with a Bentley, Maserati and Hummer parked on the side of it. He let himself in with a key that was sticking out of a flower pot where they were standing. The first set of doors put them in a foyer where more patio furniture was arranged and another set of locked doors was found. Abdul hit #958 and waited patiently for a response.

"Yessss … ," a female voice chirped on the other end of the box.

"We're here," he replied.

BZZZ! Abdul pushed the door open and again led the way. They ended up in a large room that was completely white. The walls were white, the leather sofas were white, the leather chairs were white, the marble table was white, the carpet was white, the piano was white, and all the candles scattered around the room were white. The only splash of color came from beautiful artwork and paintings hanging horizontally along the walls, and the crystal chandelier hanging from the untouchable ceiling. The sound of smooth jazz was playing softly, and suddenly she appeared, sipping on a glass of wine, looking good enough to eat.

"It's a pleasure, my beauty," she greeted, reaching for Azia's hand. "Welcome to mi casa. Make yourself at home."

Her hands felt like silk. Azia had never thought about being with another female a day in her life. But after meeting this woman, she thought anything was possible.

Her name was Gisele and she was a Brazilian goddess. She had perfect features from head to toe. If skin could melt like butter, hers definitely would. Her hair flowed down her back, and her lips were the exact shape of Angelina Jolie's. She was tall, thin, and could be easily mistaken for Adriana Lima on any given day.

Azia was momentarily sidetracked by a couple females that skated through the room to get to the pool area. They were dressed in bikini thong bottoms but no tops. Not once did they flinch when they saw that Gisele had company. They greeted Abdul and went about their business like walking around topless was an everyday thing.

"Don't mind my guests," Gisele said, watching Azia stare. "If you ever want to join the party, you're more than welcome to do so," she smiled. "Shall we?" She gestured with her hand for them to have a seat. "Can I offer you anything? Wine? Maybe something to snack on?"

"I'll take a glass of wine."

She snapped her fingers twice. "Abdul, can you grab us ladies a glass of wine?" she winked.

Gisele covered Azia's hands with her own." You're a very beautiful girl, Azia. I can make you a shitload of money if you allow me to."

Azia sat mesmerized by her voice, her touch, and her beauty. "Thank you!"

"You haven't even been here long and I'm enjoying your company." Gisele's right hand was now resting on Azia's thigh. She began to caress it gently. "I just want to make you comfortable. Don't be afraid."

Is she coming on to me? Azia sat quietly. She could feel herself getting moist between her legs. *Where the hell is that fool at with the wine?* As if on cue, Abdul appeared with two glasses filled to the brim. On any other day,

Azia would have sipped the wine. That night, she took it straight down. Both Abdul and Gisele laughed.

"You asked if you could meet her. Are you sure you were ready?" Abdul quizzed.

"I may not have been prepared, but I'm the type of person that's willing to take on new challenges." She turned from Abdul to look Gisele in the eye. "You're making me feel real good inside right now, in a way no female or man has ever done before. I'm impressed," she smiled, keeping it sweet and classy.

Gisele stood from her seat and reached out to help Azia to her feet as well. "Don't be impressed. Be as fortunate as all the rest."

By the end of the night, Azia had skinny-dipped for the first time, participated in her first threesome and drank herself to sleep. Gisele and Abdul together took her to places she had never been before sexually. That was her first time seeing Abdul with his clothes off. He was 6'2" and 215 pounds of pure muscle. There was no other word to describe how he was packing between his legs besides Mandingo. Gisele, on the other hand, was just how she imagined she'd be—one hundred percent pure satisfaction. While Abdul had Gisele in the doggy-style position, she was sucking Azia dry.

Azia didn't fight to stop her from sticking her head between her legs. She licked Azia so good she didn't want her to stop. "Damn, Gisele, baby. Where you get that tongue from?" Gisele ignored the question. She continued to lick her from her pussy all the way back to her ass crack. Azia loved every minute of it. It wasn't until Gisele started fingering Azia with two fingers while teasing her clitoris with her tongue that Azia reached her first orgasm of the night.

Then they switched positions. While Azia was riding Abdul like an American stallion, Gisele was riding his face just as freely. Azia and Gisele kissed and sucked all over each other. After Abdul was worn out, they kept it going sucking each other dry all night long. This wasn't something Azia ever visualized herself doing. Growing up, she thought messing with the same sex was gross and off-the-record. But the feeling Gisele gave her was unbelievable. No man would ever be able to make her feel like that.

■ ■ ■

"**Keemah, you** are never going to believe this shit I'm about to tell you."

Acting half interested in what her cousin was talking about, she replied, "What now, Azia?"

"What's wrong wit' you? What's the attitude for?" she questioned, looking disgusted.

"I just got a lot of shit on my mind, that's all. I'm listening. What you got to tell me?"

"I'll let you go first. It seems like your problem may be a lot more important than mine."

"I never said I wanted to talk about it," Keemah snapped.

A few people who were seated close enough to hear Keemah's last comment turned around to see who was raising their voice. The girls were sitting in IHOP. When Abdul had dropped Azia off at her car, which had been parked at Keemah's house, she decided to wake Keemah up and treat her to breakfast. Now she was sitting there wishing she'd left her ass asleep.

"Well excuse me for tryna be a friend." Azia waved her hand to get the waiter's attention. He came over to take their order. "I'll take the steak and cheese omelet and onions in my hashbrowns, please." She looked across the table at Keemah, who still had her face in the menu. "Do you know what you getting?"

She answered her question by placing her order. "I want the Belgium waffle wit' strawberries and ice cream on top, and a side of turkey sausage."

The waiter took their menus and went to put their orders in. "What? You wake up on the wrong side of the bed this morning?"

"If I woulda woke up on my own, I would probably be feeling a lot better."

"No problem! Next time I'll just leave your ass sleep!"

The two sat in silence for a little while until Keemah broke the ice. "I'm about to get evicted."

"What?"

"I'm about to get evicted," she repeated.

Azia was shocked. She didn't know times were that hard for Keemah. If she had known, she woulda been helped her out of the situation. "I told you a long time ago, Keemah. If you ever need something, ask me. Why would you wait until they're about to throw your ass out in the street to say something? I told you about that pride shit. I can't believe this. Where that nigga you be out wit' all the time? He ain't got no money to help you?"

"I ain't ask him for none."

"I can see that. That's why your ass is about to be homeless."

"Don't be smart, Azia. I didn't tell you so you can ride my back about it. I told you so you could help me. If that's what you want to do."

"Oh, so you ain't asking for my help, you just throwing it out there in case I wanna help. What type of shit is that?"

"Never mind. Just drop it. Forget I ever said something."

"Why are you so touchy about everything? Are you still upset wit' me about messing wit' Jimmy? Be honest so we can move on and get past it."

Keemah tried her best to make her lie sound believable. "Ain't nobody worried about Jimmy. He's old news. Don't I have a right to have an attitude right now? A bitch is about to be living out in the street."

Azia laughed. "You stupid." She took a sip of her orange juice to regain her composure. "First of all, you already know I ain't gonna have you living out on the streets, so stop fronting. Second of all, you have every right to be upset, but you taking it out on the wrong person. You want me to sit up here and deal wit' your nasty-ass attitude, then turn around and give you my money."

"You got a point," giggled Keemah.

"You damn right I got a point!" Azia pushed her water out of the way so the waiter could place their food on the table. When he walked away, she continued their conversation. "How much you owe?"

"Twelve-hundred dollars."

Azia accidentally spit her orange juice out. "Damn, Keemah! What the hell you been doing?"

"I missed it for two months. I really owe eighteen-hundred but I have six of my own already. I just need the other twelve."

"Oh, yeah. Your ass is going to sit and hear about my whole night, even if you don't want to, for this twelve hundred. Let me see, where shall I begin—" she teased.

Keemah's frown turned upside down. She was glad her cousin bought into her act. She wasn't about to be evicted. Mustafa's brother was taking care of her just like Rashaud was taking care of Azia. And her rent had just been paid six months in advance on the first of the month. Keemah walked around to the other side of the table to sit next to Azia. She threw her arms around her cousin, giving her a phony hug. "Aw, cousin. I love you. You always got my back."

"Whatever! Go sit your ass down so you can listen to my story," she pointed to Keemah's side of the booth.

By the time they were down to their last forkful, Azia had told the whole story. Keemah was sitting there with her eyes open as wide as they could be. "Girl, you is lying through your teeth."

"If I'm lying, pigs are flying."

"Is it true what they say? Can a female eat pussy better than a man ever will? If it is, you might have to take me wit' you next time."

"All I'ma say is the shit amazed me."

"Now you gotta take your ass home and hear his mouth. Keep my name out of it because I do not want that fool calling me wit' no questions. You better tell him you fell asleep in the car somewhere or something."

"Yeah, right. He ain't going for no shit like that."

"Well make sure you give me my money before you take your ass home because I would hate to get evicted because he put your ass in the hospital," she laughed.

Azia paid the tab and they bounced up out of there with full bellies. She stopped at the bank on the way back and withdrew the twelve hundred dollars Keemah said she needed. "Don't worry about paying me back. Just remember I got your back if no one else does."

Keemah smiled. *I wasn't paying your trifling ass back no way. Your day is quickly approaching, girlfriend.* Keemah stepped out of the car in front of her place and shut the door. She bent down to speak through the open window. "I'll call you later on to check on you."

"Alright," said Azia, making her way to what used to be home sweet home.

Her feelings for Rashaud were slowly fading. Mike and Abdul were a big part of the reason. Mike was her affection and Abdul was her excitement. She no longer got either from Rashaud. But there were other issues, too. Attention was one of them. Rashaud was so caught up in the street life, he failed to give Azia the attention she needed. Their time together started slacking and eventually fell off completely. When she was out, he was home and vice versa.

She knew he was fucking around on her but never caught him. She didn't care anyway because while he was out doing his thing, she was out doing hers. A couple days ago she went through his Blackberry when he was in the shower, reading as many texts as she could. *Hey baby— Hey love—I miss you—I want to see you—I need you— Last night felt so good—Whose pussy is that?—I love you—You better not be giving my dick away* were a few she scanned through in both his inbox and his sent mail. But she never puckered her lips up to say anything about it. Instead she continued to grind it out on her own.

CHAPTER 8
Hate On Me, Hater
"It don't matter how rich you are, when it's your time to go, you're gone."
-Detective Joseph

When Azia got home, she thought she was alone until she heard Rashaud's voice coming from the bathroom. The door was closed. She crept up and put her ear close to the door. She listened to the conversation for about five minutes before hearing him spray some air refresher and flush the toilet. She used the noise of the flushing toilet to creep away from the door without being heard. She didn't know who he was talking to, but her gut told her it was a female. He came out of the bathroom after washing his hands and found her sitting in the living room watching *Martin* on TVOne.

He flopped down on the sofa and looked at Azia like he was waiting for her to say something. "Did you have fun last night?"

"Did you?" she shot back.

"Don't play games wit' me, Azia. Where did you stay at?"

"Over Keemah's house," she lied. "If you woulda answered your phone you woulda known that."

"I didn't even know you had stayed out last night. I was just fucking wit' you."

She gave him an evil glare. "So I guess that means you stayed your ass out, too. Where were you all night?" She smirked. "Let me guess. Taking care of business, right?"

"Yup! I was taking care of business," he mocked.

She sucked her teeth, jumped to her feet and stomped past him. "You got a lot of shit wit' you, Rashaud."

She went into the bedroom and slammed the door. Thirty seconds later Rashaud left the apartment making sure he slammed the door, too. Azia walked back out into the living room. She thought he was just kidding around. She ran to the door. She opened and closed it twice before believing he was really gone. If she ever thought her heart was lying to her before, she didn't think it was lying at that moment. Rashaud didn't care anymore. She believed that if he still cared, her ass would've been hemmed up on one or all of the walls in the apartment for staying out all night. She was actually looking forward to it. When it didn't happen, she assumed her time was up.

Azia gathered as many of her clothes and shoes as she could and neatly packed them into her three-piece Louis Vuitton leather luggage set. She didn't know where she was going, all she knew was that she was getting the hell out of there. She counted the money she had saved up, which was stashed in her panty drawer: seventeen-thousand three-hundred and fifteen dollars. It would have been a lot more if she didn't have a shopping habit. She pulled the bank receipt out of her wallet when she withdrew the twelve-hundred she gave Keemah. She looked at the available balance and did the math in her head. Between her bank account and her stash, she was working with a little over twenty-three thousand. *Bet! I can work with that for now*, she thought.

She called a cab to come pick her up but when they asked where she was headed she hung up. She had no clue where she was going. It was either shack up with Abdul or possibly shack up with Mike. After debating with herself, she decided not to call either one of them. Instead she dialed the number to the cab company again. "I'm sorry, we got disconnected. I need a cab over at the Presidential Suites on City Line. I'm going to the Marriott hotel down by the airport." She was told the wait would be about thirty-five minutes. Luckily it ended up being only twenty. On her way out the door, she remembered something. *Oh, shit. Let me hit that nigga's stash.* She kicked her slides off and ran back to the bedroom only to be disappointed. After moving the dresser and checking behind the piece of wood, she saw that all the money that had been there previously was gone. *Shit! I shoulda taken some when I had the chance. What the fuck he do with all that money?* She jammed the wood back into place and rushed out the door, mad as hell. Fifteen minutes later she was pulling up to what would be her temporary home for the following days to come.

■ ■ ■

The sound of the headboard banging up against the wall was annoying the hell out of Keemah's next-door neighbors. Her and Twin, Mustafa's brother, had been going at it for the last two hours. There would be a five- to ten-minute break between sessions and they were right back at it. With Azia hanging around so often, they hadn't been able to get it in like they normally did. They had to make up for lost time. After busting a nut for the second time, Twin rolled over to catch his breath while Keemah went to wash away all the sweat and cum that was dripping down her legs. She came out of the bathroom after taking a two-minute shower. "Spark that," she said, pointing to the half-smoked blunt sitting on the nightstand.

Twin rolled over and grabbed the lighter. He took the blunt, lit it, and inhaled deeply before passing it over to her. Then he fell back onto the bed and exhaled slowly. "You's a animal girl. You know that?"

"You love this animal," she smiled, dragging on the blunt. "Have you talked to your peoples yet about the situation?"

"I talked to them a couple days ago. It's a done deal. If they were holding my brother for

ransom or something, they woulda been called by now. I know he's dead."

For so long, Twin had been in denial, hoping it was a kidnapping. But no calls ever came. As the days went by he knew that the chances of his brother being alive were slim to none. Twin put his hands over his face and let them slide slowly down to his chest. He was hurting inside. As badly as he wanted to cry, the tears wouldn't come, even when he tried. Half of him had been taken away by a stranger, and that stranger was going to pay—one way or another. "You need to start questioning that bitch. I know she knows something."

"I can't just come out and ask her. It's gonna sound too suspicious."

"I don't give a fuck what you gotta do! You need to do something before I step in and take the fuck over!" he yelled angrily.

"Don't snap at me, Twin. I ain't the one that did the shit." Keemah rolled her eyes and left the room.

He followed. "Don't walk away from me." He forced her backwards over the hallway banister. One hand was around her neck and the other was holding the banister to keep them both from falling over. She could have sworn he was about to push her over. "Don't you ever turn your back on me. Do you hear what I'm telling you?"

Keemah's eyes watered instantly. "I hear you, Twin. I'm sorry."

She looked up at him when he let her up and saw something evil in his eyes that she'd never seen before. "Now go make me something to eat." He walked back into the bedroom and she went toward the kitchen.

■ ■ ■

"I'm glad you came and pulled me out of that small-ass room. It felt like the walls were closing in on me. I don't see me staying there too long. If I'm not gonna go back home to Rashaud, I'm gonna have to find me a house, apartment, or something soon. I'm talking in a couple days soon," said Azia.

Keemah could barely hear what Azia was saying over the loud beat of the song playing. It was *Uhh Ahh* by Boyz II Men, one of her favorites. She was swaying back and forth, watching the dancers up on stage make love to the pole like it was their men. "Dayum, I need to be up in here shaking my ass. They throwing money at these tricks like it grow on trees."

Keemah and Azia had been sitting in Daddy D's strip club since nine-thirty. It was now going on eleven. Going to a female strip club had been Keemah's idea. After Azia told her about how good a night she had with Gisele, she'd been fantasizing about being with a woman. One of the dancers made her way over to their table and squeezed in between the two of them, asking if she could give one of them a lap dance. The girl wasn't the prettiest one out the bunch but she wasn't bad-looking either.

"Yeah," Azia said, pulling out a fifty-dollar bill. "You can show my cousin here some of your tricks." Azia smiled and puckered her lips up to Keemah. "Enjoy!" She left the table and headed for the bar. Azia took her drink and tipped the bartender before swaggering off wondering if Keemah was enjoying her dance. When she got back to the table, she was surprised to see what was going on. The girl had stripped out of the skimpy outfit that hid her nipples and pubic area and was licking, kissing, and grinding all over Keemah who was giving her the same action right back. Watching them was turning Azia on. She took a seat and sipped on her drink. Visions of Gisele's honey-brown skin made her drift into deep thought.

I need to call her so we can talk more about this business proposition she's talking about. She told me to call when I was ready. Shit, I'm ready now. I don't know what it consists of, but if I'm going to be pushing Bentleys and Maseratis like they are, I'm all for it. Fuck what you heard!

Gisele never took the opportunity to talk to Azia about her plans. She didn't want to give Azia too much information at once. After all, she didn't know if Azia would hop on board or decline the position. The business was illegal but in a legal kind of way. Gisele and Abdul met a few years back at a festival in South Africa. She immediately took a liking to him. His attitude was spunky, his look was right. She knew bringing him back to the states would be an investment. She spoke with one of her connections in immigration, got a green card for him and brought him home. The job she gave him was simple: keep her safe. After a year of gaining each other's trust, their relationship turned into more of a friendship. He sent for his mother when he got settled and never dreamed of returning home; he only went back to visit. Gisele taught him everything he needed to know about survival, and now she wanted to do the same for Azia.

The third song ended and so did Keemah's lap dance. She smiled over at Azia when the dancer walked away and said, "She got some moves on her."

Azia smirked. "*She* got some moves? It looks to me like you got some moves, too. You don't look like no virgin to the same-sex thing to me."

Keemah laughed. "That's because I'm not, I just ain't never tell you."

"You sneaky ho!" Azia smacked her playfully. "I knew you was just as big of a freak as me."

It was one o'clock in the morning before either girl knew it. Keemah was supposed to have called Twin to check in, but when she got to drinking and got caught up in all the fun she was having with Azia, it slipped her mind. He had called her phone several times, but she hadn't answered. "Girl, I gotta go," she said, looking at the time.

"I'm tired anyway."

The girls rose to their feet and headed for the exit. On their way out, Azia could have sworn she'd seen a ghost. She did a double-take at a car that was riding by. It went by too fast for her to chase it down to see whether or not she was tripping. She brushed it off and assumed her eyes were playing tricks on her. Keemah noticed the perplexed look on her face and questioned it. "What's wrong wit' you?"

"Nothing," she answered. She took off the six-inch stilettos that were killing her pinky toes and walked barefoot to the car. "I just thought I saw something."

"You thought you saw what?"

"I thought I saw someone I knew."

"Who?"

"Nobody. Just someone from my past."

Keemah scanned the area trying to see who she was referring to. "Are they still here?"

Irritated by all the questions, she snapped, "Why are you asking me all these damn questions?! I said it was nobody!"

But the truth was, it was somebody. She had mistaken the guy riding by for Mustafa, but it was Twin. She knew Mustafa was dead. She'd watched him take his last breath. The person in that car just reminded her of him at a quick glance, or so she thought.

Azia felt so lonely when she got back to the hotel. She couldn't believe Rashaud hadn't blown up her cell phone yet. She refused to call him. She called Mike's phone but got no answer. Then she called Abdul, who happened to be available. "What are you still doing up?" he asked.

"I was out wit' my cousin. I just got in. I meant to call you earlier to let you know where I will be staying at for a couple days."

"Where is that?"

"At the Marriott over by the airport."

"Why are you staying there? You know I wouldn't mind if you came to kick it over here with me."

"I know you wouldn't but I didn't want to burden you."

"It's no burden, Azia. I told you once before, if you need me, I'll be there. You should know the kind of person I am by now."

"I know," she sighed. "I just have a lot of things I need to sort out. One of them being my finances." She threw that in to see if he would bite.

"There's no reason for you to be struggling if you are. I introduced you to Gisele for a reason. It wasn't just so you could get your pussy eaten," he joked.

She giggled. "There's a first time for everything."

"You are right about that. The door is open for you if you're willing to step through. Just keep in mind that what we do is helpful. It's not illegal. It's not discriminating. It's not hard. It's a job. When you're ready to come on board, we can further discuss the details of it all."

"How can I come on board? You're asking me to walk blind into something I know nothing about."

"You said you're willing to take on new challenges. I'm not forcing your hand. All I'm doing is inviting you into my world. You can accept or decline. No hard feelings."

What do I have to lose? she asked herself. "I'm in."

■■■

After a little bit of coaxing I know she'll be back, she just needs some time to herself, thought Rashaud. He had come home to an empty house. When he saw that almost all of Azia's clothes were gone, he wasn't the least bit worried. With her gone he'd have a lot more time to chill and clear his head. Finding out he was about to be a father was weighing on him heavily. He couldn't figure out for the life of him how he'd ended up in such a fucked up situation. How did he end up getting a gutter-ass ho pregnant? What was he thinking? To top it off, Azia was gone. Not his boo. He couldn't let the one female he had given his heart to slip away that easily. The situation had to be dealt with. He tried talking the female into getting rid of the baby but she wasn't trying to hear it. He even considered ending her life to fix the problem. But as cold as he was, he couldn't bring himself to kill an unborn child.

"Who this?" he said answering the phone disgusted.

"We need to talk," the female on the other end advised.

He became concerned. "Talk about what? You said you keeping the baby, so what the fuck you got to say now?"

"Why you got to act all funky wit' me? You stuck so far up that conceited bitch's ass you don't know what to do. Did you tell her yet?"

"Don't worry about what I got going on over here. What you need to talk to me for?"

"I need some money."

Here we go. This is the dumb shit I'm talking about. "The only money you getting from me is abortion money. If you ain't getting one of those it ain't nothing I can help you with."

"Why can't we act civil, Rashaud?"

"I'm acting civil. You the one ain't acting civil. You tryna tear down everything I built but it ain't gonna happen."

"You call her everything? She means that much to you? How can you feel like that when I was here first?" she cried.

"You was here first but she gonna be here last. Remember that. Baby or no baby. Now if you want your baby to grow up without a daddy, that's on you. I'll take care of it but I don't want nothing to do wit' it."

"You so fucking ignorant, Rashaud. I can't believe you would stoop so low over some pussy. Pussy comes a dime a dozen and you stuck up under that bitch. She don't give a damn about you! She running wild in these streets doing her! Stop fronting like you don't know. Don't nothing get past you any other time, so I know you know, nigga! You just faking like you don't. This shit ain't gonna magically disappear. I'm carrying your baby and you treating me like I'm just a regular-ass ho from off the streets!"

"You *are* a regular-ass ho. You lazy as hell. You don't want to work. All you want to do is sit on your ass and collect money from me and welfare. If you ain't regular, then what are you?"

"Fuck you! That's why your ho is fucking Mike! If I was her, I would be, too, you no-good bastard!"

"Fuck you too, bitch!" He hung up in her ear. He got up off the sofa and went to take a leak. He was furious after that phone call. He cut the cold water on and threw some on his face. Then he went back into the living room and powered the TV on. He flicked through the channels and stopped at MTV jams. She continued to call him back-to-back for an hour straight. He ignored her calls, not answering one. She left a shit-load of messages. An hour and a half later, the TV was watching him. He had dozed off on the sofa. Around a quarter to midnight, he woke up feeling hungry for some Dungeness crabs, broccoli and corn on the cob. He didn't feel like standing in the ridiculous line at Pier 21 that's usually there around that hour. So he decided to go to The Happy End, a bar located off Woodland Avenue. That way he'd be able to get a drink while waiting for his order.

When he parked and saw how crowded the bar was, inside and out, he wished he had chosen Pier 21. But he had already parked so he stayed. Everybody was there. He gave dap to a few guys he knew from around the way and flirted with a few females. He made his way to the kitchen and had one of the guys closest to the bar order him a beer. He never noticed Tommy slouched down in the corner but Tommy saw him.

■ ■ ■

"**Son of a** bitch," the police chief cursed. "You mean to tell me can't none of you lazy pricks close any of these cases. Tell me, do you at least know if they're linked together? Do you have at least one suspect?" No one answered. "Well, fuck me. Do you pricks know anything?"

"I'm on to something chief," a young policeman yelled out from the bunch.

Completely baffled, the chief couldn't understand how someone was getting away with all these murders around the city. It was as if the perpetrator vanished as soon as they killed. "In my office! Now!" he shouted.

The Sean Kingston look-alike made his way into the chief's office. One of the other detectives was mocking the chief behind his back as they all made their way back to their desks. "In my office, now!" he repeated, whispering. His stomach was so big it jiggled when he chuckled with the rest of the detectives.

"Show me what you got," the chief demanded, taking a seat in his big leather chair. He looked over the detective's paper work. "Is this it? No way! You got to be shitting me!" He gave a pregnant pause. "Are all of these linked together or what? You're bringing this bullshit in here like you really got something." He removed his glasses from the case in his pocket and slid them onto his fat, white face. He began to read the report thoroughly. "I know who this guy is," he said, referring to Mudda. "We took him and his brother down a few years back, but they beat the case over a fucking technicality. Look at him now," he smiled. "Headless! Do you have any leads?"

"Not yet but I'm on it."

"It's been months now. How long does it take to find a suspect? Geez-laweez!" He scanned the second picture in the file. "Who's the female victim?"

"Her name is LaTonya Miller. She was gunned down in North Philly a few weeks back."

"Any suspects for this one?"

Detective Joseph stepped closer. "Not yet, but I have a few people I would like to question if that's alright with you."

"Do whatever you need to do, just don't come back until you get me some more fucking information." He balled up his meaty fist and slammed it down on his desk, stressing every word.

■ ■ ■

Tommy was throwing back shots of Grey Goose like it was going out of style. He sat and watched Rashaud's every move. Revenge was on his mind and there was no way he was going home without it. Even if it meant risking his own life. Ever since he'd opened his mouth to Stutter-man about what Busta had done, he'd been cut off completely, Busta made sure of that. The thousands of dollars that were rolling in on a daily basis came to a halt in a matter of minutes. After Busta shot him in the leg and left him to fend for himself, he had cut all ties with him. Any connect he had ever networked with was told to wash their hands of him. He felt like a lost cause. When the money stopped coming in so did his fiancé. She packed up everything—the kids, clothes, furniture and the dog—and left, leaving him with nothing. It was all over for him. The bottle had become his best friend.

Tommy had gathered the remainder of his drink and crept out the bar without being spotted by Rashuad. He found a parking spot a few cars back from where Rashaud had parked and waited patiently. As soon as he seen him exit the bar, the heat was on. He started the engine and sucked down the last of the Grey Goose, allowing it to burn his throat and chest. "Ahhhhh!" He was all riled up and ready for whatever. He grabbed his heat from the back seat and placed it on his lap, then pulled out to trail Rashaud.

It was a little after one in the morning and the streets were still alive. Hustlers and dope fiends filled the sidewalk in front of every open Chinese store. Sisters and brothers, mothers and friends occupied their doorsteps, gossiping late into the night.

Watching the street through his rearview mirror was a habit of Rashaud's. He never realized just how much he did it, but at that moment, he was glad he did.

Now it was one thing for the same car to turn down two or three of the same blocks. But when the same car turns down six or seven, that's suspicious. *Who the fuck is this following me?* He turned down a couple of random blocks just to make sure he wasn't being paranoid. The Dodge Magnum followed like metal to a magnet. *'Fuck's going on wit' this shit?*

Tommy stayed as far back as possible without losing sight of Rashaud but it wasn't far enough. Rashaud used the short time he spent at the red light on Cobbs Creek to grab his desert eagle from the back seat and his nine from the passenger seat. He turned his radio off and stuffed his cell phone into his pocket. *It ain't my time, mutherfucka. It ain't my time.*

Rashaud focused on the small groups of people lingering around. He was looking for a place to pull over where there wouldn't be so many witnesses. That opportunity came about five more blocks down. He pulled over to the side, acting like he was about to park.

When Rashaud's tail lights turned red, Tommy's adrenaline began to pump. His car came to an abrupt stop at the corner, across from where Rashaud had stopped. He blacked out and became reckless. He had almost emptied his whole clip before he realized that Rashaud was no longer in the driver's seat. Without Tommy's knowledge, Rashaud had slid out the passenger's side, but not before taking a bullet in the thigh.

"They shooting! They shooting!" Eyewitnesses scattered, not wanting to get caught up in the gun play. Some ran, while others squatted as low to the ground as they could get until the battle was over. Bullets ripped through glass, store and house windows, brick walls, stop signs and flesh. Sparks flew everywhere.

Rashaud's Cadillac absorbed most of Tommy's firepower, but Rashaud didn't let off a single shot until he saw the perfect opportunity. Tommy made the mistake of stepping around to the front of the car. Rashaud, from the ground, put his desert eagle to work. Tommy had no chance. His life ended with several shots hitting every part of his body. He had lost his life before his body crumpled to the ground.

Rashaud, in pain, limped to the nearest alley, escaping just seconds before the first cop car hit the scene. Bruised from the shattered glass and injured from the bullet, he didn't make it too far. He climbed a fence and hid in someone's backyard until the coast was clear.

"I got a fucking bullet in my arm, man! Can't you question me from the hospital?" an innocent bystander yelled out in agony. "You got all these fucking witnesses out here to tell you what went down."

Everybody in the hood knew what to tell and what not to tell. When it came to the code of the streets, if you even thought about snitching your time was up. The coward for a cop advised the ambulance to get the injured man to the hospital immediately. Anyone who had been close enough to see what happened rushed the detectives, each with a different story.

"I saw everything, my brother. Niggas was coming from all directions wit' three and four guns," one onlooker lied.

"Naw, homie. Two came from up that way," another guy pointed east. "And then the other guy came out of nowhere." He, too, was lying, giving one hell of a show.

"So do you both agree it was three gunmen?" Detective Joseph asked.

"Nope, it was more like four or five."

"Can you remember any of their faces?"

"All I can tell you is that there's some kind of sticky shit in between that crack on the sidewalk over there, 'cause that's where my face was, on the damn ground," the fake witnesses laughed and gave each other dap.

Annoyed with the two youngsters, the detective looked for someone else to question. "Excuse me, did you see anything?" he asked an elderly woman who had been awakened by the ruckus. She closed the door in his face, not mumbling one word.

"Nothing but assholes around here," the detective mumbled, then asked a fellow officer, "What you got on those tags?"

One of the first officers to hit the scene pulled his pad from the car. "I ran the tags on both cars. That Magnum is registered to a Bethany Wilkins who resides on the west side. I got a couple officers heading to the address listed on the registration now. The Cadillac is registered to a Marion Lesion. And get this, she's listed as deceased. I pulled her driving record and her birth date is February of 1917."

Detective Joseph was confused. "That would make her, like …" he thought a minute, "ninety, right? That can't be. I know she ain't driving nowhere."

The officer shrugged and pointed to where Tommy's dead body was. "I won't know which car belongs to him until I run the fingerprints."

"Get everything to me ASAP. And call me when they talk to whoever this Bethany person is," he ordered before walking back to the scene. He studied Tommy's body from head to toe. "How many he got in him," he asked the CSI unit.

"I've counted six so far but we won't know for sure until we get him up on the table."

Detective Joseph took a deep breath. He desperately wanted to know who the second gunman was. It was so frustrating he was ready to pay for the information. "It don't matter how rich you are, when it's your time to go, you're gone." He returned the officer's notepad to him. "I'm going for coffee. Call me with any updates."

CHAPTER 9
The Sun Don't Shine Forever

"The person you think is your friend just might be your enemy."
-Mike

The alarm clock went off at eight the following morning. It was Saturday. Azia rolled over to find that the nightmare that seemed so real was just a dream. She remembered being in a dark room. It was cold and quiet. There were a lot of people there but, for some reason, the only voices that could be heard were hers and Rashaud's. She remembered him asking her if she loved him. Her response was, "Not anymore." He broke down. She walked away thinking it was over, that she was rid of him for the rest of her life, but he stopped her. When she turned around, the only thing she saw was steel. She couldn't move. She held her breath and closed her eyes hoping he would disappear, but he didn't. Then the gun went off. Before knowing what happened next, the alarm clock went off. That was the first time she had ever been happy that the alarm went off on time.

She went to take a shower to relax her mind. She was missing Tonya so badly. She reminisced about how happy they had been before Rashaud came into the picture. They did everything together. They used to have fun like normal college students did. Then Rashaud came into her life and everything changed. He was sick in the head as far as she was concerned. He had turned her into somebody she wasn't. It was too late. She was too far gone and her hands were just as dirty as his. She loved him, for sure, but the whole thing was becoming too much for her to swallow.

After her shower, she sat in bed for a little while longer, thinking about the person she turns into when he's around. It was like she had an alter ego, which she later named Annie. Two people, one body, and two totally different worlds. Annie was the total opposite of Azia. They were both hustlers, but on different missions. Azia's hustle was sex for money. Annie's hustle was blood and money. The thrill it gave to hold a gun was indescribable. It made her feel like she was in charge. Her adrenaline was always up. She thought back to the first time she pulled the trigger. Visualizing the blood gushing out of Mustafa's neck sent a chill up her spine.

Her ringing phone snapped her out of the trance she was in. She cursed herself for not making sure the power was off. All she wanted to do all day was lay back and relax with no interruptions. She answered, curious to know who the unfamiliar number belonged to. Azia heard the female suck her teeth when she answered.

"Can you put Rashaud on the phone?"

"Who the hell is this?"

"Umm," she hesitated. "Can you just put him on the phone, please?"

With hesitation Azia replied, "If you want Rashaud, you need to call his goddamn phone, not mines," she warned, ending the call abruptly. She had no clue who the unidentified female was, but she wasn't going to be disrespected. She didn't give a damn if it was his momma.

Seconds later the phone rang again. "Is Rashaud there?"

Azia snapped. "How did you get this number? Call his damn cell phone if it's that important."

"Listen, I ain't got no gripe wit' you for real. It is what it is. I got what I needed to get off my chest at the card game. Just tell him that I got the proof he said he needed.

Tell him to get his money right because I ain't getting rid of it."

Azia's heart sank. She didn't know how to respond. If the girl hadn't hung up after speaking those last words she would have caught Azia speechless. Azia thought back to the conversation, word for word. Stunned, she blurted, "That's that bitch I was playing cards wit' that attacked my ass. I should kill that lying bastard. I can't believe he fucked around wit' that gutter-ass ho." She quickly switched into Annie-mode. She was ready to kill him and her. She paced back and forth in the little space available. She tried calling Rashaud several times but his voicemail continued to pick up. "Rashaud, where the hell are you at? I need you to call me right away," she said after the beep.

Azia got dressed around ten and headed out the door. She took a handful of money and went to pamper herself. The first stop was the spa. She spent two hours getting a massage and a facial. The relaxing atmosphere had her zoned out. There was no way she could stay mad in a place like that, even if she'd wanted to. She let her mind run free. An hour and a half later, she was feeling fresh and rejuvenated. Her next stop was the nail salon for a manicure and pedicure. Her hair appointment wasn't until three o'clock so she still had time to kill. While getting her feet scrubbed, she decided to try Mike again.

"Hey, stranger," he answered like she was the one ducking calls.

"You know I don't like that title. We got to come up wit' a better one than that."

"If you stop staying away from me for so long maybe we can." He was about to question her whereabouts over the past few days but decided not to. She wasn't his girl and he wasn't her man. Although he enjoyed her company, the conversation, and the sex, he kept things between them on a certain level. "Long as you cool, I'm good."

"Everything is everything," she sighed. "I just got a lot on my plate right now."

"Hopefully it's not more than you can chew."

"You know, at times your eyes can be bigger than your stomach; when you think you're hungrier than you really are. I think it's turning out to be one of those type of situations for me."

"I'm not going to pry into your business. You know if you need an ear I'm here. I'm sure everything will find a way of working itself out."

"I hope so, Mike." *For all of our sakes*, she thought. "What are you up to?"

"I'm over on 16th and Tasker at the barber shop about to get a cut."

"Can I stop through to see you?"

"That ain't a problem. Just don't bring your problems wit' you. Make sure you have that pretty smile on your face."

"I can do that. I'll be there after I leave the nail salon."

After they hung up, her thoughts of him were like an ongoing melody. Mike had tuned into her outlet. He listened to and understood her more than Rashaud had time to. Things had changed so quickly. For months, she had been feeding him people and doing whatever she could, just to keep him happy. And look what kind of thanks she got. Making a baby on her was fowl. After all they'd built together, all the pussy she'd given up to put more money in his pocket. She was feeling pimped. She recalled asking him if he was ready to have a child with her. His reply was, "I ain't having no kids right now. Are you crazy?" It was eating her up inside. She was going through so many different emotions, and she didn't know how to handle any of them. Now she was wishing she had listened to Tonya when she told her to leave him alone.

Payback had to come some way, some how. She was determined to get him back.

Mike appeared in the doorway of Jazz U Up barber shop with a cape on. This was a popular spot to get a cut, shape-up, shave, and whatever else kept a man looking right. He jogged across the street to Azia's car looking both ways. She loved seeing him and his dimples. "Hey, cutie," he greeted.

"Hey, handsome," she blushed.

He hopped into her car to get out of the way of a bus that was quickly approaching. They traded a few words, kisses and giggles. She agreed to have dinner with him later on that night. The way she was feeling about Rashaud at the moment, she planned on making it an all-nighter with him. "I'll call you around eight-thirty to let you know where to meet me," he advised.

"Okay, I'm on my way to get my hair done and then I'm heading in."

Mike voluntarily dug into his pocket and passed off three-hundred dollars to her. "This should take care of your hair and everything else you had done today. Stuff like that *you* shouldn't have to pay for."

Azia presented the palm of her hand to accept the money. She wasn't about to tell him no thank you. "I'll see you tonight," she winked.

Azia pulled off as Mike jogged back across the street. She picked up the phone to try calling Rashaud again, but still no answer. Azia's fingers dialed her salon next. "Hey, Sabrina, how many heads I have in front of me?"

"Like, two, but they only getting curled," she said.

"I'm running to the store then I'll be there. Don't give my spot away."

Azia headed for Chestnut Street to Victoria's Secret before going to get her hair tossed. On the way, she couldn't help but think to herself, *Stupid-ass nigga.*

Stupid! I can't believe he played me like this. I knew his ass was up to no good. If I had known it was going to go down like this, I woulda been got rid of his ass.

There were no available parking spaces around the store, so she parked in a no-parking zone and hit her hazard lights, thinking, *fuck it.* Of course when she came out, a blue and white piece of paper was sticking out from under her windshield wipers. She snatched the ticket and ripped it up into little pieces, just like she did with all of them. It wasn't her car so she couldn't care less. Rashaud had no real insurance on the Solara he'd bought her, so it was never replaced. He told her to give him a week to find her a new one and, in the meantime, to drive one of his. That week had now turned into months, still no car of her own, so she was stuck with a rental for now.

She arrived at Crystal Palace Hair Salon on 14th & Girard Ave. on time. She was able to get right in the shampoo chair, and by the time she was dry, she was being called over by her stylist. She walked out the door with a boost of confidence. Her hair was flowing, her nails and feet were tight and she still felt relaxed from the massage. She was good to go. She couldn't wait to try on her lingerie for the night. Looking at the time, she was glad her wardrobe was still filled with things that had never been worn before. She wouldn't have to waste any time searching for something to wear.

Not long after arriving back at the hotel, she got the call she'd been waiting on. "He-ll-o-" she said out of breath.

"Where you been all day?"

"No, the question is where you been," she spat.

"I had to take care of some business."

"What kind of business you got to take care of that keeps you from answering your phone or making calls?" She looked over at the clock and realized that time was not on her side. She changed the subject to start a quick argument. "Why you ain't tell me you had a baby on the way, Rashaud?"

He chuckled. "Who told you that?"

"The horse's mouth, that's who! When were you going to man up and keep it real? Or were you gonna try to pull the wool over my eyes wit' this one? I can't believe you! So I'm pretty sure you know we had a fight, too! Why didn't you say anything?"

He chuckled again. "You mad? I know you ain't mad for real. You think I don't know what the fuck you be doing wit' your free time? Huh?" She didn't respond. "Azia, you can't put nothing past me. I know you been creeping around wit' that nigga Mike. I'm not stupid."

She didn't know what to make of his attitude. He wasn't raising his voice like he did when he flew into one of his jealous fits. He didn't even bother to mention her moving out. Off the top of her head she tried to make it sound good. "Yeah, I was getting personal wit' him for your ass. I didn't tell you because I didn't want you to be all on my head and breathing down my neck and fucking shit up. But now I ain't doing shit for you no more. Go ask that grimey-ass ho to bait those niggas."

She hung up in his ear and ignored him when he called back. She cut the volume to low after the first couple times he called, becoming agitated by the ringtone. She reached into her bag and pulled out the first outfit she got her hands on, which happened to be a white and gold Baby Phat bubble dress. She slid on her gold pumps and grabbed an overnight bag packing it with her toothbrush, deodorant, lotion, underwear and an outfit for the following day. She had no intentions of returning that night. The night was going to be about Mike and Mike only.

Eight o'clock that evening, Azia was handing her car over to the valet. She walked through the doors of the

Chart House on Delaware Avenue anxious to see her man. He didn't know she had given him the title, but in her mind he was. The hostess took her to where he was seated out on the balcony. The view of the river was so beautiful and calming at night. Azia rose from her chair and walked over to the edge of the balcony to get a better view. Mike came up behind her and wrapped his arms around her waist. It felt so good, she wished they never had to leave.

"What are you thinking about?"

"Life," she responded.

"Talk to me, Azia. I'm tired of seeing you hold stuff in all the time. Bottling your feelings up is not going to help you. If you talk about them, I guarantee you'll feel a whole lot better, baby."

One tear trickled down her cheek. She was afraid to talk, afraid that she would break down, and she didn't want to do it in front of him. She closed her eyes and sank back into his arms. Mike clutched on to her tighter.

"Talk to me. Don't shut me out."

"I can't," she muttered. "Everything going on in my life right now is so complicated. I can't explain it. I can't talk about it. I can't respond to it. I can't even control it." She turned to look him in the eyes. "I'm not a bad person, Mike. I may make bad decisions but I'm not a bad person. I just feel so congested at times, so overwhelmed. I make moves without thinking. Some of the moves I make I regret and some I don't. I just wish I had a better understanding of what I'm supposed to be doing wit' my time here in this world. How much longer do I have? How many more mistakes will I make? How many right decisions have I made? How many of them were wrong? I just can't take it anymore."

"We all make some bad choices in life. But we learn from them. I'm going to share something wit' you that I don't share wit' a lot of people. When I was twelve years old, I watched my father rape my mother on our living room floor. After he raped her, he let two of his friends into the house to have their way wit' her. I watched them beat my mom. They ran all up in her like she was just a piece of meat. My dad sat back and watched the whole thing. He did nothing. All he did was laugh. I was young. I didn't know what was going on." He chuckled. "I was scared. I pissed my pants. You better not tell anybody that either." Azia smiled. "But the whole time, I stood there asking myself 'How can a man let this happen to his woman?' 'What could she have done so bad to deserve that?' Believe it or not, I watched for hours. I cried like a baby. I was twelve years old. I was big enough to stand up for my mom. I didn't care what she had done, no man was going to disrespect her like that—not even my father. When his friends left, he hopped his big ass on top of her again, as if she hadn't already had enough. My mom wasn't moving at all; I thought she was dead. I went into the dining room, pulled my dad's snub-nosed .38 out of a drawer, and went back into the living room. My mom still wasn't moving, but my dad was just a-humping away. I aimed a gun for the first time. He never heard me come up behind him. I got close enough to them to smell the blood that was coming out of my mother's womb and I fired. I shot him right in the head. He fell on my mother's chest. That was the first time I saw somebody dead. Shit, that was the first time I saw that much blood in person. I freaked the fuck out."

Azia's mouth was wide open. She couldn't believe Mike had just shared that kind of information with her. She wished she could open up like that to him. She wanted to tell it all—about Mudda, Mustafa, and all the other setups. But she wasn't crazy. She wasn't trying to lose him and what they had. If he ever found out she was that scandalous, he would probably kill her himself.

"I thought I had lost both of my parents until the cops came. They found me sitting on the floor holding my mom's hand wit' my left and holding the gun in my right. I found out later that she had survived all of it. It took her a while to bounce back. At one point, I remember her wishing she was dead."

"Did you ever find out what she had done to piss your father off that bad?"

He chuckled again. "She stole some money from him. It wasn't a lot of money; just a couple dollars to buy me some clothes and new shoes for school. She had asked him for it and you know what he said? He told her to buy them her fucking self. So that's what she did—took his money and went shopping. He knew damn well she wasn't working because he couldn't handle her being out in public without him. He was a straight-up asshole. He called himself teaching her a lesson. He deserved what happened to him."

"I'm surprised you're not still locked down somewhere. Did you get in any trouble?"

"I spent about a year in a juvenile detention center. That's about it. Who could blame me for defending my mother? Couldn't no judge punish me for that. They had me taking all kinds of anger management classes, like I didn't know what the hell I had done. I knew exactly what I had done. I ain't crazy."

"Damn!" Azia couldn't react. She was still stuck at the part when he pulled the trigger and killed his own father. How gangsta is that?

"I told you all of this to say that we all make choices, and not all of them are going to be good all the time. I learned from what happened to me back then. I shouldn't have killed him. If he would have lived to go to prison, he woulda suffered a lot more. But I reacted. I asked the Lord for forgiveness every night for six months straight until my mom got better."

"How is she doing now?"

"She's good. She couldn't be better. She got a nice house, drives a nice car, and got herself a nice friend that's keeping her happy. Things couldn't be better for her right now."

"Did she forgive you?"

He didn't answer the question right away, which made her assume she didn't.

"She never held it against me. She was sad that he was gone and upset when they took me away from her for a year." He shrugged. "But after that, everything was cool. We moved out here to Philly and started a new life."

"You're not from Philly?" she asked, surprised.

"I'm from Plainfield, New Jersey. That's where I grew up for the most part."

"I would've never guessed."

"Nobody knows that except my inner circle. And now you."

"Does that mean I can consider myself a part of your inner circle?"

"You know something that not all of the people in my circle know, so I guess it's only right for you to claim a spot."

She smiled. "I like that. Maybe now my name won't be stranger anymore." They both laughed. "Why is it that you don't share your story? Is it because you don't trust a lot of people?"

"*Trust* is major for me. I can count the people in my life that I trust on one hand."

"You feel comfortable having people around your empire, even if you don't trust them?"

"Help, I need. I can't build an empire on my own. But trust is something I don't have to do. You know how the streets are. You're old enough and smart enough to understand them. Now-a-days the person you think is your friend just might be your enemy. How real is that?"

"I can't argue wit' you there."

The waitress returned to check on them. "Did you guys want any dessert tonight?" she asked. "We have hot chocolate lava cake and raspberry crème brulee on the menu tonight."

Mike looked at the waitress, then at Azia. "No, thank you. I have all the dessert I need right here in my arms."

Dessert is exactly what Azia turned out to be. They got back to his place and got it in like heated animals in a jungle. R. Kelly's *Double Up* CD blasted in the background as they fucked in every part of the house. They started in the kitchen on the washing machine, then went to the dining room to the bar top, then wound up in the living room on the stairs. Next, they made their way up to his room to the balcony. Being bent over the rail and getting her back twisted out was thrilling. She felt nervous and pleasured all at the same time. Then Mike scooped her up in one motion and gave it to her hard on his bedroom floor. Rug burns would result for sure the following day. They ended in the bathroom—on the sink, on the toilet, and last but not least, in the shower. Azia was in her glory. She felt they were meant to be.

CHAPTER 10
Fighting One Battle At A Time
"Get your mind right."
-Azia

The following morning, Mike woke up to breakfast in bed. The aroma of sausages and pancake syrup hit his nose before his eyes could open. It had been a long time since he'd had a home-cooked meal. The closest he got to homemade food was at his mother's house when he finds the time to visit. Fast food during the day and fancy restaurants at night is how he'd gotten used to living. The one thing he was missing in his life was a wife to take care of him like his momma would. He had everything a man could ever wish for—a beautiful place to call home, a growing empire, fancy cars and money coming out his ass. And he'd had his share of females through the years, but sex was all it had been. They occupied his time but never filled the void in his heart. He wasn't looking for that special person to have, to hold, and to love, but that feeling arose when he met Azia. She was a good and bad girl all wrapped into one. That was what excited him the most.

Pulling her down next to him, he kissed her deeply. "What's all this for?" he asked looking down at the breakfast.

She smiled. "It's just my way of saying thank you for last night."

"For which part—dinner or dessert?"

"Both," she giggled.

"Well, I guess I'm going to have to thank you for this big breakfast then because I haven't been treated like this in a while."

"You don't have to thank me for that. I did it out of the kindness of my heart."

"And I want to do it out of the kindness of my heart as well."

"Do what?"

"I want to take you away somewhere; somewhere you can relax and clear your mind a little. I was thinking maybe Cancun, Jamaica, or maybe even Miami. As long as they got a beach, I don't care, 'cause I'm 'bout due for a vacation myself."

"Oh, Mike. Would you do that for me, for real?"

"I'm not joking."

"Well, when do we leave?"

"The sooner you book it, the sooner we can go."

Azia took the plate of food from his hands and set it on the dresser. Then she snatched the covers from his legs and hopped up on him like a rabbit in heat. She planted baby kisses all over his face saying, "Thank you—Thank you—Thank you—" each time she kissed a different spot. She ended down around his inner thighs, teasing him with baby bites, and then worked her way to his middle. She took all of him into her mouth and sucked him up like he was storing the cure to her poison.

Mike was on cloud nine. As hungry as he was, she made him forget there was a plate of food only a couple feet away. He closed his eyes and concentrated while she did her famous tricks with her tongue. "Umm—Umm—Umm—" he moaned, making love to her mouth.

It never took Azia long to bring him to his peak. It never took her long to bring anyone to their peak for that matter. She was what the hood called a PHD (Professional Head Doctor). She felt the warm sensation hit the back of her throat when he came. She swallowed, making sure there was nothing left to ooze out of the head before releasing him from her mouth.

"Azia, girl, you're one of a kind," he told her, regaining his composure.

"That's only half of me. Wait until you get to know the whole me."

Azia rushed to the computer to put together a vacation package. She searched and searched until she found something she liked. When she found it, she ran back upstairs to tell Mike about her decision. He took care of the flight and resort reservations, which were for a seven-day, six-night stay on the island of Montego Bay, Jamaica. The next morning, there was so much to do with so little time. Mike gave her money to go shopping, get her nails and feet done, and get her hair touched up. She was in her glory until her cell rang and snapped her out of the trance.

"I know you mad, but when are you bringing your ass home?"

It felt like ice had crept into her blood. "I don't have time for this, Rashaud."

"I didn't ask what you had time for. I asked when are you bringing your black ass home?"

"I'm not feeling too well right now. I'd appreciate it if you left me alone for a while. You really hurt me. I need some time to myself so I can think things through."

"That sounds like a buncha bullshit to me, but I'ma ride wit' it for now. I know I fucked up, I admit that. But don't forget who you belong to."

With confidence she replied, "That's exactly why I haven't returned, Rashaud. You act like you own me. You don't own me."

He called her every name he could possibly come up with. Bitch, slut and ho were the most frequent ones. She tried to understand where it all was coming from. He was the one that got that bitch pregnant, not her. The things he was saying cut her real deep. Each word that left his mouth made her madder and madder. She got tired of hearing his threats and allegations so she cut him off.

"That's exactly what I be talking 'bout wit' you! You got anger issues! I thought giving you this time to yourself would have given you some time to think and air things out! You the one who need to be on your knees begging me to stay, not the other way around, in case you didn't know that!" Azia took a deep breath trying to remain humble. She was sitting in the hair salon. Everybody knows gossip is the highlight of the day. "Just give me some time and let me be by myself so I can clear my head, okay? We'll talk later."

"Yeah, tell me anything to shut me up. Don't make me come find you, Azia. I mean that."

He hung up without waiting for a response to his last threat. She wasn't scared. She was sick and tired of being afraid of him. Her phone rang again, but this time it was Abdul.

"I haven't heard anything from you the last couple of days. I was calling to check on you."

"I'm fine. Thanks for checking."

"Last time we talked, you said you were ready for us to get together to discuss some business."

"I just got caught up in some personal issues. I want to be ready and focused when we meet, that's why I haven't called you yet. I'm about to go away for a few days to clear my head. I'm sure I'll be ready for you when I return. That's if the door is still open."

"Of course the door is still open. You go ahead and do what you need to do. Make sure you call me upon your return and we'll go from there."

"Sounds like a plan."

"I don't know where you're going but have fun."

"I'll try," she snickered. "Tell Gisele to be ready for her new, I can't wait to do business with her."

"I'll make sure to tell her. She's been asking for you."

Hearing that Gisele was concerned about her made her tingle on the inside. They spoke a minute longer, and then it was time for Azia to go to the shampoo bowl. She took a seat at the open bowl and began listening in on a conversation between two females near by. It was a conversation Azia wished she'd never overheard. At first she didn't know who the females were talking about, but when they mentioned a blue BMW and 20th street, which is Mike's neck of the woods, she paid a little closer attention. Azia leaned her head back into the shampoo bowl and listened quietly while her hair was being washed.

"Bitch, you lying," the one girl said with her lips tooted in the air. "His fine ass ain't got no time for you."

"I'm not lying. We're meeting up when I leave here. I should make his ass come and pick me up so I ain't got to walk home to get dressed," said the other girl.

"Yeah, tell him to come and get you. Make a believer out of me."

She can't possibly be talking about my Mike. I won't believe it. How can he be meeting up with her and he knows I'm coming back over tonight. Our damn flight leaves tomorrow. Hell no, I ain't letting that wench ruin a trip I planned. Azia was ready to sit up and tell the girl to make a believer out of her, too, but she didn't.

The female continued with her story. "We were supposed to get together the last couple of nights but he said he got tied up."

Yeah, bitch, he was tied up alright. Azia smirked and bit her tongue once again.

"He promised we'd go do something tonight because he got to go out of town for a few days. He said we gonna go down to Ruth Chris on Broad to grab a bite to eat."

"Ruth Chris!" her friend exclaimed. "They expensive as shit! Your ass better not order any steak or lobster," she joked. "You know what they say you got to do when you order high-priced shit off the menu."

"Go deep-sea diving," they said in unison and burst into laughter.

"His sexy ass can have whatever he want from me," she admitted with no hesitation.

I don't fucking believe it. She is definitely talking about my Mike. I should kick his ass. You know what? That bitch don't know who she fucking wit'. I got something for her ass. She gonna be a pissed bitch 'cause he ain't meeting up with nobody but me. Watch this shit. Azia waited until she got settled under the dryer before she made the call. The two females finished their conversation while getting their hair curled. Azia dialed Mike's number. He answered on the first ring. "What you doing, baby?"

"I'm running around collecting this money so I can get it out the way before we leave. Did you get everything you needed done?"

"For the most part. I still have to pack, but I got everything else done. I'm at the hair salon now about to get my hair done."

"That's right, get pretty for daddy, baby."

Don't baby me, you fool. "What time did you want me to come over tonight?"

"I should be home between ten and eleven."

She sucked her teeth. "That late? You know we got to get up early tomorrow. I wanted to be in bed by that time."

"I'm gonna be running all night. If you want, I can scoop you from your hotel room in the morning since you'll already be down at the airport. Or better yet, I can come and stay there when I'm finished doing what I need to do."

Naw, nigga. That ain't going to work on the kid. "I wanted to go get something to eat tonight. Do you think that's possible?"

"I can't promise you nothing but I'll try to make it happen."

She went in for the kill. "Please try, 'cause I had a taste for one of those steaks from Ruth Chris. I've been thinking about it all day." She was cracking up inside.

He paused before replying. She caught him off guard with that one. "Let me see what I can do. If I don't get finished in time, we can just order some room service when I get there."

Whatever, nigga! "Alright. Just call me when you're done."

Azia finished letting her hair dry and made her way back to the front to see if the girls were still holding the same conversation but they weren't. Now they were talking about whose video they would be in and what artist they would mess with.

These bitches are really starting to annoy me, Azia thought to herself. *Why don't they just shut the fuck up?*

"Come sit in my chair, Azia." Her stylist, Sabrina, called to her.

Mike's little fan club was finished and ready to head out the door. "I'll see you in a week unless I sweat my hair out earlier than that," his groupie said to Sabrina.

Azia rolled her eyes unnoticeably. Even if the girl's plans did go through, her date with Mike was going to get crashed before the night was over. Azia was going to make sure of it. "Who was that girl that just got out of your chair?"

"Nakita. Doesn't she talk too much? When them bitches come in here they never shut up." Azia nodded her head. "How are you getting it today?" asked Sabrina.

"Go ahead and do what you want to do wit' it. Just put it up, 'cause I'm going away and I don't feel like dealing wit' it the whole time I'm there."

"Where you going?"

Azia was hoping she would ask. "To Jamaica," she said, like it was no big deal.

"Who you going wit'? Rashaud?"

"Hell no! His ass is psycho—but that's another story for another time. I'm going wit' a friend of mines named Mike."

"He from around here?"

"He's from South Philly. He drives a blue BMW 750. You know ain't too many of those bad boys around."

"Get the hell out of here! I know exactly who you talking about. When you start messing with him?"

"We're just friends. We ain't no couple. We just be hanging out together."

Sabrina gave her the 'Mmm Hmm, whatever.'

"For real, we're just cool." Azia knew their relationship was a little deeper than *just cool*, but she didn't want to put too much of her business out there. Because if Mike was telling people they were just friends, she didn't want to make herself look like a fool and say they were more than that.

She and Sabrina talked about Mike until Azia was done and ready to get out of the chair. "I know I'll be running to you by the time I get back, so you might as well put me in your book now."

"I'll put you in for next Thursday."

"That'll work. I'll see you when I get back."

"Don't party too hard with your friend," Sabrina said sarcastically.

Azia threw up her middle finger playfully and moseyed on out the door.

"Damn, I wish I knew what time they were talking about getting together," Azia spoke aloud to no one in particular. She was driving down the street, heading for Keemah's house. This was the third rental car that Hertz had put her in since the day she left Rashaud. Not having a car of her own was really starting to bother her. Plus, the hotel and rental car bills were starting to smack her account hard. She made a mental note not to forget to call Abdul the moment she returned. It was time for some steady income to be made.

She pulled up in front of Keemah's door and honked the horn. If she had pulled up two minutes earlier, she would have bumped heads with the same ghost she thought she saw the night they were leaving the strip club, Twin. She slid out of the car and went to knock on the door. Keemah answered in nothing but a bra and boy shorts. "Where the hell is your clothes?" Azia asked with her face balled up.

"This is my house. I can walk around butt naked if I wanted to," Keemah responded. She stood aside and let Azia in. But before following her inside, she stuck her head out the door to see if Twin had pulled off or not. She saw the empty space two spots away from her house where his car had been parked. *Damn, that was close!*

Azia had already positioned herself in front of the TV. She flipped through the channels waiting for Keemah to come inside. "What are you doing tonight?"

"Resting! Hanging out wit' your ass all the time, I don't seem to get any."

"You can rest when you get old. Right now I need you to find some energy for me. I want to go down Ruth Chris to get something to eat."

"I don't feel like getting dressed for that type of atmosphere. I don't even think I have anything to wear period. I need to go do some laundry."

"C'mon, Keemah. Come hang out wit' me before I go away."

"Away? Where you going and who you going wit'?"

"Mike is taking me to Jamaica. We leave in the morning," she sang with a sparkle in her eyes. Keemah sat there, wishing it was her getting ready for a trip. Then Azia said, "I need to go to Ruth Chris to see about something."

"See about what?" Azia told her about the conversation she'd overheard in the salon. After hearing that, Keemah was down to go. She was down for anything involving drama. She had been that way since they were children. "What you gonna do if he is there wit' her?"

"Just make it known that he ain't as slick as he think he is."

"He ain't your man. Technically he ain't got to explain nothing to you."

"Don't hit me wit' no technicalities. I ain't tryna hear none of that."

Keemah made her way up the stairs to find something to put on. "Like I said, he ain't your man."

Azia sensed a bit of jealousy in Keemah's voice. She wasn't ready to go through the same crap she had gone through with Tonya when it came to Rashaud. "Just hurry up so we can go."

■ ■ ■

Helena was sitting in her bedroom with tears falling from her eyes, listening to the harsh words coming out of Busta's mouth. After a night filled with heated sex, they woke up arguing, and she was getting sick of it. She turned her naked body to face him in the bed. "Busta, I told you! It's not your baby! I know its Rashaud's baby! You can sit up here and spit fire at me all you want, but the end result is still going to be the same!"

"You don't know who baby it is on some real shit! You just guessing!"

She frowned. "I'm not guessing. I know for sure. We started messing around after I found out I was pregnant. I just ain't tell you."

Busta became disgusted. "Why the fuck you wait until now to tell me?!"

"Because I was feeling you and didn't want to lose you! You make me feel so much better than Rashaud does. I'd rather be wit' you, but I know that wit' me carrying his child, it'll never happen." She played her part well and Busta was being suckered right in to it.

He came in close enough to hug her. "Go get an abortion and we'll make it happen. I love you, girl. What Rashaud says doesn't matter. Get rid of the baby and have mine. He don't want you to have his baby no way."

That was not what she was trying to hear. There was no way in hell she was getting rid of the baby, though she wasn't sure if it was his or Rashaud's. She was only messing around with Busta because he kept her bills paid and made her feel good inside, unlike Rashaud. But he wasn't the one she wanted to be with. She was going to use the pregnancy to her full advantage, assuming that Rashaud would come around and start treating her differently once he knew she was carrying his seed.

"I can't get rid of this baby, Busta. I'm not strong enough to willingly kill an unborn child," she lied, knowing damn well that if she aborted this baby, it would be number three.

Busta released her from his arms. "Well, it ain't nothing I can do then. I'm not gonna keep fucking and taking care of you while you carrying another nigga's child. That ain't happening. Go right on ahead and be stupid, 'cause you already know he ain't gonna treat you like I do. He don't want your ass and he ain't leaving Azia, so you can forget about it. If you thinking otherwise, then your dumb ass gonna be sitting here all by yourself, you and your bastard child."

"He ain't got to take care of me and neither do you! Fuck that! I can fend for myself! Get the fuck out wit' your ignorant ass!" She hopped out of bed and threw his clothes on his head. "Now you want to flip the script 'cause I said it ain't your baby! I thought we were better than that!"

"You were just a piece of pussy. I don't know what made you think otherwise." She sat with a look of shock on her face. "Don't give me that look. You fucking me and my best friend. How can it ever be more than that?"

"You were damn sure taking care of me like it was more than that."

"I don't mind paying for the pussy when it's good."

"Nigga, you full of shit! You were just sitting up here talking about killing his child and having yours! Now you feeling some kind of way because you know Rashaud is who I really wanna be wit' ! Get to stepping—!"

The way Busta grabbed her around her neck was lethal. He watched her complexion turn from caramel to purple within seconds. The blows she was trying to throw didn't faze him one bit. He was ready to end her and the child's life. It wasn't his baby so it didn't matter to him. Several seconds after debating with himself, he released his grip.

Helena fell out of the bed, gasping for air. It took her a couple minutes to find enough air and energy to try to kick him out of her house again. In no rush, Busta put his clothes on. He eyed her severely. He was hurting inside but would never let it be known. He cursed himself for falling for her in the first place. What was supposed to have been a night of fun turned into months of passion. "I wonder what Rashaud gonna say about the possibility that the baby's mine," he grunted.

"It ain't yours! I told you, I was already—"

"Bitch, stop the lies," he spat, cutting her off. "That's what you want me to think, but I ain't stupid. We didn't start fucking too long after ya'll did so you ain't really sure. You want the baby to be his—fine. I'm gonna roll wit' that. But you better not call my phone ever again wit' that crying shit. I'm washing my hands of you. Go let welfare pay some of these bills, get your hair done and clothe you, 'cause you ain't my problem no more." He exited the room and never looked back.

■ ■ ■

Mike and Nakita were sitting at the table looking over their menus. Mike was used to the sophisticated establishment they were in. Nakita, on the other hand, wasn't used to it at all. The most expensive place she'd ever been in the city was probably Chickie and Pete's. She looked over the entrée section, then the appetizer section, then back to the entrée section. After reviewing the prices, she didn't know which side she should order from. She didn't want it to look like this was all new to her, but she told on herself when she realized the sides had to be ordered separately.

She looked up at Mike and asked, "The entrées don't include sides?" Mike shook his head no. "For that price, they just ought to."

Mike chuckled to himself. "Don't worry about the price. Just order whatever you want."

She looked the menu over for ten more minutes before deciding on the filet and shrimp with a side of broccoli. Mike ordered the Porterhouse steak for two. His plan was to eat one half and save the second for Azia. He was going to tell her he picked it up to surprise her, knowing how bad she'd been craving it. But his plan was nipped in the bud when he saw her approaching his table. He cleared his throat and started fidgeting in his seat. By the time he thought of getting up to go to the bathroom to avoid the confrontation between the two girls, it was too late. She had already reached their table.

Nakita knew something was off by the way Mike was acting. When she looked to her side she saw Azia standing at the table. She recognized her immediately from the salon. Her first thought was that she had a question about her hair or something. "Can I help you?"

Azia stared down at her without blinking. "No, you can't help me," she said, then turned to Mike. "But he can."

"What you doing here?"

"I was going to ask you the same question. Shouldn't you be getting ready for our trip? Oh, my bad, I forgot you supposed to be running around collecting the money." She smacked the side of her leg like she got the answer right. "Yeah, that's what it was."

"What are you doing here, Azia?"

"I told you I wanted some Ruth Chris. The plan was for me and my cousin to grab a bite to eat, and then I was heading back to the hotel to wait on you."

Nakita sat quietly for as long as she could until she remembered she had been talking to her girlfriend about Mike and where he was taking her while Azia was getting her hair washed. She chuckled. "You funny," she barked.

"I'm not here for you, so you can save your comments." Not once did Azia raise her voice or act out-of-pocket with either one of them. She knew how to get her point across without making a scene, especially in classy places.

Nakita was not on the same page. She kept it hood no matter where she went. "You coming in here like this shit is coincidental." Her voice went up a notch with each sentence. "This ain't no coincidence! You heard me talking about coming here wit' him!"

Other guests started to look in their direction.

"Keep your voice down," Mike insisted.

Azia looked over at Mike and pointed to Nakita. "She right. I did hear her say you were bringing her here. That's why I'm here. But now that I see and hear what kind of chick she is, I'm embarrassed. I shouldn't have wasted my time. 'Cause she damn sure ain't no competition. We ain't even on the same level."

Nakita stood. "What you tryna say? What you mean I ain't on your level?"

Azia took a step back. "Pssshhh...Do I really have to answer that? You jumping out of chairs like you ready to fight. Look around you. This ain't Burger King. I came here to confront him, not you. So you can have a seat and mind your business."

Mike was tired of hearing them go back and forth. After the hostess came over to ask them to keep their voices down, it had become embarrassing. "Azia, go wait for me outside. I'll be out there in a minute," he demanded.

Azia looked at the girl one more time before stepping off. She grabbed Keemah's hand and they headed out the front door. All the guests who were already seated looked at them like they had stolen something when they walked back through the restaurant. Less than five minutes after they hit the front pavement, Mike stormed out. He got so close to Azia she could smell the wine on his breath. His hands remained at his side. "What you call yourself doing? You're better than this."

"How can you lie to me? And how can you brush me off when I say I want to get something to eat so you can go be wit' another chick? What tip you on?"

"Are you tryna mess up our plans to go away together? Is that what you want to do?"

"No!" She gritted her teeth. "I wanted to spend tonight wit' you. I don't care if we'll be together for the next week, I wanted tonight and I couldn't get it because you'd rather be wit' a class-C type broad. Get your mind right."

"Take your ass to the room and I'm on my way." Azia turned her head away from him. He snatched it back his way. "Drop your cousin off and go straight to the hotel. Do you hear me?"

"I hear you," she whimpered.

"I'll be there within the next hour."

"So what does that mean? Are you going to finish your little date or what?"

His facial expression said it all. Azia knew it was time to get her black ass out of dodge if she still wanted to make it to Jamaica the next day. She and Keemah jumped in the car and sped off. Mike stood outside for a minute to calm his nerves. He laughed to himself, thinking about how bold Azia was for pulling a stunt like that. He actually found it flattering, but he would never tell her that.

As for Nakita, her part of the game was over. She had really embarrassed herself. If she'd had any sense at all she would have sat there with her mouth shut and let him handle it. When he strolled back inside, he stopped at the hostess' station and asked for their meals to be boxed. When he got to the table, Nakita had already started on her food. She looked up at him with attitude but said nothing. Mike took a seat, folded his arms, and didn't touch his food.

"Are you going to eat?"

"Naw, I'm cool. Go ahead and finish yours."

Five minutes later, the waiter was heading toward their table with boxes. Did you still want to wrap everything?" Mike nodded yes. The waiter took Mike's plate from in front of him and slid everything neatly into the take-home container. Then he looked over at Nakita who was stuffing a forkful of food into her mouth. "Did you want yours to go as well?"

Mike answered for her. "Yes, you can wrap hers, too."

The waiter hesitated because of the look she gave him, but then he went ahead and took her plate. Mike paid the bill and hauled ass out of there, trying to get her home as soon as possible. If he could have flown or clicked his heels to get there any quicker he would have.

CHAPTER 11
Negril, Jamaica
"You choose your friends, not your family."

They woke up early the next morning to make sure they didn't miss their flight to Negril, Jamaica. The airport was jam-packed. Luckily for them, the ticket counter at Air Jamaica wasn't crowded at all. They checked their baggage and made their way to the security checkpoint. This was Azia's first time flying. She'd been out of the state before but had always driven where she needed to go. She looked around, amazed at how much they put you through before letting you past security. She had to remove everything from the feet up. She removed her Gucci stilettos, belt, cell phone, watch and earrings, placing it all in the plastic container and pushing it onto the belt with her carry-on luggage. Mike was behind her, complaining because he had a lot more to remove. First were his sneakers, watch, chain, cell phone, two-way pager, earrings and rings. But when he walked through, the censor sounded so he had to go back.

"I took everything off," he said, tossing his hands in the air.

"Did you remove your belt sir?"

He looked down and realized that it was still on.

"This is a metal detector it detects all medal," she stated, sarcastically.

He dismissed the sarcasm. If I had been the streets she would have gotten an ear full. He tossed it up onto the belt and walked through, looking annoyed, like it was one of their faults he had forgotten to remove it. "Now I gotta put all this shit back on," he mumbled.

Azia waited patiently on the side until he finished.

They headed for Gate 67. Azia was excited. Mike, on the other hand, was tired. After he got to the hotel the night before, he spent all night trying to explain himself to Azia, like he had been caught having an affair. After a while, he realized he was working too hard. They were about to go on a seven-day, all-expense-paid trip, courtesy of him! So why the hell should he be sweating? Her ass had better find a way to suck it up and move on.

The flight lasted about three hours and fifty-five minutes. Azia opened her eyes when she heard the sound of a bell ring over the top of her head. It was the signal to fasten your seatbelt. Then she heard the voice of the captain through the speaker welcoming everyone to the land of the pretty white sand. Azia did as she was told by the flight attendant and brought her seat to the upright position. Mike was out cold. He had slept the whole way. The flight attendant nudged him to get his attention. He popped up and looked at her like she was crazy, forgetting where he was until he turned to his left and saw Azia staring out the small window. He was still acting cranky, but she didn't care. She had every intention of making him forget all about last night.

Both of them had jet lag by the time they retrieved their bags from the baggage claim. Azia was looking forward to a stretch limo waiting outside to take them away. She was disappointed when Mike whistled for the young Jamaican Rasta to bring his cab over to pick them up. Without realizing it, she rolled her eyes and slid into the hot back seat. Mike slid in beside her. Rasta-man tossed their luggage into the trunk and ran around to the driver's side. "Where to, mon?" he asked.

They listened to Jamaican tunes for the entire ride, one song after the other. By the time they reached the resort, Azia was rocking to the beat and getting in the groove of the whole island thing. The minute she stepped foot out of the taxi, she chose to let all her worries melt away in the calming waters. For the first time since she could remember, she felt free and alive. Sandals Negril Beach Resort and Spa truly lets you taste and touch the very essence of Jamaica. It was perfect, inside and out.

They experienced nothing but Caribbean hospitality. When they entered the elegantly rustic, jewel-like lobby, they immediately came face-to-face with a beach so magnificent it took their breath away. It was a half-mile of pearl-white sand that arched in a perfect crescent. It was kissed by the translucent, turquoise water of the Caribbean Sea. The spectacular sight of the aquamarine water greeted you from every corner of the resort. No matter where you were on the property, you would never be more than a few steps away from the sea.

The lush gardens, the staff's easygoing warmth, and the soothing sound of the waves put them in a carefree state of mind. Azia looked on admiringly as they further explored the place. The natural beauty and the laid-back vibe meshed effortlessly throughout the five-star resort. Azia paid close attention to the design details that brought the establishment to a whole new level of magnificence. It was designed to provide maximum access to the glorious surroundings of the island, allowing anyone who has ever visited to experience the wonders of unspoiled sand and blossoming gardens as only Adam and Eve could have. It felt like paradise.

After checking in, Azia and Mike were escorted up to the beachfront, penthouse, one-bedroom, swim-up river suite. Azia had never seen anything so breathtaking before. The elegant world on the inside and the tropical world on the outside lived together harmoniously. In their particular suite, they were able to swim right up to their patio. In all her twenty-one years of living, Azia had never seen anything like it. It was heart-melting.

Azia took Mike's hand and guided him out to the deck. "It's so beautiful here. I can't believe how peaceful and calming it is. I never knew a place like this existed."

He placed a gentle kiss on her forehead. "This is exactly what you need."

The pool featured hand-cut glass tile and elegant chaise lounge chairs formed from bamboo. Inside the suite was an expansive living room, complete with a 42-inch plasma television. There were custom furnishings and tropically inspired décor all around. The spacious bedroom featured a 37-inch plasma television; a four-poster, mahogany bed; a marvelous bathroom with marble and hand-cut mosaic tile accents; and a Jacuzzi tub. It also contained his and her vanities.

Each and every day, they made sure they watched the sun sink into a blaze of flaming ocean off the tip of Jamaica's westernmost point. They sipped tropical drinks all day, every day to keep their moods afloat. On the first night, they decided to stay in and focus their attention on nothing but one another. The following day, they took a catamaran ride along the coast and gazed out at seven miles of white sand glory, and green cliffs dotted with cottages and buildings that ranged from old-fashioned to exotic. Later that night, after having a candle-lit dinner, they swayed to the ever-present and utterly unique rhythms of Negril's maverick soul music. The days to follow consisted of them swimming, kayaking, windsurfing, snorkeling, jet-skiing, parasailing, and enjoying spa treatments out on the beach. Mike also rented a speedboat for them so they could test the waters. Azia couldn't get enough. It felt too surreal to her. Each night she made a wish upon a star, then let the rhythms of the ocean stir the private passions of her dreams.

"Mike, do you trust me?" she asked.

They were having dinner at the Bayside Restaurant on their last night there. The estate was open on all sides, providing a panoramic view of the island as it sparkled under the moonlight. Mike took a moment to think while listening to the live band that had been entertaining them while they ate.

"What made you ask me a question like that?"

"Because it's something I need to know."

The sincerity in her eyes made him wonder. Mike was falling for Azia but didn't want to admit it to himself or anyone else. As much as he tried to keep the game square with her, she was reeling him in more and more each day. He decided to keep it real with her, because when in doubt, the truth shall set you free. "No, I don't trust you," he admitted. He knew she wasn't as innocent as she pretended to be. But something about her made him not want to let go.

Azia felt her heart stop. She blinked hard. A sour taste formed in her mouth and her jaws locked. She was not expecting to hear that. He could've said anything except no. "Well, why do you do the things you do for me? Why did you allow me into your home? Why do you continue to lead me on like you do?" She sounded as if the tears were going to fall at any given second.

"Azia, baby, we discussed this before. It takes a lot for me to trust someone. I don't go running around putting my trust in any and everybody. It's a process wit' me. You have to give me a reason to trust you. You have to make me understand why I should trust you—"

She interrupted him. "What am I to you?"

"You're my friend," he stated without hesitation. "I love spending time wit' you. I enjoy your company. You make me laugh and you give me something to look forward to when we're together."

She looked down at the table, then back up at him. "I always thought friends were people you could trust."

Mike shook his head. "Some friends will get you hurt. You'll see first-hand one day, I guarantee you. It happens to the best of us. My own cousin crossed me. At one point, I thought he was the *only* person I could trust until he proved me wrong. He let me down. But you know how the saying goes: You choose your friends, not your family. I chose you. I want you to be a part of my life. I want you to continue to be exactly who you are. Don't fake it wit' me. I want the real you, not the fake you. That's the only way we'll grow together—"

Again, she interrupted him. "Why are you hesitating?"

"I'm not hesitating, I just don't want to rush things. When you rush things, they end up exploding in your face. Just be easy, baby girl, and see where life takes us. Only time will show us what the outcome will be."

He slid back in his chair and stood up. He walked around to the other side of the table and reached out for Azia's hand. She didn't know if she wanted to accept or decline it. She was still stuck on his lack of trust for her. How could he let her get so close to him if he had trust issues? She couldn't understand it for the life of her. Seeing her hesitation brought him in closer. Again, he reached for her hand. This time she wasted no time in accepting it.

He led the way out to the beach where they took a long walk, letting the sand tickle their toes. They stood silently, listening to the waves make their own music. Mike stood behind Azia with his arms wrapped around her shoulders. She was facing the ocean, taking in the beauty of it all. The setting sun looked like it was descending into the water.

Azia could feel Mike growing aroused through his linen pants, which blew in the wind. She was already hot and horny, ready to make love right there on the sand. Mike walked her over to a pit that was used to build fires. He took Azia's hands and started to softly kiss her neck and graze her nipples with his hands. For a minute she thought she had moaned out loud. She let her head fall back invitingly. He licked and sucked all over her neck, around to and down her back, tonguing any part of her skin that the dress couldn't cover, and then back around to her nipples. He teased them repeatedly through the thin cotton material. Stationing himself in front of her, he lifted the front of her sundress and palmed her wetness with his hand. He smiled. She wasn't wearing any panties. He began to fondle her clit, making her yearn for more. There were people out but not that many. Either way, it didn't matter. Azia was ready for Mike and didn't care who was watching. After letting the straps from her dress fall to the sides, Mike uncovered both of her breasts, licked and bit softly on her nipples while she played with herself and him. He was rock hard.

"I want you so bad," she moaned.

Mike was ready to give it to her. He turned her backwards with little force and bent her over. He slid inside of her with ease. She was dripping wet. He stroked for a few minutes until he felt himself about to cum. He pulled out, not ready for it to be over yet.

Azia screamed out softly, "Please, baby, don't stop! I'm about to cum! Please put it back in!"

He ignored her pleas and spun her to face him. He stuck his tongue out and she sucked on it like it was a peach. Then he dropped to his knees and put his head underneath her dress. She kept her balance by holding on to his head. In what seemed like a split second, she had cum all over his face, her knees buckled. He stood up and held her to keep her from falling. He began to plant baby kisses all over her face. She tried to drop to her knees but he stopped her.

"I want to taste you," she said.

"No. This is your time."

Mike gripped Azia's booty with both hands and lifted her. She wrapped her legs around his waist and he lowered her down on what felt like brick to her. She used his neck and shoulders as leverage. He kept a firm grip on her ass as he guided her up and down, feeling her insides tremble. She closed her eyes, taking one breath at a time. Her second orgasm was better than the first, but now she wanted him to feel some satisfaction. "Baby, I want to make you feel good."

"You have to wait because I'm not done making you feel good."

Azia lowered her feet to the ground and Mike kissed her passionately, pulling gently on her hair. He moved from her mouth to nibble on her ears. He was making her feel so good. All of a sudden Azia felt her juices flowing down her legs. She had cum again, without being penetrated. That had never happened to her before. She spoke softly into Mike's ear. "Mike, I'm cumming again." Her right leg was shaking. He took the head of his penis and rubbed it against her soft skin. She wanted him so badly but he wouldn't submit himself to her just yet. He straightened himself up. "C'mon, let's go," he ordered, sweeping her up into his arms.

Mike carried Azia from the beach back to the resort. Other couples looked on and smiled at them as he carried her through the lobby and up to their suite. When they entered the room, Mike undressed Azia and then himself. Both of them naked, he took her hand and led her to the bathroom where they took a steam-filled shower together. He soaped her body and she soaped his in return. Azia placed her head on his chest and wrapped her arms around Mike, letting the spray of the water use her back as a dartboard. The emotions flowing through her were flawless. She wished they could stay in Jamaica together forever.

She picked her head up from his chest and looked in his eyes. "Can you wait for me in the room?"

Mike climbed out of the shower to give Azia a few minutes to herself. She waited for him to leave, then climbed out of the shower and dried off. She lotioned every single part of her body with ultra-softening body butter from Victoria Secret. The vanilla scent made her want to taste herself. She couldn't wait any longer. She was ready for Mike to put every last inch of himself inside of her. She grabbed her white tank top and pulled it over her head. Then she stepped into a pair of blue, lace, Brazilian-cut panties that slipped between her butt cheeks, and a pair of pumps. She re-pinned her hair up in a bun, leaving a few strands hanging, and took a minute to look herself over in the mirror smiling back at the reflection. There were no flaws. She was all pure and natural beauty.

Mike heard the door open. He sat up on the bed with a towel around his waist. He had the room lit up with candles. The sliding patio door was wide open, allowing the warm breeze to blow through every so often. When Azia stepped into the room he froze. He knew she was gorgeous but damn. She had a nigga shook. He couldn't utter a word. She walked over to him like she was on a catwalk, never missing a beat. His manhood wasted no time rising to the occasion. He stood up, took her hand, and spun her around. The way the lace panties fit her ass was thrilling. He was ready to stop holding back. He attempted to guide her onto the bed but she stopped him.

"You had your turn," she said, removing his towel and laying him back on the bed. "It's my turn now."

He smiled.

Azia started at his feet. It messed him up a little bit when she started licking between his toes. He'd never had a woman do that before. He wanted to tell her to stop but it felt too good. Her soft tongue slid between his toes like a snake through grass. Then she sucked each toe, one at a time. She moved up from his ankles to his thighs, licking here and kissing there, making him squirm. She stopped licking him for a minute and caressed his inner thighs to relax him. His eyes were glued shut. She resumed licking the inside and outside of his thighs, then skipped his groin area and licked all around his belly button and up his chest, sitting directly on his dick. She began to grind softly. He gripped her ass, making the grind more powerful, while she kissed him tenderly around his nipples, neck and face.

Azia took Mike's hands off of her and guided them back to his sides. She slid back down to his groin area and took all of him inside her mouth. She cupped his balls and licked him good. Then she noticed the complimentary bottle of Jamaican rum on the nightstand. She freed him from her mouth and got up.

Mike's eyes opened instantly when he felt the draft. "Where you going?"

She answered his question by cracking open the bottle. "Just relax," she insisted.

Azia poured the rum all over his stomach and slurped it up with her soft, perky lips. This was different for her, but so was Mike. He was doing things to her that no man had ever done so she wanted to do the same in return. Once the alcohol entered her system, it made her hornier. Before getting back into position, she gulped down a shot straight from the bottle and passed it to him. He didn't normally mess with rum like that, but he didn't want to dampen the mood, so he took some to the head and slammed the bottle back down on the nightstand. Azia pushed him back down by the chest. He grabbed a pillow and placed it behind his head so he could watch her work. She began to lick all around his stomach and inside his navel. The smell of the rum had her hot as hell. She cupped his balls again with one hand and put both of them into her mouth. The dance she did with her tongue was unbelievable. He couldn't take it. He was about to nut off of that alone.

"Shit, Azia," he whimpered, fighting to get her to release him.

She did, but only because she wasn't ready for him to cum just yet. She put all seven inches of him back into her mouth and deep-throated him like never before. She was amazed herself. He tried his best to keep his eyes open, but it felt too good. His eyelids opened and closed like he was going in and out of consciousness. Every now and then, Azia glanced up, without stopping, to catch his expressions. Then she felt him throb. He was pulsing inside of her mouth. She knew he was about to explode. He grabbed the back of her head tightly and began to fuck her mouth. Seconds later, he let out a long sigh of relief. She let his cum slide out from between her lips like drool. She hopped up from the bed, grabbed the bottle of rum, and took it to the head. She was gone.

Mike sat on the edge of the bed and watched her drink rum like it was Kool-Aid. She looked like an angel, even drunk. He studied her shapely hips, thick thighs and apple-round bottom. Her pussy looked extra fat through her lace panties now that it was completely bald. He looked to the floor and was turned on by the pumps she was wearing. He wanted to tear her pussy up with her wearing nothing but those.

"C'mere," he said, taking the bottle and setting it down. She stood in front of him, her belly in his face. He began to lick Azia all over her belly and her head began to spin. He slid her panties down her thighs to the floor. She stepped out of them one foot at a time. Then he stood up and lifted her tank top over her head, letting it fall to the floor along with everything else. "Turn around and lay down," he demanded. She spread herself across the bed. He began to massage her head, neck, back, ass and thighs. Then she felt his warm lips venture up and down her back. He positioned her on her knees. Azia arched her back just how Mike liked it. He took two fingers and slid them inside of her. She moaned softly. While his fingers went to work, so did his tongue. He licked up and down the crack of her ass repeatedly. It couldn't have been more than two minutes before she was cumming and her juices were running down his hand.

Mike turned Azia over onto her back and put his fingers into her mouth so she could taste herself. Then he climbed on top of her and entered her. She sank her nails into his back as he stroked his way in and out of her, rhythmically. She was no lazy lover. She used her flexible body moves, even while she was on the bottom. When she came, her pussy muscles gripped him like a pit bull locking its jaws on its prey. His speed picked up. She knew he wasn't far from his own orgasm. His heavy breathing in her ear helped to bring her to yet another one before it was over. It was as if they were racing to see who would win. Azia twirled her waist left while he stroked right, both of them desperate to reach their peak. And when they did, the feeling was phenomenal.

CHAPTER 12
Sent From Heaven
"The grass isn't always greener on the other side."
-Abdul

Keemah and Twin were snuggled up in the middle section at The Bridge cinema deluxe watching *Ocean's Thirteen* on the big screen. The film was good, but not better than *Eleven* or *Twelve*. Keemah was barely paying attention to the movie. Her mind was on Azia and how her trip was going. That added extra bitterness to all of the animosity she currently held in her heart for Azia. She wanted to be the one going away on vacations and living the glamorous life, but instead it was her cousin. She thought about making a move on Mike out of spite but then she considered the consequences. If he decided to snitch on her, she knew things would turn ugly and end the phony friendship she and Azia had. She couldn't have that. What would she tell Twin? "Hey, babe, by the way, I made a move on Azia's man, that's why she doesn't fuck wit' me anymore." She couldn't risk losing her own man and ruining whatever it was he was cooking up. Instead she thought about Rashaud. She knew it would be easy to move on him. She remembered the way he used to stare her down and lick his lips at her when Azia wasn't around. She knew he wouldn't run back and tell because he wouldn't want to mess up his chances at getting Azia back. It didn't matter to Keemah if Azia never found out. She just wanted to feel the satisfaction of sleeping with her cousin's man. Azia had done it to her so she figured, *anything she can do I can do better.*

"What you in deep thought about?" whispered Twin.

"Shhh..." she shushed him. "It's nothing."

They watched the rest of the movie in silence. Afterward, they headed for the lounge, which was connected to the theatre, to fall back in the relaxing area. Keemah ordered a shrimp martini appetizer and a Long Island iced tea while Twin settled for a vodka and cranberry. Keemah was glad the crowd was light that night. She didn't want to be there in the first place. The only reason she agreed to go to the lounge was so she wouldn't have to hear Twin whine and complain. She would rather have been home getting her back blown out. Twin was a beast in bed. His head game was vicious and his stroke game was impeccable. He had yet to fail her.

Twin rose from his seat when he saw a friend of his enter the lounge. They greeted one another with a half hug and a pound. "What up, Mike? How was Jamaica?" Twin asked, happy to see that his connect was back in town.

Keemah didn't look up until she heard Mike's name. *It can't be,* she thought before spinning around. She almost fell out of her seat when their eyes met briefly. Mike remembered her face but couldn't recall where he'd seen her before. She wasn't about to refresh his memory. Her heart was racing. She damn near broke her neck trying to look over his shoulders. She just knew Azia was tagging along behind him. It would be over if Azia caught her and Twin together. There would be no kind of explanation to give. After seeing that the female Mike was with wasn't her cousin, she exhaled deeply. Keemah politely said hello and turned back around to finish her meal and drink. *How the fuck can the world be this small? And who the hell is this new chick he wit'?* It wasn't the same girl from the restaurant. *Damn! That nigga don't waste any time, does he? I wonder if he remembers who I am. I wonder if he knows what's going on. What if he knows I'm planning to set my own cousin up? How would that make me look? If he does know, he's just as scandalous as I am because he spends just as much time with her as I do. Naw, he can't possibly know. If he does, he's doing a hell of a job of acting. Twin, hurry up and sit your ass down so I can question you.* She waited impatiently as the two men talked a few feet away.

"Jamaica was beautiful man. I wish I coulda stayed longer."

"I'm glad you didn't 'cause a nigga running short on that white girl," Twin said, referring to the cocaine Mike supplied him with every couple of weeks.

Twin and Mustafa were two of Mike's most consistent buyers. Over the years, their business relationship grew to a point where Mike began to front six bricks at a time. And just like clockwork, two weeks later they were back with a duffle bag filled with cash in exchange for another six. No matter what they had to do, Twin and Mustafa made sure they kept up their end of the deal. They had the streets locked down from Atlanta to New York, and their distribution level was at an all-time high. Even with the disappearance of Mustafa, business between Mike and Twin remained the same.

"Business still flowing I take it," Mike smiled.

"That ain't gonna change. You know how I get down. I just wish I still had my brother by my side to enjoy the fruits of labor wit' me."

Mike cocked his head to the side. "You still ain't heard nothing yet?" Twin shook his head. "That's the part of the game I don't like. I don't mean to talk like your brother is dead. Shit, I hope he somewhere breathing. You know that's my nigga."

"I doubt it man. It ain't looking good."

"In these streets, secrets don't go untold forever. Ain't no such thing as taking it to the grave. Somebody bound to slip up and say something, so just keep your ears open and I'll make sure I do the same." Mike gave Twin another semi-hug and nodded at Keemah. "Homegirl is over there looking lonely. Go do your thing and make sure you hit me tomorrow so we can handle that," he advised.

"I'll do that." Twin joined Keemah and ordered another vodka and cranberry. "You've been in deep thought all night. What's up wit' you?"

Keemah kept her focus on the television that had been entertaining her while Twin and Mike conversed. "I know him." She took another sip of her drink.

Twin instantly thought the worse. "Don't tell me you used to fuck him."

"No!" she spat with her nose turned up, as if she would never subject herself to Mike. "Why that got to be your first reaction every time I say I know somebody?"

He disregarded the question. "How you know him?"

"I've seen him around before."

"Just because you seen him around don't mean you know him," Twin smirked.

"You right," she smirked back. "But I know someone that knows him very well."

"Who?" Twin asked, anxiously awaiting the answer. When it came he thought his ears were deceiving him.

"Azia. He came to pick her up from Annette's the night we were up there playing cards."

Twin became enraged. "And you just telling me this now?!"

"How the hell was I supposed to know you knew him?! I didn't know he was your connect! You don't tell me shit! You only tell me what you want me to know!"

Twin stood. "Who the hell is you raising your voice at in here?!"

"I'm not raising my voice." Keemah froze, hoping she wasn't about to get her ass kicked out in public. *If this nigga hit me, this gonna be the day I smack his ass right back.* "What are you getting bent out of shape for? I'm telling you now because I thought you should know."

Twin's whole mood had transformed. "Get your shit and let's go."

This dude be tripping. I don't know what the hell he mad at me for. I didn't know, thought Keemah, collecting her belongings from the table.

She wasn't moving fast enough for Twin so he snatched her up out of the chair. "I said bring your ass on."

Mike never noticed what was going on at the other end of the bar. He was too wrapped up in the beauty he had on his arm for the night. After dropping Azia off at the hotel, Mike went about his business, getting back into the swing of things on the streets. His seven-day getaway was nice, but it made him miss out on more money than he'd thought it would. His voicemail was full by the time he touched down in Philly; all missed calls from the selected few he chose to deal with when it came down to business.

He was comfortable with where he stood financially, but more money was always good. The operation he ran was simple: Wash my back and I'll wash yours; cross me and I'll shut you down. He knew how to run the game without getting his hands dirty and keep everyone under him satisfied. He had built a street team to maintain his empire while he ran things from behind the scenes. He invested in daycares, hair salons and barbershops, as well as after-hour joints around the city. That helped turn his dirty money into clean money.

On top of that, he was the most desired by all the ladies. But while all of that was good, his latest project was what he was anxiously awaiting to finish. It was going to be called KoKa's Bar and Grill, named after and run by his mother. This was going to be a restaurant like no other, at least no other in the city of Philadelphia. It had been a year since he'd drawn up the floor plans and bought the land where it would be built in center city. The wait was almost over. It was his most prized secret and the grand opening was approaching fast. He already knew it was going to be major. As long as things continued to flow smoothly, there were no worries. But nothing in life ran smoothly without some bumps along the way, not even for the street king.

■ ■ ■

"You have to weigh your options. Sometimes you got to go with what you think is best for you at the time because following your heart can get you heartbroken. I'm telling you from experience—getting your heart broken is not a good feeling."

Abdul and Azia were out and about, looking at different houses for sale. While she had been in Jamaica, he had taken it upon himself to set up an appointment with a realtor to see what was up for grabs in the Montgomery County area. Azia was enjoying the house hunt. The homes out there were beautiful. They looked like they were built especially for families.

"I hear you, Abdul," she said in response to the last comment he'd made. After sharing the highlights of her trip, she broke down and told him all about the problems she'd been having with Rashaud. Sometime in the recent past, Abdul had emerged as a trusted confidant and good friend. Azia was glad she'd gotten the chance to get to know him. Even after hearing about the ethics she chose to use to make her way through college, Abdul never judged her. He taught her things she failed to understand on her own. He stressed the importance of investing and business management. Keeping up with her finances and budgeting were not Azia's specialties. As fast as she received money, she spent it. After her tuition fees were taken care of, the rest went to support her shopping habit. The more she listened to Abdul's intelligence, the more she wanted to learn.

"I just don't know what to do anymore. Rashaud's not going to stay away for too much longer. I just pray he don't resurface anytime soon. But knowing him, I'm sure he will." She sighed. "Then, on the other hand, I'm really feeling Mike. He's the one that makes me feel appreciated. I'm happy when I'm wit' him."

"The grass isn't always greener on the other side, Azia."

She thought silently before continuing. "The grass may not be greener, but it may be more groomed. As far as Rashaud is concerned, I don't even know why I still care. After what he did to me? I must be losing my mind."

"I wouldn't say that. You're human, and we as humans have feelings that are sometimes uncontrollable. According to what you told me, you and Rashaud have a bond. Ya'll built a relationship around some deep dark secrets as you called them. Now, I don't know what those secrets are, but they must mean a lot to you."

Hell yeah, they mean a lot to me! And they would to you, too, if you knew what the hell those secrets were! she thought. *You would probably kick my ass out of this car right now without stopping if you knew how much of a bad girl I really am.*

"I think you need to worry about *you* and get *you* together before you think about anyone else. That's why I have you out here today. You're wasting unnecessary money on a hotel room and rental cars. That money could be going toward a mortgage and car note. At least you'd be able to call something your own. This will be the first step toward finding yourself. Who's the real Azia? Will she please stand up?" Azia giggled. "There's that pretty smile."

They pulled up to the last house they were scheduled to see that day. As Azia climbed out of the car, a chill crept through her veins. She looked up at the house and before going inside, turned to Abdul and said, "This is it. This is the one."

Azia took one look at the house and knew it was the one for her. There were acres of perfect landscape and trimmed trees. It was no surprise that the inside of the house was just as immaculate as the outside. Past the grand, two-story foyer to the left was an oversized private study with a full bath, perfect for a home office or library. To the right was a spacious living room that featured a gas fireplace, and an elegant dining room that opened into a well-equipped kitchen, complete with a large, center island and a walk-in pantry. The laundry room was conveniently located diagonally from the kitchen. Further down was a unique doublewide staircase that served as the center point of the home. Upstairs there were three bedrooms and two bathrooms. The master suite had a walk-in closet; a private, oversized bathroom with a corner soaking tub; a stand-in shower; and a deck in the back. The other two bedrooms shared another bathroom. There was also a guest bedroom located on the lower level, which included a recreation room, a half bath, and the entrance to a two-car garage.

"I'm scared to ask how much it costs. I know this house is out of my league," said Azia.

"Nothing is out of your league when you're dealing with me. You know I'm going to take care of you," he smiled.

Yeah, okay. I appreciate the offer, but don't think your ass is getting a key. "Abdul, I appreciate you tryna help me and all, but as bad as I want to live the life you and Gisele are living, we both know the truth. I'm not on that level."

"I'm trying to get you there if you would allow me to. Stop complaining and don't worry about it. If you want this house, you got it—compliments of Gisele and me. You can consider it a welcome aboard present if you want. The mortgage will be taken care of every month. All we ask is that you join our team of advocates. Leave everything else up to us."

Why do I feel like I'm about to sell my soul?

"I've been paying close attention to you ever since the day we met. I know you got what it takes to survive in the game."

He spread his arms out from his chest. "Isn't this the way you've always dreamed of living? It's at your fingertips. It's up to you to follow suit."

Azia thought for a minute. "What's the catch? You're not just going to give me a house this big and tell me to consider it a damn present. A car, maybe, but not a half million-dollar home." She looked confused. "What are ya'll really into?"

"Azia, sweetheart, you're either in or you're not."

She was too money-hungry and materialistic to decline an offer like that. She was down for whatever to get what she wanted. If she had to suck or fuck a hundred men, two at a time, six a day, she was all for it. If she was going to be called a whore, she wasn't going to be a broke one.

"I'm down. But you got to tell me more."

"Gisele will teach you everything you need to know," he smiled. "C'mon, let's get the paperwork started on your new home."

CHAPTER 13
Thirsty For More
"Game over!"
-Busta

Attempting to take his mind off Azia for the umpteenth time, Rashaud was sitting in the back of his car getting head from his soon-to-be baby momma. She was slurping him down real good in an attempt to make him wife her. The car was filled with smoke. He let his head rest on the back of the seat and closed his eyes as he continued to drag on the end of his blunt. Azia was all he could see. He felt her presence even though she was nowhere around. "Damn, girl! Suck that dick!" he demanded, fucking her mouth with force. He was in the zone. He grabbed the back of Helena's head and jammed himself into the back of her throat. Seconds away from erupting, two of his guys ran up and started banging on the car window, startling them both.

"Argh! Bitch!" he shouted, yanking her head away from his meat.

Helena had accidentally sunk her teeth into him when she jumped from the banging on the window. "I'm sorry! They scared the shit out of me!"

He rubbed the soreness before rolling the window down just a crack. "'Fuck ya'll niggas want?"

They peeked into the cracked window. "Yo, Rashaud," one guy said, looking over at Helena. "We need to holla at you man. It's important, dogg."

"I'll be out in a minute," he advised, still rubbing himself. "And don't bang on my window like that no more, muthafuckas."

The guys strolled off and waited for him up the block on the steps of an abandoned storefront.

"I'll be back in a minute," he told her. Rashaud climbed out the car to fix his pants and headed to where the youngsters were. "What the hell ya'll got to tell me? I should fuck ya dumb asses up for fucking up my nut."

They laughed. "Yo, dogg," the slinky one started, "That nigga Busta going off the deep end. Word got back that he tryna find Stutter-man to kill that nigga for running off at the mouth. I know that's your man and everything, but c'mon! Stutter-man don't deserve that!"

The heavier of the two cut in. "I mean, we don't know what the circumstances are, but I know Stutter-man ain't no snitch."

Rashaud stood quietly with his arms folded, listening to the two plead Stutter-man's case.

"I heard Busta been riding up and down these blocks, night and day, tryna get at that nigga. Ever since Tommy got laid out, he's been tripping over that shit."

"I caught him walking down the block the other night wit' his gun in his hand, talking to his self. I stopped him for a second." He demonstrated the move on his friend. "I was like, 'Busta, you a'ight?' He looked at me wit' death in his eyes. I let the nigga go and got the hell up out of Dodge. I ain't want no parts of that."

Rashaud hadn't talked to Busta since the day he met up with him and admitted his guilt in the shootout. He knew Busta would have found out whether he came clean or not because his car was all over the news. Luckily for him, he had no priors so his prints weren't in the system. They had nothing on him so they couldn't come after him. Busta, on the other hand, wasn't feeling the fact that he had killed his little cousin. "You shoulda let me handle it!" Busta had said. But Rashaud had already given him a chance to handle it and he had let Tommy slide. So as far as Rashaud was concerned, he just did what he had to do to save his own life.

"Make sure ya'll keep your ears open for me and let me know what the deal is," Rashaud stated. "Call me as soon as anything happen around this mutherfucka. I don't care if a nigga get caught pissing on the wall, I wanna know about it."

The youngsters nodded their heads in agreement. "A'ight, we out. You can go bust ya nut now," they joked.

Rashaud hopped into the driver's seat and started the engine. Helena was still sitting in the back seat, waiting patiently to finish what she had started. "Hop up front," he told her.

"Why? Where are we going?" she asked, climbing into the front seat.

"I'm taking your ass home. I got some business to handle."

"I don't wanna go home. Why can't I go to your apartment? I wanna wake up to you in the morning, Rashaud." She leaned over to rub on his thigh. "I know you want me to finish what I started."

He was back at attention like a rocket counting down for lift off. Momentarily, he thought about fucking her brains out right there in the car. The thought of how much wetter she'd been since becoming pregnant had him anxious to fill her warm insides. But he had some other shit to worry about first. He needed to go holla at Busta to see if he could talk some sense into him. There was no need for Stutter-man to die, especially if what Tommy told him wasn't true. Stutter-man was only following Rashaud's orders when he told what he'd heard. The longer Rashaud thought about it, the more things didn't make sense. He was starting to wonder if Tommy had told the truth. Did Busta really kill Tonya? If so, what reason did he have to end that girl's life? They had only been in the same room two or three times as far as he knew. Something was being left out and he was determined to get down to the bottom of it. Everything that's done in the dark is destined to come to light sooner or later.

"Don't be going through my shit either," Rashaud said, letting Tonya in his front door. "I'll be back in a little while." He locked the door behind him and headed out to find Busta to put a stop to the madness. Unfortunately for Stutter-man, Rashaud got there too late.

■ ■ ■

Nothing but loud laughter and shouting could be heard through the barbershop doors.

"I need that ho in my life," one of the customers yelled.

"I don't need her, I just want her to teach my girl some of those moves. Shit, I'm 'bout to go pay somebody to find her ass," another shouted.

"She taking the dick like a horse. The bitch ain't even moaning. Look how wide he got her asshole open."

Everyone stopped what they were doing to come closer to the 19" flat screen that was mouned to the wall.

"I ain't came across a chick yet that can take it like she taking it."

The guys inside the shop were so into the porno that was playing that they never noticed Busta come in. On the screen was an Asian girl riding one guy backwards in her ass while the other guy pounded away at her kitty cat.

Busta got the call he'd been waiting for. Now that Stutter-man was back in town, it was time to put his soul to rest. Busta felt like Tommy's murder was all his fault and someone had to pay. If Stutter-man would have just kept his mouth shut, his life wouldn't be in danger. Busta spied through the shop window for a few seconds before making his move. He spotted the chair Stutter-man occupied, then made sure there weren't too many people surrounding the door. He grinned when he saw everyone gathered around the small TV, aroused by the adult flick. Covered from head to toe, wearing some dirty work boots, and revealing nothing but his eyes, Busta jogged up the two front steps and through the entrance.

Stutter-man was sitting in one of the barber's chairs getting a shape-up. After getting a phone call from a friend of his from around the way who advised him that everything was cool, Stutter-man had come back to Philly, under the impression that the situation had been taken care of. He'd thought it was just a big misunderstanding. What he didn't know was that Busta was the one who had arranged the call.

"Dayyuummm!" a couple of guys blurted in unison, staring at the screen. The three entertainers had switched positions and were going at it nonstop.

In the blink of an eye everyone's demeanor changed.

POW! POW! POW! Two rounds landed in the side of Stutter-man's head and one hit the mirror behind the barber's station. Everyone ducked trying to find any available way to take cover. The first thing they thought is that it was a stick-up. That was until they saw Busta backing out the door after painting the walls with Stutter-man's brains. He never flinched or said a word. He came in, did what he had to do, and rolled out. Stutter-man didn't have a chance. He was slumped over the side of the chair, hanging almost to the floor. Blood had dripped from his head down his cape and was now running onto the floor. When the coast was clear, everyone got up. They spoke in hushed tones, staring at the unbelievable sight of the stale body. That was the last of Stutter-man. The game was definitely over for him!

■ ■ ■

"Joseph, we got another one," the detective said, throwing his gun into his holster. He swung his jacket over his shoulders in a rush to get to the scene of the latest incident. "We got a hot one down on 20th street."

Detective Joseph's chin dropped to his chest. He was pissed to have another murder to deal with. He could barely keep up with the ones he had sitting I front of him. He slammed the paperwork down on the junky desk and flung his chair out of the cubicle. "What the fuck now, Charlie?"

"Don't know, but I just got the call."

The detectives pulled up to the scene almost twenty minutes later. They would've gotten there sooner if they hadn't stopped at Dunkin Donuts on the way. The crowd was thick when they arrived. They could barely drive up to the block because of all the people gathered around in the streets and sidewalks. The barbershop was taped off with yellow crime scene tape to keep back anyone who didn't have a badge. The body hadn't been touched. When the detectives walked up the steps into the shop, the first thing they noticed was what was playing on the television. The owner of the shop was so caught up in what had just happened, it hadn't occurred to him to stop the DVD player. Detective Joseph chuckled and pointed to the screen. "That's a bad bitch." Then he focused his attention on Stutter-man. "They're getting younger and younger every day. Any witnesses?"

"Nobody's coming forward."

"You mean to tell me that a man can get his goddamn brains blown out in a barbershop and nobody sees a thing. Hell no! Get me the owner!" The owner was pointed out. Detective Joseph walked out of the shop and headed toward him. From the look on the owner's face, he knew he wasn't going to get much. "Are you the owner?" Detective Joseph asked, whipping out his notepad.

"Yeah, this my shop."

"State your name."

"I already gave them all my information, showed them all my papers. I answered all their questions so I don't see no point in going through all of it again."

Detective Joseph looked up from his pad. "I asked you to state your name."

"Marcus Grimes," he spat.

"Were you here when the shooting occurred?"

"Yeah!"

"Can you tell me what happened?"

"No!"

Again Detective Joseph looked up from his pad. "You wanna be a wise ass? I can be a wise ass with you and shut this place down. How's that for business?"

"Look man, I ain't see shit. A nigga came in blasting and I hit the floor. That's all I can tell you. It was a dozen other muthafuckas in there. Why can't you go harass one of them?"

"Are they out here?"

"I guess. Shit, I don't know. You got to search through all these other nosy muthafuckas out here."

"Well since you can't point none of them out for me to question, I guess it's me and you buddy." He looked over at Charlie and said, "This one's coming with us. He said he would love to answer any questions we have."

"I ain't say that," frowned Marcus. "I can't leave my shop open like this."

"Don't worry about it. They'll be in there for a while. C'mon and take a ride with us."

Unwillingly, the young man did what he was told. He climbed into the back of the squad car talking the entire time and hoping everyone around was listening. "I ain't got nothing to say so I don't know why ya'll draggin' me away from my place of business. I don't know who did the shit. I ain't got nothing for ya'll. You're wasting all of our time." He didn't want word to get back that he was volunteering the least bit of information, because in the hood, snitches get stitches.

■ ■ ■

Gisele was excited to hear that Azia was joining her team of angels. When Abdul brought her to the house, she was waiting down by the pool in a bikini and wearing a rose-pink, satin robe that blew open every time the slightest breeze hit it. She was resting on one of the lounge chairs around the fifteen-thousand-dollar, heated swimming pool. Azia used the light that reflected from inside the pool to safely make her way over to her. "Hey, baby," she greeted with a bird peck on Gisele's lips.

"Azia," she smiled. "So we meet again."

"I told you we would. Were you doubting me?"

"That doesn't matter now does it? I'm just glad to see you made a believer out of me. I've been waiting on you."

"I had some personal issues to deal with. But now I'm ready to do what I have to do."

Gisele chuckled. "You make me want to eat you up right here and now. But because Abdul tells me you're anxious to know about our operation, I guess I have to hold off until later." Azia grinned. "I was told that you loved the last house you saw."

"It's beautiful."

"That one was my favorite, too. Did Abdul tell you that as long as you're a part of our family everything will be taken care of?"

"Yeah, he told me something like that."

"Good! I just want to make sure we're on the same page. I have something else for you." She used her arm to roll onto her side and grab a bag from beside the chair. Azia almost drooled when Gisele's robe slid open and revealed her silky right leg and ass cheek. She watched as Gisele pulled some keys out of the bag and swung the robe closed. "These are for you. It's time to turn that rental in and start pushing your own ride."

The first thing that came to Azia's mind was a Maserati like the one she'd seen in the driveway. If the key in her hand was to the ignition of a powerful, yet elegant vehicle like that, she didn't know what she would do. She tried to remain as cool and collected as possible. "Which car would this be for?"

"Abdul will show it to you on the way out. But that's not important. The few questions I have for you are."

"I'm sure I'll have answers for you."

"I like that, my darling," she winked. "How familiar are you with escort services?"

Shit, I hope that ain't what I done got myself into. "I've heard about them before, but that's about it besides what I see on TV." Having sex with men for money was one thing. Having to escort them to dinner or parties before doing so was another. *That would be too much unnecessary time spent. Just bust a quick one and let me go on about my business.*

"Abdul, would you mind getting us a couple of glasses of wine, please?" Gisele asked. "Bring the whole bottle back when you come, darling."

Here we go again, thought Azia, remembering what the wine had done to her the last time. It seemed quicker and more effective than any liquor she'd known. "Is that the kind of business you run?"

"Not exactly. I like to call it Operation Satisfaction. We have clients come in from all over. They love to spend time with beautiful young ladies like you and I. I mean, look at us, who wouldn't?" Azia blushed. "The way the business works is simple. All you have to worry about doing is delivering yourself however you see fit, and then delivering my package back to me."

Azia was puzzled. "Delivering myself how I see fit. What you mean by that?"

"Listen, we don't allow any of our angels to get their hands dirty with our product. What's ordered is delivered ahead of time. All I need you to do is collect what's owed to me, and your take is five percent."

"Wait," Azia started piecing things together. "Let me get this straight. You want me to meet up wit' your clients, fuck them, collect the money, and bring it back to you. So you're something like a pimp is what you're telling me. How beneficial is that? I'm sorry, but I'm not one to get pimped. I've been doing just fine on my own."

Gisele laughed. "Maturity, Azia. Open up your mind and listen to what I'm saying to you. You have to be on a more mature level to really understand the beauty behind this opportunity. I'm not trying to pimp you. All I need is an angel in disguise."

"I hear what you're saying but it's not making much sense to me."

"That's because you're not reading between the lines. I'm trying to explain it to you. I don't want to give you too much at one time."

"Well, if you want me to be down wit' your operation, quote-unquote," she said, making air quotes, "Give it to me raw. You have to explain everything to me from start to finish. I need to know what I'm getting myself into."

"You're on a need-to-know basis, Azia." Gisele sat upright in her chair, frustrated. She hadn't been expecting the hundred and one questions. Azia was annoying, but Gisele couldn't blame her. Her questions showed that she was on top of her game. All the other angels that had been brought on board over the years just hopped on the bandwagon, no questions asked. As long as there was money involved, everything was good in their eyes. But Azia, she was different. She was special and she knew it. She was smart, but nosy. That night was the beginning of a long courtship for them both.

"I'm going to do something I never do. I'm going to give you the low down."

Abdul was standing a few feet away, holding a bottle of wine in his hand. Azia's back was to him. He shook his head repeatedly, trying to stop Gisele from spilling the beans. He didn't think Azia was ready to know the business, but it wasn't his choice. Gisele was the only one who had the option to pick and choose who to bring on and who should know what.

She winked her eye at him and continued talking to her protégé. "Now I want you to understand that nobody else besides Abdul knows my operation. Nobody! But I feel like you're special, so I'm willing to share it with you. But keep in mind, Azia—if you try to or ever think about crossing me, that'll be the end of your life."

The devilish look in Gisele's eyes was threatening. Azia listened silently with open ears. She had already assumed drugs were tied into it somewhere along the line, she was just waiting to see how she could slide in and somehow change that five percent she was being offered to fifty percent.

"Are you sure you want me to continue?" Azia nodded, her eyes wide open. Gisele lit a Black & Mild apple tipped cigar, inhaled, and blew it out slowly. "I'm running a heroin operation. I have a connection that sends me shipments like clockwork. Where from is something you don't need to know. It's smuggled in on boats and then delivered to me by either Amtrak or U-haul.

Azia wasn't surprised to hear that drugs were being smuggled into the states but she was surprised at how Gisele made it sound like taking candy from a baby. "How do they get away with bringing it on the waters? And how do they get it on the trains? I know security is airtight now after 9-11."

"It's called connections, my dear. It's not what you know, it's who you know." Gisele continued to drag on the thin, sweet-tasting cigar. "The drop comes in from Florida by a couple of guys—always the same two because you know I don't trust many. Two fine-ass Italians," she grinned.

"So the work comes in from Cuba?"

"Don't get ahead of yourself. Assuming does nothing but make an ass out of you."

Gisele sucked in the last of her cigar until it burned down to the filter. "The product is delivered in advance. You'll never see it, you'll never get your hands dirty. All I'm asking you to do is meet up with the client to collect what's due. Whatever else happens within that time is up to you. I'm not asking you to sleep with anyone, although I must say my clients tip very well," she smirked. "I just need someone to play the field. My days of hustling and bustling are over. I've scuffled long enough in these streets to make it where I am right now. If you let me guide you, I can make all this happen for you as well."

"I'm not feeling that five percent. I feel like I'm the one being put in jeopardy."

"Ain't no deal ever this sweet. I'll be paying your rent, car note, and putting a few extra dollars in your pocket. I'll even pay your school expenses if needed. It's not a big deal to me because I know my money is guaranteed."

The mention of school put Azia into a daze. With everything going on, she hadn't thought about registering for the next semester and it was quickly approaching. "What if I want to get my hands dirty? What if I'm willing to do more to get more?"

"Let's take this thing one day at a time. There's really nothing more for you to do except sit there and be pretty. You say you've been doing that on your own all this time anyway. But you've never done it with my caliber of people."

Fuck it, I'm game, she thought. "I have another question for you. The work you got coming in, how much you getting it for?"

"Almost nothing!" she exclaimed. "I don't even have to be greedy and break it down. I sell it pure, right off the boat for a good price. I have steady clients, loyal ones, who would be foolish to go anywhere else. Nobody's prices top mine."

"Where do I sign?" she joked.

Gisele stood up from her chair and dropped her robe. "You can start right here." She untied her bikini stop and let it fall to the ground. Then she walked over to Azia and shoved her soft, tender breast into Azia's mouth, thinking, *damn, this young chick got me open.*

CHAPTER 14
Am I My Brother's Keeper?
"Just pay attention sometimes."
-Bilaal

Rashaud arrived on the scene surprised to see all the yellow tape and police surrounding the area. He parked a few blocks away and walked over to mix in with the crowd. There was no need to ask who the victim was because Stutter-man's body hadn't been removed yet. Looking straight through the open barbershop door, Rashaud couldn't believe his eyes. When he saw the dirty black and white Fila's on the feet of the dead man, he knew exactly who had been murdered. He tried to inch in as close as he could get without being noticed. He was wearing a baseball cap pulled so far down it damn near covered his eyes. He raised the brim a little to see who he could pull away from the scene for information. "Yo, come holla at me," he said quietly to a fat, freckled-faced man, then proceeded to walk away.

"Is that you, Rashaud?" the fat, freckled man asked.

"Nigga, shut ya mouth and come holla at me."

Freckle-face followed Rashaud back to his car. "What the hell happened in there?"

"I don't know. I heard somebody ran up in the shop and blew Stutter-man's brains out. They don't know who it was because he was covered up." Rashaud already thought Busta was the culprit but refused to admit it to the man he was talking to.

"I know they saying more than that. Give me the low down, nigga."

"Dogg, that's all I heard. They was up in there watching a flick and dude came out of nowhere blasting. He never said a word. He came in, did what he had to do, and was out."

"Is that what you heard or was your monkey ass up in there when it happened?"

The guy thought about lying for a moment but decided against it. "Yeah, man, I was up in there. That's how I know wasn't nothing said. But my ass ran to the back when I heard the first shot, so I ain't see nothing," he stressed.

"Yeah, whatever nigga. Busta been through here today?"

"Earlier." Freckle-face's hands and nose began to sweat. The sound of Busta's name made him nervous.

"How long was he out here?"

Why the hell he got to be questioning me? I do not want these niggas to even think I know more than I need to know, he thought before responding. "You know what? I couldn't even tell you 'cause I bounced after I came up a couple dollars in the crap game."

"If you see him before I do, tell him to call me ASAP."

Rashaud climbed into his car and sat meditating for a moment. He called Busta's cell several times but didn't get an answer. The first place he thought to look was Biggs' spot, but when he pulled up, it was pitch black and bore no signs of occupancy. "Where the fuck this dude at?" he spoke aloud to no one in particular. Then he sped out of the lot, giving up for the night. He would just have to wait for Busta to return his call—if he ever did.

When Rashaud returned to his apartment, Helena was asleep. As he stood beside the bed examining her thin body, he couldn't help but chuckle. She was wearing Azia's silk nightgown, the same one he'd thrown on her the day he had to rush her to the hospital. Thinking about Azia made him want to call her. He got undressed and walked out to the living room. He hit the power button on the TV remote, flopped down in the chaise lounge, and attempted to dial her number. She answered on the third ring sounding like she'd had one too many drinks. "Where you at all drunk and shit?"

"At a party," she lied. She was still wrapped up in her private party with Gisele and Abdul. "Wassup?"

"I was calling to check up on you but I take it you alright," he spat.

"I'm cool. How about yourself?"

"I'm patiently waiting for you to walk back into my life. I don't know how much longer you think I'm going to be this patient, but I hope you plan to make a move real soon."

Azia saw Abdul approaching her. He had just finished with Gisele and was on his way to come work on her. She rushed the conversation. "We'll see, Rashaud. I'll talk to you some more about it tomorrow."

"Why it sound like you rushing me off the phone?"

Abdul had already entered her from behind. He was working in a slow, circular motion, trying to keep things easy until she ended the call.

He fit perfectly and felt so good inside of her. "I'm not rushing you off but I do have to go." She was trying her best not to moan in his ear.

"Make sure your ass calls me, too. Or I'll be sure to come and find you."

Helena listened to the whole conversation without Rashaud's knowledge. She hated Azia with a passion. She didn't understand what it was about her that had her man so gone. Azia was nothing but a slut in her eyes. Someway, somehow she had to make Rashaud realize that she was the better one for him. She believed that once the baby arrived, that would be a good start, but what could she do in the meantime? That was something she was determined to figure out. "Hey, baby," she said, walking over to him.

"I thought you were asleep."

"I was until you woke me up. Who were you yelling at?"

"Nobody."

"It didn't sound like nobody to me."

He disregarded the comment. "Why you got that on?"

"What?"

"You know what the hell I'm talking 'bout."

She pinched a small piece of the nightgown and said, "What? This?"

"Yeah, that," he smirked.

"I needed something to sleep in. I figured since she ain't here to wear it no more I could take over. You probably bought it anyway."

"See, you thinking too hard and making irrational decisions. You thought you could take over," he mocked. "Take that shit off."

Helena sucked her teeth, slipped the gown up over her head, and tossed it on the floor.

"Now come here and finish sucking daddy's dick."

■ ■ ■

The following morning, Keemah woke up to a snoring Twin. She rolled out of bed holding her side where he had punched her repeatedly in the ribs the night before when they got home. Twin was good at whipping her butt without leaving any visible evidence. She began to wonder if it was even worth it. Yeah, he kept her bills paid and she stayed looking fly, but the way he beat her last night was unacceptable.

And for what? He went on some kind of Bitch-I'm-going-to-beat-your-ass-because-she's-your-cousin frenzy. Half of the things he said to her last night made her rethink setting Azia up. "Ya'll bitches are blood, so I know ya'll just alike," was one of the comments he'd made. "You'd probably turn on me for that ho," was another. If Twin had those kind of thoughts in his head, there was no way he was going to allow her to live. He was just using her to get at Azia, and he was going to handle one then the other.

The thought of sticking by his side for so long and agreeing to set up her own blood for him had her mind twisted. She was jealous of Azia and mad that she had taken her man a while back, but was it really worth ending Azia's life? A smile crept across Keemah's face as she stared at her reflection in the bathroom mirror. She was reminiscing about the old days and how tight she and Azia used to be. No matter what, her cousin always had her back. *What am I doing? This nigga in here beating my ass like he Harpo or somebody, for no good reason at all, and he expect me to ride out with him. I know he plan on doing one or two things as soon as he gets his so-called revenge for his brother—he's either gonna jump ship and say fuck me, or he's gonna kill my ass to make sure he don't leave no witnesses behind. Maybe I'm playing on the wrong side of the fence. Maybe it's time for me to switch teams. If I had any faith in him I would continue to stick by his side. But this nigga got me paranoid. I got to get him before he get me. It's time to turn the tables.*

Keemah heard the unsteady hallway floorboards squeak, which was a sign that Twin was awake. She put some toothpaste on her toothbrush, acting as if she hadn't been in deep thought just a minute ago.

"Good morning," he greeted, gripping her up in a bear hug from behind.

"Ouch!" she exaggerated when he squeezed tighter.

He had all but forgotten about the effect all those vodka and cranberries had on him the night before. He had become emotionally distraught and took it out on the thing standing closest to him—her. Now he was feeling bad. "I'm sorry, baby. I just had so much on my mind last night. I think I had too much to drink." She gave him the "whatever" look. "I'm dead serious. I'll make it up to you," he said rubbing her side.

It's a little too late for that, my nigga, was what she wanted to say. But instead she took a deep breath and sighed. "I hear you."

Keemah cooked a hot meal and went back upstairs to rest. Twin stayed downstairs and decided to make a couple of calls. One of his calls was to Mike but he got his voicemail. "Yo, Mike, it's Twin. Holla at me when you get this. I wanted to know what time you tryna bump heads. A'ight!" He scrolled through his contacts and stopped on Bilaal B. He pressed the talk button and listened as the phone played Lil Wayne's *Fireman* instead of a normal ring.

"Do you ever sleep?" the groggy voice answered.

"I see you do," Twin replied. "Don't you know hustlers never sleep?"

"Well this is one hustler that do. It don't make no sense for us all to be up and out at the same time. When ya'll decide to rest, then I'll go and chase the paper ya'll missing out on, youngblood," the man stated. They shared a laugh. "What could you possibly want wit' me this early?"

"Something been on my mind and I can't seem to shake it."

"What is it, youngblood?"

"My brother."

"We discussed this already, Twin. I know you feeling like half of you is missing, but what can we do besides try to take down the muthafuckas that took him down? You got to be patient, youngblood."

"I've been patient, and you not letting me make a move on that bitch. I know she had something to do wit' it. Why won't you give me the go-ahead?"

Bilaal was the man back in Atlanta. Nobody made a move without his say-so. He was the Godfather of the streets. Although Mustafa disappeared up north, Twin still respected Bilaal's take on the situation. He knew that if he made a move without Bilaal's knowledge, Bilaal would get word and take it as disrespect. Not only was Bilaal the head man in charge down south, his name rang bells in other cities, Philly being one of them. Mike was one of the people on Bilaal's list of resources, and even though he had mad love for the twins, Mike was somebody Bilaal was not willing to cross.

"What do you wanna do? Go and kill the girl without finding out who was really behind it? You know if she had anything to do wit' it, she wasn't in on it alone. Let me finish doing some digging and when I feel as though we need to make a move, that's when things will pop off, youngblood. Don't keep questioning my judgment. I'm starting to get a little offended."

"I'm not questioning your judgment. I'm just tryna understand your point of view, that's all. I'll fall back and wait for the green light."

"You said that once before and now you're on my phone, early in the morning, whining like a little bitch."

"That's because I got some other shit on my mind, too."

"Well, come out wit' it. I ain't got time to sit on the phone and play head games wit' you. I got two fine bunnies here waiting to put me back to sleep."

Twin smiled. That was just like Bilaal; always had at least two on his arm at one time. "Do you know who Mike's girl is?"

"Mike ain't got a girl, youngblood. That brother is too into getting this money to think about settling down. What would make you think otherwise?"

"'Cause my chick told me he's fucking wit' her cousin."

"Her cousin?! The same cousin you say is involved in this whole Mustafa thing?"

"Yeah, she's the one."

"Let me tell you something about our man Mike. If he had the slightest inkling that she had something to do wit' it, she damn sure wouldn't be up under his arm if what you saying is true. He's probably just fucking the girl anyway. I don't see it being any deeper than that. If you feel any different then go ahead and approach him like a man and find out what's up. But keep in mind that when you confront a nigga like him, it's like stepping to a powerful nigga like myself. You better make sure you stay in your place and don't cross the line. I'm sure he'll keep it real wit' you. And another thing—you better keep your eye on that chick you shackin' up wit' too. She seem a little suspect to me. She might be telling you what she want you to know instead of everything you need to know.

"She cool. I got her under my strap for now. When all is taken care of she'll be dealt with. I need her for the moment, not a lifetime."

"Stop talking and listen. Ya brother was a hardheaded ass too. You don't have to come back wit' a answer every time somebody says something to you. Just pay attention sometimes. I hope she ain't there wit' you if you talking like that. Don't you know females are like mice? They sneaky as hell and hear every goddamn thing. "

"She's sleep—"

"Just listen to what I'm telling you, muthafucka! Now I'm growing impatient wit' your ass! Just sit down and chill the fuck out!"

"I hear you, Bilaal," Twin said, but it was really going in one ear and out the other. If he had been paying closer attention to the words coming out of the wise man's mouth, things for him could have turned out a whole lot differently.

■ ■ ■

The interrogation room was as cold as ice. Busta felt like he was sitting in a refrigerator. There was nothing in the room besides one steel desk and two chairs. He had been in that room for a while now, saying the same thing over and over again. "If you charging me wit' something, charge me and let me call my lawyer. If not, let me the hell up out this joint."

Detectives Joseph and Charlie tried playing good cop–bad cop but it didn't work. Busta wouldn't utter a word. They had nothing on him for real. They had just brought him in for questioning because someone mentioned that he had been around the neighborhood looking for Stutter-man. Seeing how hard and how much of an ass he was, the detectives went to plan B. They assumed that if he sat in there long enough he would bend, so they turned the air conditioner up and waited it out. But to no avail. Plan B didn't work either.

"Ya'll can hold me in here for as long as you want. I ain't cracking," he yelled, looking at the one-way mirror. "Where the fuck's my lawyer?"

The detectives looked at one another and then back through the mirror. Detective Joseph spoke first. "What are we gonna do with this asshole? We can't hold him forever."

"I know he knows something. Your guy ain't giving up any more information?"

"I got what I could out of him. I had to twist his arm to get this asshole's name. And I could tell, after he said it, that he was petrified. This guy has some kind of control over all the little youngsters around there. Ain't none of them willing to talk."

"Well, we can't hold him forever. What you want to do?"

Detective Joseph tossed his hands into the air. "Let the prick go." He turned and stormed out of the room.

Busta walked out of the precinct thinking, *you dirty bastards.* He was heated. After Marcus mentioned his name, they picked him up. That's why Rashaud couldn't find him. Busta wondered who had enough guts to mention his name. There was no one who could identify him because he made sure he revealed as little as possible. Then he began to curse himself for asking so many people where Stutter-man was and when he was coming back, so they probably put two and two together. But they knew how deadly Busta was. So even if they knew for a fact that he committed the crime, there was no way anyone should have willingly given up the information. If he ever found out who did, he wouldn't think twice before stepping to them.

BEEP-BEEP. Busta scanned the area trying to find the car that was honking. When he saw that it was Rashaud his blood began to boil. It took every bit of strength he had to keep a straight face. He walked up to the car slowly and bent down to talk through the window.

"Hop in," suggested Rashaud.

Busta opened the door and climbed in. He shut the door and looked straight ahead without saying a word. The pain in his aunt's voice crying for the loss of her son echoed through his head. She cried to Busta, asking him to find whoever it was that killed Tommy. Busta looked her dead in the eyes and responded, "I will," even though he didn't have to do any searching. Rashaud had already admitted his guilt, but Busta couldn't tell his aunt that. If she found out that her son had been killed by someone she claimed as her own, she would probably have a nervous breakdown. And what would she think of Busta if he allowed it to happen without fixing the problem? That was not a lecture he was trying to hear. In the back of his mind, he wanted to correct the problem before laying it on her hard.

"What were they in there talking about?"

"Bullshit!"

"Who gave them your name?"

"I don't know."

"I got a call from Auntie this morning. She said they came and hemmed you up. I didn't want to come inside—you know I don't fuck wit' the police like that. So I waited outside. The only way you gonna catch me up in there is in handcuffs," Rashaud joked.

Busta wasn't in a joking mood. He had just sat in a cold-ass interrogation room for over twelve hours, and he was ready to explode. "Yo, man, just take me home."

"What's wrong wit' you?"

"Try sitting your ass in that icebox for twelve hours and then ask me that question again."

"Damn, dogg. I ain't have your ass sitting in there. Don't take the shit out on me." Rashaud knew Busta was still upset about losing his cousin but he didn't know it was threatening their brotherhood. Tommy was fake and Busta knew it so he didn't think it would come to the point where his life would be jeopardized behind the situation.

Rashaud pulled up to Busta's house, not feeling where the conversation was headed. He parked in front of Busta's door and killed the engine so they could finish talking. Neither of them yelled, screamed or raised their voices. They both remained humble, keeping the respect level at a high. But deep down inside, both had thrown up their invisible guards. Things were not the same.

"Yo, Busta, I apologize for taking your cousin away from you, but if the shoe was on the other foot, you woulda did what you had to do, too. I didn't go after Tommy. He came after me on some Scarface-type shit," he chuckled, trying to lighten the mood. "The nigga started blasting at me like he was really a gangsta! And don't forget—I got shot, too." Rashaud looked at Busta and waited for some feedback but Busta never cracked a smile or said a word. Tapping Busta lightly on his arm Rashaud said, "Well, tell me this. What was I supposed to do when the nigga ran up on me? Was I supposed to let him kill me? Was I supposed to take one for the family? Hell no! If you think that's how I ride, you sick in the head." He used his finger to poke himself in the head as he spoke his last comment.

"I hear all you saying, Rashaud, but the shit don't mean nothing to me. None of it! So however you feel about me and however I feel about you is what it is." Busta's voice became firm. "My cousin is dead because of me. My aunt is left childless because of me. I got to live wit' that shit every day."

"Why are you blaming yourself? I'm lost 'cause I can't figure the shit out. Help me understand why all this happened because of you."

Busta blacked out. "Because I said so! I was the one that told him about me killing Tonya! That shit wasn't a rumor! What, you thought he grabbed the shit out the air?! No! I told him I blasted that bitch, so it is my fault! If I wouldn't have said it, he wouldn't have had anything to tell! Did I break it down clear enough for you or are you still lost?!"

Rashaud was stuck on stupid. "You did what? What the hell you kill that girl for, man? What she ever done to you?"

"That bitch ain't do shit to me! But that other bitch … " he stated, referring to Azia. "She the one I was after! I thought her ass was the one driving that night when I unloaded!"

"Say what?" Rashaud couldn't believe what he was hearing. He felt like Busta had spit acid in his face. His best friend, someone close enough to be called a brother, tried to kill the one woman that meant the world to him. "You tried to kill my girl, Busta?"

"She ain't just your girl, she everybody's girl. What make you think you so special?"

"You tried to kill my girl, Busta?"

"My answer ain't gonna change. I don't care how many times you ask me. Yeah, I was trying to off that no-good-ass trick—"

BOOM! Just like that the conversation was ended. Rashaud put a single bullet between the eyes of his brother from another mother. Busta's limp body fell back against the passenger side door. He had been running off at the mouth so much, he never saw Rashaud reach for the caliber. Blood and brains were splattered all over the inside of the car, as well as all over Rashaud's face and clothing. Rashaud leaned across the seat, opened the door, and kicked Busta out onto the ground. "I bet you wish you woulda changed your answer now, pussy!"

CHAPTER 15
A Change Of Plans
"Sorry ain't do it, I did."
-Keemah

Twin showered and dressed and was ready to meet up with Mike as planned. He walked into the bedroom to see if Keemah was still sleeping and she was. Or at least that's what she wanted him to think. He planted a kiss on her cheek and whispered, "I'm leaving," in her ear before departing. As soon as she heard the door shut, she crept out of bed and tippy-toed to the window. She peeked through the curtain to make sure he had pulled off. When he did, she hopped back into the bed and grabbed the cordless from its base. She sat still for a moment in deep thought, biting down on her bottom lip. She was nervous. Her face was contorted. She dialed Azia twice before getting an answer.

"What you want, girl?" Azia yawned.

"I wanted to see what you were doing."

"It sound like something is wrong." Azia sat up in the bed, now fully awake. "You okay?"

"No, Azia, I'm not okay. I have something really serious to talk to you about."

"Wassup?"

"We need to talk in-person."

"I'll be running around all day tryna find some furniture for my new house. You can join me if you want to."

"Your new house?! You ain't tell me you found something!"

"It came about all of a sudden. I'll fill you in on that later though."

"Where you at?"

"I'm still staying at the hotel for now. I'll probably check out of here in the next couple days."

"I'm about to get dressed. I'll meet you at the room in about an hour."

"Make it two hours, bitch. You forgot you just woke me up?"

Keemah sucked her teeth. "I'll be there in two hours, Azia. I'm not tryna sit around in that stuffy-ass room either so be ready."

■ ■ ■

Mike and Twin met at the 7-Eleven on Washington Avenue. They greeted each other with their normal brotherly hug then stepped into the store, chitchatting. Mike walked over to the coffee station and made a cup while Twin bought some small stuff at the counter. Whenever they met out in public it was always at a store. It looked less suspicious than just swapping and pulling off.

"Ring me up one of those, too," Mike said, pointing to a pack of Orbit chewing gum.

The Indian man rang everything up and gave each of them their items. Mike headed out first, scanning the area for any extra eyes. Feeling at ease, he hit the button for his trunk and it popped open. Twin's car was parked right next to his. When Twin came out of the store, he went straight for his back passenger-side door and grabbed the money bag. In one swift motion, he tossed it into Mike's trunk and grabbed the duffle bag that contained the six keys. Mike slammed his trunk shut and gave Twin a hard stare. "You alright? You seem a bit out of it today."

Twin held no punches. "I got something on my mind that ain't sitting well wit' me."

"What might that be?" Mike asked, puzzled.

"What you know about that chick Azia you be dealing with?"

How the fuck he know about Azia? he wondered. "What you mean what I know about her?"

"What you know about her?"

Twin's attitude wasn't sitting well with Mike at all. His personal life and whoever he was fucking was none of Twin's business. He tried to remember when he had ever brought Azia around Twin but couldn't think of a time. Then, at that very moment, he placed Keemah's face. He chuckled. "That's where I know her from."

"Who?" Twin asked.

"The chick you were wit' last night. I couldn't remember where I'd seen her before but now I remember."

"That's Azia's cousin."

"Oh, yeah, I know. But what I want to know is why you questioning me about her."

"I'm gonna come out and be straight up about it. I think she had something to do wit' my brother. She got to know something."

"Why would you think that?"

"Because she was the last person to be seen wit' him. And a few different people verified that."

Mike nodded his head and played with his chin like he always did when he was in deep thought. "I'm not gonna sit up here and say it ain't true, 'cause anything is possible in this day and age. But I will say I don't see her doing no shit like that."

"That's what you think, but my gut's telling me otherwise."

"If you so sure, why haven't you made a move on her yet?"

"Because I'm waiting on the go-ahead from Bilaal. He told me to chill out and lay low until he digs a little deeper into the situation."

Again Mike chuckled. "If that's what Bilaal said then I suggest you listen."

"Do you suggest I listen because you feeling her?"

Mike stopped himself from putting his hands around Twin's neck. This wasn't the place or time. He was already upset he was standing around listening to nonsense while being dirty. "Don't worry about what the fuck I'm doing. And the next time you got some shit to get off your chest, make sure you come correct wit' me. If you bring the same attitude you bringing to me now, we're gonna have a big misunderstanding. Ya dig me?"

Twin nodded his head and climbed into his car thinking, *I will end both yours and that bitch's life if I have to, mutherfucka.*

■ ■ ■

"**Damn, Azia girl!** How many more stores are you going to look in?" asked Keemah.

The girls had been out all day shopping for furniture. They had been to Ikea, Wal-Mart, Dane Décor, Minima, and Jerusalem Furniture, picking out what Azia needed for each room. She was surprised to find everything she was looking for. Azia was so excited to furnish the house, she crammed it all in one day. Keemah tried to be excited for her cousin, but something heavier was weighing on her mind. She had suddenly developed a case of guilt.

"Ooohhh! Ain't these cute, Keemah?" Azia was in a zone, not realizing how impatient her cousin had become.

"Yeah, it's nice," she said lackadaisically.

"What's wrong wit' you? You wanted to come, remember? I bet when you see the house, your ass is going to be tryna move in. Lighten up, I'm almost done."

Almost done end up being two hours later. Azia scheduled all her deliveries for the same day to kill all her birds with one stone. Keemah trailed behind her cousin aimlessly. She still hadn't come clean about her reason for being there, but Azia was so caught up in her own thing, she had forgotten to ask.

"You want to go get something to eat?"

"No, I want to go see this extraordinary house you keep talking about."

"Good, 'cause I can't wait for you to see it," Azia said excitedly, stepping into her new 08' Lexus GS. Every time she sat in it, the new car smell reminded her how far she'd come.

"You still ain't told me how you got this new car and house," stated Keemah, popping MJB's CD into the disc changer. "You need to share that information so I can get on my grind."

Azia wanted to spill everything to her cousin but went with her better judgment. Keemah was on a need-to-know basis, and what Azia was doing she didn't need to know. "Let's just say I know how to work my middle."

Both girls laughed.

"Well, teach me, ho. Don't be working the middle by your damn self if I can be getting gifts like this, too."

"When the time presents itself, I'll put you down. But for now—whatever you need, you know I'm here for you."

The sincerity in Azia's voice made Keemah believe that what she was about to do was the right thing. "Azia, remember I said I needed to talk to you?" she asked, turning the volume down.

"Damn, I forgot. I was so caught up in the day."

Keemah hesitated. "I don't know where to begin."

"The beginning will work."

"I don't know," she said, taking a deep breath. "What I'm about to tell you is gonna spin you through a loop. I just hope we can move past it afterwards."

Azia's heart sped up. Her insides felt itchy because she knew something terribly wrong was about to be revealed. "What is it, Keemah?"

"Azia, you know how close—"

She interrupted. "Don't give me the history speech. Tell me like it is."

Keemah took another deep breath. "Before I break it down, I need you to know that whatever happens between us, I will always have love for you."

"Did you sleep wit' Rashaud?"

"No!"

"Mike?"

"No! It ain't nothing like that."

Azia released a sigh of relief. "Well, I can probably handle anything else."

"It's going to be a lot to handle. I won't even fault you if you wash your hands of me."

"What did you do?"

Tears fell from Keemah's eyes. "I know about Mustafa. I know you set him up."

Azia almost hit the car in front of her at the red light. She hit the brakes so fast both she and Keemah jerked hard in their seats. She looked her cousin in the eyes. "Who told you something like that?" Keemah didn't respond. "Who told you that, Keemah?"

"His twin brother."

Azia was baffled. "Who's his twin brother?"

"They call him Twin. We've been messing around for a while now. He's the one I was wit' down in Atlantic City the night his brother disappeared."

"What?!" Azia panicked. "Why would he think I had something to do wit' it?!"

"Because everyone says you were the last one to be seen wit' him."

"Yeah, we went to the hotel and got it in but he dropped me off after that!" She made her story sound so convincing.

"Twin thinks you set his brother up. I never defended you, I just went along wit' it."

"Why hasn't he come to question me? I woulda told him what happened that night."

"In his mind, he already knows what went down. He said if you ain't do it then you know who did. He wanted me to get closer to you to reel you in for him."

"Please don't tell me that. We blood. I know you wouldn't do me like that."

"Azia, at the time I had so much hatred built up for you. I told him I would. I wanted to get you back for what you did to me."

"I hurt you that bad?! Look me in the eye and tell me I hurt you bad enough for you to set me up and let a nigga kill me!"

"He wasn't gonna kill you," she lied. "He said he just wanted to scare you into telling him where his brother was."

"What?! That nigga was gonna kill me and you know it! If he believed I had something to do wit' his brother's disappearance he was going to black out, and you ain't gonna tell me otherwise!" Keemah sat quietly. "I can't believe you! After all I've done for you!"

"Stop acting like you so innocent, Azia! Don't forget—not only did you sleep wit' my man, you took him away from me and used him up like a bad habit. How do you think that made me feel?!"

Azia made a sharp U-turn and pulled over on the side of the road. She forced the car into park, hopped out, ran around to the passenger side, and yanked Keemah out of the car by her shirt. "I know exactly how it felt! It felt like the time you let three girls jump my ass while you ran home like a bitch! It felt like the time you told your mom I was stealing money from her purse when all the while it was you! I can go on and on if you want me to!"

Keemah had forgotten all about the harsh things she had done to Azia in the past.

"You cut me deep wit' this one! I want to fuck you up right now but I feel too numb to make a move! Stay the hell away from me!"

"Azia!" Keemah went to reach for her arm.

BOP! Azia landed a closed fist to Keemah's right eye. She staggered back, tripped over the curb, and landed on the ground. "I said stay the fuck away from me, bitch!" Azia spit on her and walked back around to the driver's side of the car. "If you know like I know, you better watch your back."

"But I just wanted to be honest wit' you," Keemah said with tears in her eyes, still on the ground. "I'll do whatever you need me to do. We can take him out together."

Azia didn't respond. She sped off, leaving a cloud of dust in Keemah's face. She was too through with her. Mike told her that she would find out first-hand that the one she trusted most would be the one to stab her in the back. Just when she thought she'd won back the love of her cousin, the only family member she ever really cared for after losing her mother. The pain was too much to bear. All of the emotions bottled up inside of her broke through and she began to sob hysterically. She was glad she didn't have the chance to take Keemah's snake-ass to her new house. All the trust was gone. She was also glad she went against her instincts. She had been thinking about turning Keemah on to Gisele to help her get a few extra dollars. But Keemah's struggle was no longer her responsibility. The only thing on her mind was retaliation. She wanted to settle the score.

She looked down at her ringing phone. As if on cue, Rashaud was calling. "Where are you?" cried Azia.

"We need to talk. Meet me over at Biggs' spot in an hour."

"Where you at now?"

"Stop asking so many damn questions and just do what the fuck I'm telling you to do!"

"Fine!" she yelled and shoved the Blackberry into the cup holder. She made a quick turn to hop on the expressway. *How did I get myself tied up in this shit? I can't believe his brother been scoping me out all this time. I wonder why he hasn't gripped me up yet. Maybe Keemah's exaggerating. Maybe he doesn't think I did it and just wants to ask me a few questions.* Thought after thought turned over in Azia's mind all the way to the chop shop.

When Azia got to Biggs', Rashaud was the first person she saw. He was standing in the door of the garage smoking a blunt. He had changed out of the t-shirt stained with Busta's blood and washed all traces of his blood off his skin. Azia pulled into the lot slowly. She parked and hopped out.

"Don't park out there. Drive it in here," he ordered, moving out of the way.

Azia got back in and drove the car into the garage. Rashaud pulled the garage door back down to the ground. She sat in the car until Rashaud came around and opened her door. Still, she didn't get out.

"Get out!"

She jumped out with her lips poked out. She knew something was wrong with Rashaud, but she swore her problem was a whole lot worse.

Rashaud stared at the car for a minute and asked, "Whose car is this?"

"It's a rental," she lied.

He didn't believe her and made a mental note to grill her about it later. "Busta's dead." He had no intentions on beating around the bush. He wanted to tell her exactly what he did and why he did it. "I killed him."

Azia was at a loss for words. She felt lightheaded and her mouth was dry. "What you do that for?"

"I was hoping you asked me that," he snickered. "I did it for you."

She shook her head in disbelief. "Why would you kill him, Rashaud? What the fuck you do that for? Have you really lost your mind?"

"Bitch!" he said, gripping Azia by the shirt. He slammed her into the car door. "I said I did it for you and that's all you can come up with?! I killed my brother over you! You better appreciate that shit!"

This nigga done lost it! He must be on something. Azia tried her best to calm him. "Okay, baby. Let me go so we can talk about it."

He released her and they walked over to the round table and took a seat.

"What happened, Rashaud?"

"I don't know what he was thinking. I didn't mean to do it, I just snapped." His eyes looked dazed as he stared down at the floor without blinking. "I just reacted."

"Reacted to what?"

"He killed Tonya."

Azia didn't believe it. "No," she said, shaking her head. "What reason would he have to kill Tonya? He didn't even know her like that."

Rashaud looked up from the floor. "He wasn't tryna kill her. He was after you."

It felt like a frog had leaped down Azia's throat as she swallowed. "He tried to kill me? Rashaud, what are you saying?"

"I ain't stutter. He was tryna kill you. He thought you were the one driving the car that night, not Tonya."

Hearing that opened up a new can of worms. Not only did she feel guilty for not having had the chance to make peace with her friend after the argument they had before she died, now she was hearing that Tonya's death was supposed to have been hers. Her head was spinning as fast as a merry-go-round. "He couldn't have hated me that much, Rashaud. Why would he try to hurt you like that?"

"He thought he was doing me a favor but the shit backfired on his ass." He jumped up from his chair, ran up to a cement wall, and sent his fist into it. The skin on his knuckles broke and he began to bleed. He shook his hand trying to shake the pain and the tingling sensation away.

Azia ran to him. "What are you doing?!" She grabbed his hand and studied the bloody bruise. "Oh, Rashaud. I'm so sorry you had to kill him. But why did you do it for me?"

He pinched her cheeks with his thumb and index finger so hard her lips poked out. "Don't you know how much I love you? I told you I would do anything for you. That nigga tried to take you away from me. I don't give a fuck about nobody else when it comes down to you. Remember that!"

He let her face go and gripped her into a bear hug. She didn't know whether to be flattered or afraid. He had killed his best friend over her. It didn't matter how much she wanted to be free of him, how could she now? If she puckered her lips up to tell him that it was over, she would be sealing her own death.

"Did anyone see you?" She was hoping someone had. That way there would be the possibility of imprisonment for him.

"I don't know, but I don't give a fuck."

"You need to lay low and let things cool off for a while. Why don't you go away somewhere and chill out."

"I plan to, but you coming wit' me."

"Huh? I can't come wit' you. School is about to start back up. I have responsibilities here I need to tend to."

"Like them other niggas you fucking, right? It's not an option, Azia. If I said you rolling out wit' me then that's what it is."

She sucked her teeth. "You already got me tied up in enough bullshit! I'm not tryna go wit' you to be tied up in more!" When she noticed Rashaud stepping in closer, she blurted out, "That nigga Mustafa got a brother that had Keemah spying on me! He knows I had something to do wit' it! I got enough shit on my plate right now! What if he goes to the cops and they come questioning me?!"

"When you find all this out?"

"A little while ago. Keemah finally came clean and told me everything. She said he didn't want to kill me, just question me about his brother's whereabouts."

"That's a bunch of bullshit."

"That's exactly what I said."

"If he wanted to go to the cops he woulda did that already. They ain't never gonna find that body no way."

"Where is it?"

"You don't need to know all that. If somebody comes asking, then you really ain't got no information to tell 'cause you don't know."

"I was ready to kill my cousin. I can't believe she stooped that low."

"I told you before to watch that bitch but you always thinking I'm being paranoid. I know fake when I see it. She jealous of you and would do anything to take your spot."

"What am I supposed to do?"

"Where she go?"

"I don't know. I left her back on Passyunk Avenue somewhere. I told her to stay the hell away from me."

"Naw, that ain't the right move. She came clean for a reason. Who is his brother?"

"She said they call him Twin. Him and Mustafa are twins."

"You got to keep Keemah in your corner right now. Dude must be on her bad side, that's why she turned on him. We got to use it to our advantage. Call her up and tell her you want to talk."

"I can't talk to her right now. The thought of seeing her or hearing her voice is making me sick to my stomach."

"Put that pride shit aside and make the call. I wasn't asking you to do it, I was telling you to do it."

"She probably won't answer no way," said Azia, going to retrieve her cell phone from the car. She dialed Keemah's number with attitude. "Hey, Keemah, where you at?"

"Sitting in McDonald's over at the plaza," she answered.

"We need to talk."

Keemah hesitated. "I don't think we need to talk right now. You want to fight and I ain't for all that, Azia. I just wanted to open your eyes to something. I admit I was wrong, but you ain't tryna hear I'm sorry 'cause sorry ain't do it, I did."

"Yeah, yeah, I hear all that." Rashaud nudged at her to drop the nasty attitude. "I need to know more. You said we can set him up together so I need to come up wit' a plan before he get at me. If you sorry like you say you are, then I know you still wit' it."

"Come pick me up and we'll take it from there."

"Alright. I'll be there in about fifteen minutes."

Azia tossed the phone back into the car. She looked over at Rashaud and said, "Done."

CHAPTER 16
THE BUSINESS

"I'm married to the game."

-Mike-

Mike was in a daze slouched down on the small antique sofa inside of his mother's home. Ms. Koka knew there was something on her son's mind. After she called his name several times and snapped her fingers in front of his face, he snapped back to reality. "I heard you the first time," he spat.

Ms. Koka stood in front of her son with her hands on her hips. "Boy, who you talking to like that?! You must've gone and bumped your head!"

He rose from the sofa. "My bad, Ma. I just got a lot on my mind."

"I hope it ain't business-related. You got enough on your plate right now with this club alone. You don't need anything extra adding on to the headaches you already got." She lit a cigarette. "What's going on with you?"

He waved the smoke out of his face. "I wish you'd shake that habit. I'm tired of seeing you destroy your lungs."

"I didn't ask you that, I asked you what's up. Talk to me."

"Nothing I can't handle." He headed to the kitchen with his mother on his heels, yapping away. "Ma, I said I can handle it. It ain't nothing for you to get so worked up over." He leaned into the refrigerator and pulled out the orange juice. He unscrewed the cap and took the bottle to the head.

Ms. Koka popped him in the top of his head and tried to snatch the bottle from his hand. "I told you about drinking out my shit! Get a damn glass!" she shouted.

Mike screwed the cap back on and swallowed the last gulp. "I'm finished."

"Stop doing that shit, Mike. You ain't the only one that drinks orange juice in here. We don't know where your filthy lips been or who they been kissing." She rolled her eyes and continued to puff on her Newport. She took a seat at the kitchen table and pulled some papers out of a manila folder. "Here," she shoved the papers at him.

They were papers that included a deed for the new establishment, a liquor license, and receipts for everything that had been purchased to furnish the place. "Damn, Ma. You know we mapped out a budget. Don't try to kill my pockets."

"Oh, boy, please! You know you're gonna get all that back in no time. I'm the one running around, sweating my behind off, tryna make the place look like something. I'm not tryna hear your mouth." She flipped open a catalog from BDS and showed him the booths, bar, chairs, and tables she'd picked out. He gave his approval on them all. "I knew you would like them," Ms. Koka smiled. "Your momma got taste."

"Is everybody that got their hand in this doing their part and helping out like they suppose to? I'm not one for slackers."

"Everybody is doing their job, Mike. You just finish focusing on what you got going on and I'll handle the rest." Mike hugged his mom and let her know how much he appreciated her holding him down through the years. "I'll be glad when you find yourself a wife to hold you down so I can take a break." They both laughed. "I'm laughing but I ain't joking. You not tired of being lonely yet?"

"I'm married to the game, Ma. You already know that."

"The game won't last forever. You're doing what you need to do now so you won't have to continue to be a pawn in the game, right?" He nodded. "I'm not trying to rush you into a relationship. Lord knows the woman that tries to come and snatch my baby up will have to go through me first. But I don't want to see you alone forever. I want some grandkids to run around and tear my house up so I can whip their little butts," she giggled. "Son, you work hard and you deserve the best. When you do decide to settle down, just make sure it's not with one of those little hoochie-mommas that think they can turn from hood to fabulous overnight on account of you. Make sure their heart is for you and only you."

"That's easier said than done, Ma. You tell me how I'm supposed to know if a chick is for me or not. Ya'll too tricky. How will I know if her heart is where she says it is? I sit and listen to the lines these females lay on me time after time, and

I realize they're all the same. I'm not even gonna front, Ma. I'm feeling this one chick. She got that ready to ride attitude and she smart. She's in school, handling her own and everything. But she's sneaky. It's something about her that turns me on like no one ever did, but at the same time, it's something about her that drives me away and makes me keep my guard up. I'm not looking for someone that's made for TV, I need someone that I can love and build a family wit'."

"If your gut is telling you she ain't the one, then she ain't the one, baby. That's probably your little head speaking for you instead of the big one," she chuckled.

"Naw. The sex is good but it's more to her than that. My gut ain't telling me she's not the one, that's what scares me. The shit that goes on in these streets is telling me to brush her off and leave her where she at. I don't know what it is. She a good girl, I know she is. I think she just got caught up in some bad ways."

"I want to meet this girl. I'll tell you if her little fast ass is sneaky or not. My third eye never lies."

"You so silly," he laughed.

"I got to watch out for you 'cause you're all I have in this world. I mean, don't get me wrong, I love Anthony. But you're my heart and I'm your soul. Don't you ever forget that."

Mike looked his mother in the eyes and said, "I never will."

■ ■ ■

Azia and Rashaud pulled into the McDonald's parking lot and waited for Keemah to come out. When she saw the car pull up, she grabbed her sandwich and headed out the door. Seeing Rashaud in the passenger seat made her hesitant. She walked around to Azia's side. The window came down slowly.

"Where are we going?" Keemah asked.

"Just get in the car, Keemah," Azia answered.

Going against her better judgment, she climbed into the back and they pulled off.

Rashaud turned counter-clockwise in his seat and said, "Wassup?"

"What's up wit' what?"

"Don't play stupid. Who the hell is this nigga looking for Azia?"

Keemah didn't know whether or not Azia had told Rashaud the whole story but she wasn't about to keep any more secrets. If Rashaud didn't know Azia had been messing around on him he was about to find out. "His name is Twin. Azia was fucking around wit' his brother, Mustafa."

Rashaud focused his attention on Azia. "Who's Mustafa?"

Azia was steering the car with her left hand and twirling her hair with her right, playing along. "He was just a friend, Rashaud. It wasn't like that."

"Well, whoever this Twin cat is is thinking otherwise. Why would he be looking for you about his brother? I'm finding that hard to understand."

Keemah butted in. "He think she knows where he's at. He's been missing for a good while now. Nobody called for ransom money or anything. He just vanished into thin air."

Rashaud turned his body toward the back seat again. "So don't nobody really know what the fuck happened. Ya'll are just guessing and pointing fingers right now. How could you agree to set your own cousin up and you don't even know what really happened? Explain that to me."

Keemah shrugged her shoulders. "I wasn't thinking. He had my mind all twisted. He made me believe she had something to do wit' it because she was the last one wit' him. But I came to my senses. I know she wouldn't be involved in nothing like that. Not Azia."

"You came to your senses? That shit right there don't even sound kosher to me."

"What you mean?"

"I ain't stutter. All of a sudden you want to play Captain Save-a-Ho like you got her back but you really a snake at heart. Ain't no way I'm going to help set up my own family and still be able to sleep at night."

"I thought about that, and I wasn't sleeping at night. Every time me and Azia got together I wanted to tell her but I didn't know how."

"Guilt makes you tilt." Azia agreed. "So what's up wit' this fool? What's his plan?"

"I don't know but I heard him talking on the phone this morning about it. He was pissed off, too. Whoever he was talking to told him not to make a move until they said so."

Damn, who else is in on this? Both Azia and Rashaud wondered.

"Well, something got to happen before he gets the go-ahead to come at my neck," suggested Azia. "I can't believe my name is caught up in the middle of all this."

"If you weren't fucking another nigga it wouldn't be," Rashaud spat.

Azia took her eyes off the road momentarily and smirked at Rashaud. "Don't go there."

"I'm going to map something out," Rashaud explained. "Until then, keep an eye on this cat and tap into all his conversations to find out what his moves are going to be. You gotta act like everything is still cool wit' ya'll. Ain't nothing changed, and don't act out of place. You gotta pay attention. Do you hear me?"

"I hear you," Keemah said.

Azia dropped Rashaud back off at the chop shop then headed to the hotel where Keemah car was parked. They rode the whole way in silence—no tunes, no conversation. Azia had nothing to say and Keemah was too scared to say anything. She knew she couldn't beat her cousin. That was proven throughout the years when they had their little tussles here and there. But little did Keemah know that fighting was the last thing on Azia's mind. Azia was ready to take her .25 pistol from under her seat and put a bullet in Keemah's heart. She imagined it, play-by-play, over and over again in her head. It was hard to believe that the cousin she would've laid down her life for let dick and envy dominate her. But Azia couldn't kill her. Keemah was worth more to her alive. Azia needed to get close enough to Twin to catch him before he caught her, and there was no one better to bait him than Keemah.

"Azia, I wish you would say something," said Keemah, exiting the car in the hotel parking lot.

Azia killed the engine and climbed out. "I don't know what came over you, but dick ain't worth forsaking your own blood. I ain't got shit else to say to you right now."

"I'll make it up to you. I promise."

Azia squinted her eyes, thinking, *Oh, bitch, best believe. I'm going to make it up to your funky ass, too.*

■ ■ ■

"He just left here! Dammit! How did he end up with his brains on the ground that quick?" asked Detective Joseph.

"It happened right in front of the house where we picked him up at. Whoever did it got to have some big balls to do it in broad daylight." Detective Charlie shook his head. "I couldn't believe it myself."

The news of Busta's murder had been circling the precinct for hours. He was pronounced dead on arrival at Hahnemann University Hospital. The bullet found in his head was linked back to Tommy's and Tonya's murders. Rashaud and Busta had never had a problem switching guns with one another, but when Rashaud took Tommy out, he had no idea that the gun he used had Tonya's blood on it, too.

The detectives stood around trying to figure it all out but couldn't. They were scratching at a brick wall. "I can't stand here and keep doing nothing about this shit. They're making us look like clowns. We can't even piece together one murder. This is bull," complained Detective Joseph.

A chubby, white, slue-footed cop said, "You go out and chase those baboons all you want. I'll be here waiting on you to get back empty-handed like you always do." He flopped down in his chair, kicked both feet up on his desk, and threw his hands behind his head. His discolored smile revealed what years of drinking coffee could do to your teeth.

"Well, keep your big ass in here then, muthafucka. Some of us take our work seriously."

Slue-foot wasn't offended. That was how they all talked to each other. "Too seriously. Let them finish killing each other. In the end, it'll be less work for us."

"Let's go, Charlie. Let these assholes sit in here and finish jerking each other off."

The two detectives exited the building again, on the hunt for answers and suspects.

■ ■ ■

Later that night, Mike stepped out of his green Denali rocking a nicely fitted white, Armani v-neck t-shirt; a pair of faded blue jeans; some black, Prada, striped sneakers; and his Prada shades. The diamond bezel watch he had on captured the attention of many who stood around waiting to get into Solo Night Club, one of the city's most exclusive clubs. Everyone out there was dressed to kill. Luxury cars were piled almost on top of each other and traffic was backed up. Mike could hear the music pumping inside the club all the way outside. He was accompanied by Camel, the muscle of his empire, and Kane, one of his closest friends. The three of them bypassed the line and stepped to the front where they gave dap to all the bouncers at the door. Mike removed his shades and made his way inside.

On their way in, they heard a few guys yell out, "Yo, why the fuck them niggas getting in wit' white t-shirts on?"

One of the too-muscular bouncers replied, "'Cause them niggas is VIP and you ain't, that's why. Now get the fuck out the line." Mike, Camel and Kane laughed and moved on.

The place was popping, shoulder-to-shoulder. Everyone had come out to congratulate Anthony "The Messenger" Thompson, a well-known boxer, on his sixth round TKO victory. There were a number of celebrities, big-time hustlers, gangstas and wankstas in the building from the surrounding Tri-State area. Mike didn't do the club scene too often. He knew that when folks got to drinking, there no telling what would happen by the end of the night. Feeling how hot and humid the place was made him wish he had stayed home. It took two days for Kane to finally talk him into going.

Mike threw his shades back on and walked toward the dimly lit dance floor. He scanned the place, nodding his head at familiar faces and studying unfamiliar ones. One of the things he hated about clubs was the way you could feel the heavy bass from the music in your bones. He became tense. When he saw the man of the hour passing through, he took a minute to pay his respects.

"Wassup, Messenger," he said, gently tossing his arm around the young champ's shoulders. The sound of 50 Cent's *In Da Club* slightly overpowered their conversation. "I didn't get to come check you out the other night, but I heard you put a beating on that nigga."

"You know. That's what I do," Messenger smiled.

"Well, congrats, my man. Make sure you get a bottle on me before I leave."

"Fo' sho!" The Messenger walked off to finish hosting and entertaining all those who had come out to celebrate with him.

Mike turned to Kane. "I'm heading to the bar." Then he tapped Camel who was leaning up against a pole with his arms folded. His body was stiff and his face was expressionless. "You can relax a little bit, Camel. Damn."

"I don't relax," Camel admitted. "I stay focused."

"Whatever. I'm about to go to the bar. C'mon," he ordered.

They headed to the bar while Kane stayed back, flirting with any female that walked by wearing close to nothing. When they walked past the lounge area, Mike stopped dead in his tracks. He shifted and took two breaths without blinking. He got upset when he thought he saw someone that looked like Azia from the side. He walked a little further into the lounge to get a better look. It was definitely her. She was sitting between Gisele and Abdul having the time of her life. She was watching two of Gisele's angels give the spectators something to talk about. They were bumping, grinding, kissing, licking and pouring champagne all over one another. All the guys standing around cheered them on.

Mike concentrated on the smile Azia was wearing. Every time Abdul leaned over and whispered something in her ear, she lit up and burst into laughter. He became more pissed after watching her stroke Abdul's cheek and give him a lap dance. He was ready to go yank her from the sofa and drag her slinky ass out by the neck. But of course he would never put himself on blast like that. Instead, he shot her one last glare and proceeded to the bar.

"Ain't that your girl over there?" asked Camel, adding insult to injury.

"You might want to rethink your question 'cause you already know my girl wouldn't be caught in a place like this."

Camel adjusted his position. "Okay. Well ain't that the bitch you fucking over there?"

"If that's what you want to call it."

"Looks like she into some wild shit. Them bitches over there getting it in," he grinned, ready to make his way back to finish watching along with everyone else.

Mike ordered them both a drink and leaned his back up against the bar. He continued to watch Azia out the corner of his eye. Every move she made, his eyes caught it. Camel caught him a couple of times but said nothing. He spent the most time with Mike so he already knew what it was hitting for. No matter how many negative things he or anyone else had to say about Azia, his friend neglected to listen.

"Ya'll niggas ain't order me a drink?" asked Kane. He squeezed between Mike and Camel and ordered one. Then he turned around and tried to focus on what the crowd in the corner was so hype about. "Fuck's going on over there?"

"Some lesbian chicks getting it in," said Camel.

"Oh yeah? Is that so?" Kane took his beer from the bartender, tipped him, and headed to the back to find out if there was any truth to what Camel had said.

Ten minutes later he was back with an earful. "Yo, Mike! Your girl is back there bumping heads wit' some faggot-ass nigga. You seen her?"

"I ain't stunting that shit," he flagged.

"Naw, let's go handle that," his trigger-happy friend suggested.

"Let that chick be, Kane. If I ain't mad, why you mad? You act like she sucking your dick at night. Leave that shit alone."

"I already pulled her cards. She knows you here, so I'm sure she'll be over in a minute," he advised. "But, woo-wee, those are some bad bitches she over there wit. She need to put a brother down wit' some of that pussy. They over there doing some freaky shit. I ain't never had no shit like that done to me before."

Mike chuckled just before Azia reached them. He couldn't help but notice how well she was put together. She had on a fire-print, silk, halter dress with a detachable black, leather corset belt purchased from the House of Dereon. The dress was so long it hid the sandals she was wearing, which matched the dress perfectly. The way the soft material of her dress clung to her body aroused him and his boys. She knew just how to keep things classy and sexy at the same time.

"Hello, fellas," she greeted with a smile. She walked over to Mike and stood toe-to-toe with him. She clutched the bottom of his shirt and said, "I miss you."

He could smell the liquor on her breath. He took her hands and removed them from his shirt in a respectful way. "Do you think you've had enough to drink?"

She cocked her head to the side. "Aww, you care about me?"

He refused to stand there and entertain her sarcasm. He gulped down the rest of his drink and turned to walk away. She grabbed his arm. He turned to her and said, "Yo, holla at me when you sober."

Azia didn't know what the attitude was about but she wasn't going to let it affect her night. Whatever he had seen— if he'd seen anything—was strictly business, not pleasure. "C'mon, Mike. Don't treat me like that."

"Go finish doing ya thing, baby girl. I'm good." He waved his hand for Kane and Camel to follow.

Azia smirked as she watched them fade into the crowd. For the rest of the night she mingled and networked with Gisele by her side. All the love everyone showed her on the strength of Gisele was blissful. She smiled at everyone Gisele introduced her to, trying her best to stay focused, but her mind was on the other side of town. She couldn't stop thinking about Mike and his sudden change of attitude. Before they left Jamaica, he clarified that they were just friends so why was he tripping? She couldn't figure it out. She wanted to be his, but he didn't want to rush things. She decided to roll with it since Rashaud was back in the picture. She had to fall back where Mike was concerned for a little while. The last thing she wanted was for Rashaud to find out they'd become close. He might've tried to put the whole idea of setting Mike up back into play and she couldn't have that.

The more she drank, the more she felt the liquor gaining control of her actions. She was good and twisted. She continued to bounce her way around the club. Her clientele went from one handful to two handfuls in a matter of hours. She had all the high rollers ready to submit to her desires. Azia was a handful and she knew it. "You ain't a trip, you a whole damn vacation" is what Rashaud always told her, and it wasn't a lie. She knew just what to say to men and in which direction to swing her ass to get their undivided attention. Gisele had taken her maturity to the next level. It wasn't about how many men she slept with or how much she got paid. What mattered at the end of the day was how many of them walked away respecting her hustle.

Azia and Mike locked eyes from across the club just as Gisele approached her with the man of the hour. She took her focus off of Mike and smiled when The Messenger brought her hand to his lips.

"I heard some wonderful things about you," he smiled. "Gisele and I go way back."

"I'm glad to finally get the chance to meet the champ. I've been trying to catch up wit' you all night but you were too busy floating around so I let you be."

"Trust me," he said, looking her up and down, "I woulda put what I was doing on hold to spend a minute or two wit' you."

"I'm glad to know you woulda stopped, but I'm worth more than a minute or two. If Gisele told you anything I'm sure she told you that."

The Messenger laughed. He looked over at Gisele, who was smiling herself, and said, "You were right. She does remind me of you a lot," he winked.

Gisele nodded. "This one here is my pride and joy," she grinned, patting Azia softly on the butt.

Azia spoke up. "Congratulations on your win. Maybe one day I can be in the front row cheering you on," she hinted.

"Maybe so." The Messenger looked over at Gisele and said, "Whoever said beauty is of the essence didn't lie. We'll be in touch."

Azia was caught up in the moment. She didn't know what it was about The Messenger, but he had her gone. She could tell by that short conversation that he was well-mannered. That alone hit a spot. And the neatly twisted locks in his head were a complete turn on. It didn't take long for her to forget about Mike, who was still watching from afar. She felt a pair of eyes burning holes through her skin. She looked from left to right to see if Mike was still around but he was gone. "Gisele, I'm heading home for the night. I'll see you tomorrow."

"Oh no, darling. You have work to do." She pointed over at a tall, thin, muscular man who had his eyes glued on them both. He was the true meaning of dark and lovely. "He's been waiting for you all night."

Azia knew she'd seen his face somewhere before. "Who is he?"

"A very wealthy man."

By the end of the night, she found out that the man was the owner of one of Philadelphia's top venues. She stared at him for a while before making a move. He looked much thinner as she got closer, but he was still fine. When he gawked at her with his puppy dog eyes she became wet instantly. The liquor helped. She walked up to him and said, "I hear you been waiting for me." He nodded his head. *He so goddamn sexy*, she thought. She turned around and scanned her surroundings, making sure Mike was still nowhere around. She did not need him thinking she was some kind of groupie.

He squeezed her thigh and asked, "How much longer you gonna keep me waiting?"

By the time they reached his hotel room, Azia was ready for him to be all over her. She was ready to go against the rules and stick her tongue down his throat. She fell into his arms when he started rubbing all over her breasts down to her butt.

She let him pull her dress over her head and put his wet tongue all over her neck. She shivered and panted for air. He pulled her thong off and wiggled his nose between her thighs. "Oh, baby," she sighed.

She could feel the heat from his breath warming her clit. He planted baby kisses all around her middle but never stuck his tongue out. He blew on her clit for a few seconds, then stood up and began to undress. Azia felt robbed. She had been ready to get her clit licked and sucked from front to back, left to right, up and down.

"Lay back on the bed," he demanded.

She sat down and slid back in the darkness. She didn't get a chance to feel or see what would be coming next. She watched his silhouette roll a condom on before climbing on top of her. When he entered her, she was so disappointed. It was one thing for a man to slip in that easily because she was just that wet, but it was another thing for him to slip in that easily because he was just that small.

"You feel that dick?" he asked, squirming around on top of her.

"Oh yeah, daddy, I feel all that," she said, rolling her eyes to the back of her head.

"Get on top and show me how to ride this monkey."

Ride this monkey, she reiterated to herself. *Is he serious?* If it hadn't been so dark, he would have caught the frown on her face. Azia climbed on top and did the satisfying job she always did when in control. She rode the hell out of him until he begged her to stop. There was no fun in it for her, but knowing he was wealthy was enough to keep her amped. Not too longer after, she was back in the missionary position praying it would all be over soon.

It hadn't been that long at all since Gisele had brought Azia on, and the funds were rolling in like water. She got spoiled real quick. The agreement Azia and Gisele had jumped from five percent to ten percent. That was because Azia took on a little more responsibility than the others. On a good week, pulling in at least three jobs got her close to ten grand. Getting tipped by the ones she chose to give her goods away to was extra. As long as she kept them happy, in all fairness she had to admit, they did the same.

Thirty minutes later, Mr. Ride This Money was rolling off of her, trying to catch his breath. "Gisele, Gisele, Gisele," he repeated as if she was there. "Where do you find them?"

"I'll take that as a compliment," Azia said, climbing from the bed. She went to soap a washcloth and began to clean herself up.

"I'm afraid to admit you might be the best so far."

"Good things come wit' time." Azia tossed the dress back over her head. Spending quality time afterwards wasn't something she was into. "I wish I could stay and play some more, but we both know Gisele's waiting for her share of the pie."

He hopped off the bed like a bunny rabbit and hit the light to the lamp on the desk. He glided across the green carpet toward the dresser with his pencil dick flapping from side to side. He wasn't the least bit ashamed. Azia giggled to herself. He pulled out a medium-sized, leather sports case from the drawer that was small enough to carry by hand. "There's fifty-five grand in there. Tell her that when I finish testing the product, I'll give her the other twenty." He leaned over and grabbed his pants from the floor. He reached into his pocket and pulled out a wad of cash. "This is a little something extra for your time."

Azia didn't think twice before counting the money right away. "Thank you," she said looking up at him, satisfied with the extra two thousand he'd given her.

CHAPTER 17
Thou Shalt Not Steal
"Being greedy is a very unhealthy way to live."
-Azia

A couple more weeks flew by and August was nearing. Keemah stepped onto her porch to check out the weather and felt like a fish stick frying in hot oil. It felt like hell had taken over. There was no better way to describe it. Her mood had been shaky ever since her run-in with Azia. She hadn't heard from her cousin since that day. Every time the phone rang she hoped it was her cousin. At night she tossed and turned, getting no sleep at all. Guilt made her tilt. Keemah hoped this was something they could move past. But knowing Azia, she would be sure to get her back one day, someway, somehow. It was much easier to forgive than to forget.

It bothered her more and more to know that Twin had no intentions on keeping her around. It would either be him or her. Of course, out of selfishness, she chose herself. Then she began to think about everything her cousin had going for her. She didn't know where Azia was getting all that money from, but she wanted some of it. If her cousin found it in her heart to let bygones be bygones, the first question on her list would be *how can I be down?*

Keemah crawled back into bed trying to keep from waking Twin but failed.

"Why you up so early?" he asked.

Everything about him was becoming annoying. His words stuck her like a sharp object. "I wasn't sleepy." She tried to remain as humble as possible.

He attempted to roll on top of her but she held him back at arms distance. "Not right now."

"What you mean not right now?"

"I got cramps," she lied. "My period is about to come on."

That excuse always worked with Twin. He hated the sight of a bloody pad. Whenever it was that time of the month, he slept on the sofa or in the other room because he was afraid she might leak on him at some point in the night.

"You know you ain't got to say it but once," he said, sliding out of bed. "Make sure you let me know when that shit start running out of you."

Keemah rolled her eyes. "Grow up!"

"Whateva!"

He hopped like a kangaroo on one foot, jamming one leg into his jeans, then the other. He tossed his black t-shirt over his bare shoulder, walked over to the window and peeked out. "Yo, what's ya plans for the day?"

"I ain't got no plans."

"I'm not feeling your funky-ass attitude. I don't know what done crawled up ya ass, but you better pick that shit out and keep it moving before I do it." He slid the t-shirt over his head as he spoke. It had a picture of Mustafa on the front. Over the picture was R.I.P. and under it was *wherever you are.* Keemah studied the shirt for a moment. She looked Twin up and down. There was no denying that he was sexy. She was horny as hell and mad that she lied about having cramps. Now she was thinking she'd better get it in every chance she got because any given day could be his last. Just when she was ready to throw in the towel and snatch his clothes off, his phone rang. He walked out of the room talking in whispers.

Keemah leaped off the bed. "Why the hell you running?!" He put his finger up to his lips. "Ain't no be quiet! Who the hell is that on the phone, Twin?!"

"Hold on," he said into the phone before dropping it down to his side. "Calm your ass down, girl! What the hell is wrong wit' you?"

"You the one tipping out of here when your phone rings! Wassup wit' that?!"

"It's my damn momma," he lied.

"Ppsshhhh…" she flagged him. "Well, let me talk to her then!"

"For what?!"

Keemah tried to snatch the phone. Twin snatched his hand away. "Give me the phone!" she ordered.

Without returning to the call to say good-bye respectfully, he pressed the end button.

"What the hell you hang up for?!" Keemah stood with her hands on her hips, looking angry. "You are such a liar! Who was that on the phone?!"

"Girl, you tripping!" Twin attempted to head down the steps but Keemah was so far up on his back a piece of paper couldn't have slid through. "Ay, Keemah! Go the fuck 'head wit' that dumb shit!" He pushed her away. She pushed back. This went on twice more before he smacked her. She held her face, trying to calm the sting. "Have my shit packed by the time I get back so I can roll the fuck up out of here, you dumb-ass bitch!"

"No! *You* the dumb ass!" She shouted at the top of her lungs. "Pack ya own shit and get the hell out *now*! Ain't no need for you to come back!"

He opened the front door, spun around in her direction, and ran his tongue across his teeth. "You heard what I said! Make sure it's done!" He stepped out the door into the hot heat and went about his business.

"I'm going to make sure it's done, alright," she mumbled to herself. "His stinking ass didn't even wash his face or brush his teeth."

That afternoon, Keemah tried contacting Azia several times but kept going straight to her voicemail. Impatiently waiting for her to stop by or return her call, Keemah was more than pissed off. She got dressed and headed out the door on a mission. If they were going to set Twin up it had to be soon. She was losing it with each passing second.

Her first stop was the Marriott. She took a chance and asked if Azia had checked out yet. The chubby Puerto Rican woman at the front desk said that she had. Keemah stormed out of the hotel on the hunt, like she was a lioness stalking her prey. Her next stop was the apartment on City Line Avenue. After snooping through some mail in the hotel room, she finally found out where Azia and Rashaid were shacking up. Since Azia was ignoring her calls, she knew there was a good chance that he knew her whereabouts. She exited off the 76 expressway without giving a warning call. She parked her Altima, hopped out, and sashayed into the building like she owned one of the suites. "Can I help you?" asked one of the workers.

"No, I know where I'm going."

She took the elevator up to the right floor and moseyed down the hall to their unit. She took a minute to make herself look more presentable before knocking. Loud, old-school rap could be heard on the other side of the door.

Rashaud was sitting on the sofa with his feet propped up. His face twisted when he heard the door. He grabbed his 9mm before stepping to the peephole. *What this ho want?* he thought, turning the knob. He opened the door and stood silently. She had seen Rashaud plenty of times before, but seeing him now, up close and personal, aroused her. He had on a wifebeater, revealing what few muscles he had. You could tell he did a few push-ups at least twice a week.

She blinked a couple more times before breaking the ice. "Hey, Rashaud. Where's Azia?"

Rashaud stood aside to let her in. He closed the door behind them. She glanced back long enough to see the lust in his eyes. It was a little uncomfortable but exciting. "Where she at? In the room?"

Rashaud leaned against the door and replied, "I don't know. You tell me."

Keemah stood there silently. A very sexual vibe was flowing through the room. As often as she had visualized her and Rashaud making out to spite Azia, the actual opportunity presenting itself created some tension.

"You gonna tell me or what?" Rashaud said.

"Tell Azia to call me. Me and Twin about to be on the outs so whatever she want to do need to be handled now," Keemah said, sweeping past him. Rashaud stepped in front of her and began to smile. "What's the matter wit' you, boy? Is you crazy? Move and tell Azia to call me, please."

"I know where she at. I'm just fucking wit' you." Rashaud licked his lips looking smoother than LL Cool J, undressing her with his eyes. "You know you's a sheisty-ass bitch, but I like that. You and your cousin are two of a kind," he laughed.

"Fuck you," she growled.

He aggressively pulled her to him by the hips, stopping when their bodies were only centimeters away. He whispered, "Don't you wanna know why your cousin chose me?" He forced her hand to his thickness, moaned and nibbled at her ear.

Keemah lost all train of thought for a second. *Damn, this nigga look good, feel good. What would Azia do in a situation like this?*

"I can see it written all over your face," Rashaud teased, taking full advantage of her weakness. "I know you want me. I can tell by how you looking at me right now."

It was so true. *Azia did it to me. What the hell? I might as well get in where I fit in. Hold up! Let me get my ass out of here. For all I know, they're tryna set me up,* she thought, and took a step back.

He smirked and his shoulders relaxed. "You want it or it wouldn't have taken you that long to step off." Again, he forced her hand to his groin. "Feel all of it."

Her heart raced a million times faster than usual. She tried to get out the door. "Move out my way, boy."

He stepped to the side to let her pass—or so she thought. When she reached for the doorknob, he came from behind, putting soft bites all over her neck and grabbing her throbbing wet kitty. He could feel the heat through her fishnet and lace cheeky panties. She surrendered, letting him take control.

"I knew you wanted me. Stop playing and give me this pussy." Rashaud snickered, undoing his jeans and pulling his zipper south all in one motion. His left hand was positioned up on the door; his right hand did all the work.

"Please, just stop. Please stop," Keemah moaned, which, in his mind, meant keep going.

"You want me to stop?" he whispered hotly in her ear. "If you want me to stop, make me stop." He yanked her panties down from underneath her skirt, flipping the skirt above her waist.

He bent her over against the door after seeing how much she was enjoying his hands invading her essence. She shifted from her left leg to her right eagerly, invitingly. He grasped himself firmly, patted it against her ass, and then jammed it inside her. "You wanted all this up in you, didn't you?"

"Yes … please … don't stop," she moaned.

It felt so good she was as loose as a goose. She was moaning, cursing, and cooing, "Damn, Rashaud!" like it was her very own chant. The more he drilled in and out of her crying womb, the harder she threw it back. She pushed her face into the door, muffling her sounds of satisfaction, and played with her clit. Feelings of guilt came and went. The sound of her body banging against the door drove him wild.

"Fucking bitch. You like this dick don't you?"

Keemah was in a zone. She more than liked it. She was ready to call it her own. She found herself comparing him to Twin. Their stroke game was one in the same but Rashaud had him beat in the size department.

"Answer me when I'm talking to you!" he ordered, pumping harder and harder until she cried out for him to stop.

He ignored her pleas. It got to the point where he was slamming into her so hard, the door became her head's punching bag.

"You're hurting me!" she whined.

A few minutes later he was ready to erupt. But before letting loose, he pulled out and shoved Keemah's body to the floor by her head. She sucked him like she was trying to find a cure for the sick.

"That's how you do it! Deep throat that shit!" he groaned between pauses. "Here it come. Get that shit. All of it, you hear me?" Seconds later he came all over Keemah's face and mouth. Watching her slurp it up reminded him of Azia. Keemah didn't feel as good as her cousin, but she sure knew how to suck a mean one.

Rashaud snatched a towel that was hanging on the back of a chair and wiped up any remaining cum. Then he flopped back down onto the sofa, grabbed the remote, and gave her the "Ok, get the fuck out" look.

"So that's it?" Keemah asked, straightening her clothes and feeling stupid and disrespected.

He didn't even look in her direction. "I'll tell Azia to call you. Ain't that what you came here for?"

Keemah sucked her teeth and stormed out the door.

Rashaud smiled, thinking, *stupid-ass trick.*

■ ■ ■

Azia was sitting with three of the other angels, feeling awkward. They were all gathered out back around the pool area at Gisele's home, listening to her give the most threatening lecture they'd ever gotten—except for Azia. She didn't think anyone could frighten her more than Rashaud had when he pulled Mudda's bloody head from the gym bag. And there was no reason for her to panic because she wasn't guilty of stealing anything. Her involvement was just a big misunderstanding.

Gisele was pacing back and forth, cursing under her breath. She was outraged. Over three thousand dollars had gone missing. She was determined to find out why, how, and when it had happened, and who the culprit was. "I do everything for you bitches and you steal from me." She sighed deeply. It sounded like air being slowly released from a balloon. "From me? You steal from your own mother? Three thousand dollars ain't shit. I wipe my ass with that every day. So if you were going to risk your life, you should've risked it for a hell of a lot more."

"But, Gisele—" one of the girls began.

"Don't!" Gisele held up her hand and clawed at her like she was reaching for death. "When I talk, you listen." Suddenly, she pulled a brown, leather Gucci bag from out of nowhere. It seemed to materialize in mid-air. She turned it over and let all of its contents fall to the ground. Hundreds of dollars wrapped in bundles hit the ground, bouncing over top of one another.

Abdul and a handsome Italian stranger were standing in the shadows quietly. The unfamiliar Italian was sophisticatedly put together. He had on a pair of off-white, Armani, linen trousers; what looked like an off-white silk shirt; and some brown open-toe sandals. There was a diamond stud the size of a dime in his right ear, a rose gold chain with diamonds hanging heavily from his neck, and a rose gold diamond-encrusted watch to set off his look. Azia believed it was safe to assume that he was one of the men who came to make the drops on a weekly basis.

When Gisele let the bag fall to the ground on top of the money, the sound startled Azia. She snapped out of it and gave Gisele her undivided attention. "I don't even know where to begin. How do I handle a situation like this? Never have I had to decide before. Everyone knows not to steal from me," she said. "Azia!"

"Azia?!" repeated Azia, like she had heard wrong. Gisele couldn't be calling her out from the bunch! Light whispering could be heard amongst the other girls. Azia jumped to her feet, ready to plead her case. "Gisele, you know I would never do nothing like that to you." As tough as Azia thought she was, there wasn't one nerve in her body that could be accounted for. She was terrified.

"Come here a minute," ordered Gisele.

Azia walked slowly over to her and stopped when she was an arm's length away.

"Tell me how I should handle the thieving-ass trick."

Azia's eyes widened, her body relaxed, and her mind was set free. She didn't know which one of the girls Gisele was talking about, but all of them could go to hell if it was left up to her. She was no longer mixed in or tied to the situation at hand so she didn't give a damn. Azia stared at the remaining three females, feeling powerful. She had always been the outcast of the bunch. It was not a secret that she'd become Gisele's favorite. Her eyes scanned from left to right, looking each girl in the eye. "I would really like to know which one tried you like that," she said.

Gisele walked over to Lisa, the smallest but thickest of the angels. She gripped up Lisa's Latino frame from her seat by her throat. The other two girls flinched and rushed to get out of striking distance.

Azia was amazed to see this dark side of Gisele. Her stance was priceless.

Gisele manhandled the poor girl like a fifty-cent candy bar. "Did you think I wouldn't notice?"

"I-I-I," was all she could get out. She stumbled over her words.

"That wasn't a question I needed answered." Gisele looked over at Abdul who had crept from out the darkness. "Get rid of this lying whore." She threw Lisa into his arms.

Get rid of her? thought Azia. *Now didn't she ask me what she should do about it? Shit, I was tryna get my hands dirty.*

"Azia, don't look so upset. What's on your mind?"

She watched as the girl tried to fight off both Abdul and the Italian, but to no avail. "I'm just enjoying the show," she admitted.

"Hold on. Bring her ass back over here for a minute." Gisele reached behind her back where she had a small .22 handgun secretly stashed away underneath a two-piece jumpsuit. "I don't like to get my hands dirty, but you are getting under my skin, little girl. You should have just gone quietly."

POP! The bullet ripped through the girl's right eye. Her blood splattered on all that was near, including the Italian.

"Damn, Gisele," he stated in the sexiest voice Azia had ever heard. "I just bought this damn outfit." Those were the only words he spoke before helping Abdul wrap the body in a trash bag and haul it out.

The other two angels cringed in their seats, their insides trembling. Never before had they seen someone murdered before their eyes. It was all unreal to them. Gisele sensed the uneasiness in them both, which concerned her. "Do I have to worry about hearing what happened tonight ever again?"

Without hesitation, they both shook their heads no.

Then she looked over at Azia who stood firm. The bloodshed hadn't moved her one bit. She still looked the same, breathed the same, walked the same, and talked the same. She was a soldier for real, and although Gisele figured she would stand strong, that was the first night she actually felt it in her bones. "I see I don't have to ask you. I know that you know what time it is," she winked.

Azia nodded and winked back.

"All that on the ground goes to you."

Azia looked stunned and so did the other two angels. Some of the profits in that bag belonged to them. One angel attempted to say something but decided against it when Gisele shot her the "I wish you would" look. "You have something to say, angel?" Gisele asked, placing her pistol back in its hiding space.

The young angel shook her head no.

"I didn't think so." Gisele scooped up the Gucci bag from the ground, tossed it to Azia, and disappeared into the shadows, leaving the three angels alone.

Azia collected all the money from the ground and put it back into the bag. She debated in her mind whether or not to keep it all for herself or give the other girls at least their portion of the pie. *Fuck them hos*, she thought. She watched them watch her every move. When she moved left or right, their eyes did, too, like owls up in a tree. After getting every last dollar up, she walked over to where the angels were seated. *I shouldn't give you hating-ass bitches nothing*, her eyes read. She dropped the bag onto a chair and grabbed out enough money to cover the five percent owed to them. She contemplated for another moment, and then passed the funds over.

"Why don't we just split what's in there between the three of us?" one of them ventured.

"You would like that, wouldn't you?" smirked Azia. "I don't think so."

The angel who had spoken rolled her eyes and another sucked her teeth, hopping to her feet.

"I know damn well you ain't feeling froggy, cause if you are you better leap high, bitch." Azia stood guard waiting for the female to make any sudden moves toward her.

The angel who'd hopped up said nothing. Instead she dropped her shorts and shirt to the ground and dived into the pool like a professional swimmer.

"Now you bitches wanna be my friend," Azia mumbled to the one who'd previously spoken. "Finish hating on me like you always do." She snatched the bag and sashayed inside the house.

Gisele was upstairs on her bedroom's balcony looking out over her angels without their knowledge. She wanted to see if her newest protégé would pass or flunk her test. When she'd told Azia to keep the money, she wanted to see what she would do with it—share it or be greedy and keep it all. Watching her distribute some to the other angels made her proud. She passed the test with flying colors. Had she kept it and walked off the property, it would have shown Gisele that Azia was all for self. Anyone with that type of mentality wasn't welcome in her Operation.

Just as Gisele stepped off the balcony, Azia appeared in the doorway of her bedroom. "Am I interrupting?"

Gisele waved her in. "No, come on inside."

Azia walked into the room and placed the bag on what looked like an island filled with different perfumes, jewelry and scented lotion sets. She looked over her shoulder at Gisele who was only inches away. "I don't know why you offered this to me, but it was unnecessary." She nudged at the bag.

Gisele's face wore a look of surprise. She checked Azia's to see if there was anything hidden behind her actions.

Azia sensed her concern. "You take good care of me, Gisele. I don't want you to think I'm taking advantage of you in any way."

"You're a very smart girl, Azia."

"I am smart, but this has more to do wit' being greedy. That, I am not. Being greedy is a very unhealthy way to live." She smiled, turned, and headed for the door.

Gisele proudly watched Azia walk away. She felt like a proud parent at her daughter's high school graduation. Azia had taken it a step further than expected. But Azia was smart for real. She knew exactly what she was doing. Making a move like that would allow Gisele to feel more comfortable with her and gain more trust. She could feel Gisele's eyes on her back until she was no longer in sight. She never turned back, just grinned all the way to the car.

Gisele walked over to her oversized King bed, grabbed the phone, and fell back, allowing the soft mattress and pillows to swallow her thin frame. She placed a call to Abdul to make sure he and the Italian handled everything they needed to handle as far as Lisa's body was concerned.

"It's done!" he assured her.

"Tell Benny I want him to stick around for a couple of days. I think it's about time that he met our new friend."

"Are you sure?"

She looked over at her nightstand at a picture of her and Azia that had been taken the night they'd gone to Solo. "After tonight, I'm positive."

CHAPTER 18
As Quick As They Rise They Shall Fall
"Backstabbers, they smile in your face."
-Twin

"Why you ain't been answering your phone?! Me and Keemah been tryna call you all night! Where the hell you at?!" Rashaud raged through the phone without coming up for air

Azia had just climbed into her car. She hadn't even had a chance to bring the engine to life before the phone rang. "I was taking care of some business, damn! Stop riding my back! Where you at?"

"I'm at Keemah's house. Meet us over here," he ordered.

Keemah's house, she thought. "What the hell you doing over there?"

"Just bring your ass on. Dude is on his way back from Atlanta. We need to handle him tonight if it's gonna get done."

"You got a plan or what?"

"Don't worry about it. I'll figure something out."

I bet you will," she smirked. "You always do."

Twenty-five minutes later Azia was ringing Keemah's doorbell. She could hear light chitchatting and snickering on the other side of the door. Her face became tight. She pressed her ear firmly against the cold steel to catch what was being said. The more snickering she heard, the harder she pushed her ear against the door. She started banging wildly on the door, like she was the police.

The door flew open.

"Damn, what the hell took you so long to answer?" she questioned.

Rashaud was sitting in a chair up under the window.

"How long you been out there?" Keemah asked, nervously.

"I've been ringing the bell forever."

"The bell doesn't work."

"What the hell is all the giggling and snickering for?"

Rashaud cut in quickly, changing the topic of discussion. "Where you been?"

"Don't answer my question wit' a question. This ain't jeopardy. You the same one that hate when I do that shit." She could smell a mixture of marijuana, cheap liquor, and cigarette smoke in the air. "Ya'll suppose to be looking out for this nigga and ya'll in here having private parties. I can step if you need me to."

"Go 'head wit' that nonsense, Azia." Keemah took a seat across from them both. "So how we gonna do this?"

Rashaud laid down the rules briefly. Azia's role was to play like she was high, drunk and disoriented. Keemah's role was to play like she was delivering the package—signed, sealed and delivered.

Keemah's phone began to wiggle across the table, distracting them all from their thoughts. "It's him," she said, looking down at the screen. "What you want me to say?"

Rashaud jumped up. "Just tell the nigga you already packed his shit and he need to come get it or you'll feed it to the dogs."

Keemah answered the phone and did what she was told to do. Her heart felt like a brick. She thought she was prepared for what was about to go down, but with Twin only minutes away from death, she realized it was no game. She had made a deal with the devil and there was no turning back. "He said he coming down Grays Ferry Avenue."

"Cool! I'm gonna chill in the basement until he gets inside. Make sure he ain't got no heat on him. Play ya part, Keemah. Don't bitch up. If you do, that nigga gonna kill you," Rashaud warned to put fear in her heart. He headed to the basement.

Azia dragged her body across the floor and followed him. She had other things on her mind, like how Rashaud ended up at Keemah's house before she did. She wasted no time questioning him about it. "What the hell were you doing in here wit' her, Rashaud?"

"Are you serious? We in here staking a nigga out and that's all you thinking about? How about you check ya gat and go upstairs to get into position so we can lay this dude down before he lay you down."

Azia could see straight through Rashaud. He was hiding something and she knew it. She decided to sweep it under the rug until she handled her business. After that night, it wouldn't matter if Rashaud and Keemah had something going on. What mattered was that Twin got dealt with. It was time for him to join his brother. She chucked up the stairs to Keemah's bedroom and stripped down to her undergarments. She discreetly slid the curtain back and peeked through the dusty blinds. *Damn, do her lazy ass ever clean?* She asked herself.

Keemah opened the basement door and yelled softly to Rashaud, "Here he comes." She left the door ajar and ran across the squeaky living room floor and halfway up the stairs.

When Twin entered the house, he and Keemah locked eyes. He closed the door and took a few more steps. He scanned the room briefly. There was nothing packed as far as he could see. He glanced back up at Keemah who was sitting on a step. He sniffed and scanned the area, sniffed and scanned.

"Who you been in here smoking wit'? I thought you said you had my stuff packed for me?"

She grinned. "I got something better."

He was all ears. "What's that?"

"Come and see for yourself."

He climbed three steps and stopped. "What am I coming to see?"

"I told you I would do something for you, and I'm a woman of my word. Even though me and you ain't on the up and up right now, I still want to show you I got your back."

Twin was curious to know what kind of present was waiting for him in the darkness. "What? You finally giving me my threesome?" he smirked.

"Something like that," she winked.

He cocked his head to the side. "Wassup, Keemah? What you got going on?"

She held out her hand. "Come and see."

Rashaud listened closely at the top of the basement stairs. He was waiting on his cue. When he heard the two of them walk up the rest of the steps, he crept out quietly like a snake slithering through grass. His gun was unlocked and loaded, his adrenaline was pumping hard, and he was waiting patiently to meet his mark.

Azia was spread across the bed looking edible. The room wasn't fully lit, but Twin knew exactly who she was. He couldn't believe his eyes. He had her right there in front of him. She was beautiful. He had always wondered what had made his brother slip up and leave his guard down, and now he had a chance to see it first-hand. She looked like an angel. "What's wrong wit' her?"

"I slipped something in her drink. We was smoking some weed, too, so she's done. You can do whatever you want to do to her. She ain't gonna know or remember nothing."

"She ain't no good to me like this. I need to question her, not sit here and look at her."

"Lust over her is more like it. I can see it written all over your face," she spat.

Azia tried her best not to laugh. She couldn't believe how jealous her cousin was acting, even in a situation like that. She tried not to move a muscle or blink; she concentrated really hard. Because of the way her body was sprawled out and positioned on the bed, Twin had no idea what was hiding beneath the thin, white, down comforter.

He walked a little closer to further admire her beautiful, silky skin. He became aroused when he noticed her nipples pushing through the teddy she was wearing. Her breasts were the size of melons—not too big, not too small. They were just right. He sat down beside her on the bed, then took his hand and ran it down her thigh. Her skin was as soft as cotton candy. Mesmerized, he turned to look at Keemah and asked, "So what you telling me? She mines for the night?"

Rashaud was already creeping his way upstairs. He couldn't see what was going on in the room, but he could hear it very well. *This dude better not be feeling up on my girl,* he thought.

With his back toward Azia and his face scrunched up, Twin asked, "Are you gonna answer my question?"

Suddenly, he felt a quick movement behind him. Azia sat up like Dracula rising from his coffin and said, "No, mutherfucka, I am." She had the gun jammed into the side of his neck.

Twin jumped up and stumbled back into the dresser. When he turned to his right, Keemah was there. When he turned to his left, there was Rashaud, holding his heat close enough to touch the tip of his nose. He surrendered, throwing his hands in the air. "Alright, man. We good."

Azia hopped off the bed and slipped back into her clothes. "Cut the light on, Keemah," she ordered.

Keemah didn't budge. She was frozen in place.

"Cut on the fucking light!" repeated Azia.

Azia waving her gun brought her out of her petrified state. She speed-walked to the other side of the room and hit the switch.

Azia stared Twin down. It felt weird seeing how identical the two brothers were. She had seen twins before, but had never looked in the face of one whose sibling she'd help kill. It scared her for a second, but then she bounced back. "Let's take him to the basement."

Twin looked over at Keemah and smirked. "I shoulda slumped ya ass when I had the chance, you shady bitch." He knew better than to trust a chick from Philly. They were known for setting people up. Why did he think she was any different?

"Well, it's too late now, ain't it?"

Rashaud intervened. "Cut all the small talk and go turn the music up."

Keemah flew downstairs and turned the bass of the stereo system past twenty. Azia and Rashaud escorted Twin down the steps.

Along the way, Twin decided to make a joke out of the situation. He started singing the 1972 hit record *Back Stabbers* by the O'Jays. "They smile in your face, when all the time they wanna take your place—them back stabbers—backstabbers ..."

Rashaud mugged him in the back of the head. "Shut the fuck up, clown, and keep moving."

Shutting up wasn't an option for Twin. "I just wanna know where my brother at."

"How should we know where the hell—" Azia began.

Twin cut her lie short. "Do you really think you gonna keep getting away wit' the bullshit you be doing? You can't rob niggas like us and get away wit' it? You shoulda done ya homework before making a big move like that. How the fuck you sleep at night?"

"Like a baby," she sneered. "Now keep the fuck moving!"

Cautiously, Keemah followed them into the basement. She was way past tense. The creaking sound on the fifth wooden stair on the way down to the basement startled her. She couldn't remember the last time she'd visited the dusty place. Everything she needed was on the second and third floors. The sight of the cobwebs and spiders made her cringe. "Can we do this somewhere else?" she whined, brushing herself off every time she took another step.

Azia and Rashaud glanced back at the same time. "Get your ass down here," Rashaud ordered.

Tupac's *All Eyes On Me* rattled the walls like a California earthquake. Keemah was surprised that her annoying neighbors hadn't come over to ask her to turn down the ruckus. Then it dawned on her that, even if they tried, she wouldn't be able to hear the door.

Rashaud clicked on a small lamp that was sitting in the corner on a broken down wicker table. The lamp barely gave off enough light to see. "This all the light you got down here?" he asked. Keemah nodded her head. "Run upstairs and get me another lamp or something. I can barely see this nigga." Keemah climbed the steps two at a time. "Don't make any sudden moves, my man, or I'm gonna blow ya head off," Rashaud threatened Twin, then said to Azia, "Keep an eye on him."

Twin was trying to figure a way out of there. Time was racing against him, but there was one thing he still had on his side—the .38 hidden under his oversized shirt.

Keemah had forgotten what Rashaud told her to do. She had been so jealous of Twin's reaction to Azia's nakedness she totally forgot to give him a hug and check for a gun. There was at least a thirty percent chance of him making it out of there alive. It was two against one. He excluded Keemah, knowing she didn't have a weapon. *How the fuck am I gonna get my gun without them seeing me?* As if the Lord had answered his prayer, the opportunity presented itself.

"So how you end up here before me, Rashaud? Are you gonna answer the question or keep brushing me off?" Azia asked.

"What are you talking about?! This ain't the time to play questions!"

"I don't give a damn what time you think it is! I wanna know how your ass got here before I knew what the hell was going on! When did ya'll become so close?!"

Keemah caught the end of their conversation. She ran back down the steps with a light bulb in her hand. "I ain't got another lamp. Just put this new bulb in." She handed it to Rashaud.

Rashaud walked past Twin and directed his comment to Azia. "Keep the gun on him. If you even hear him breathe when I switch out this bulb, shoot his ass." He stopped at the table with his back to them, turned back for a split second, and then proceeded to untwist the bulb.

When the light went out, there was still a little light from one of the streetlights shining through the small basement windows. As quickly and as quietly as possible, Twin eased his right arm behind his back in an attempt to pull his weapon. The minute Azia took her eyes off of him to look evilly at Keemah was all the time he needed.

The light came on and Twin's gun was already drawn. Azia was the first to catch a bullet. *POP!* "Aaahhh!" she screamed, buckling to the floor. The bullet tore through the skin of her left shoulder. If he had a second more to get a better aim, he would have shot her in the heart. Luckily for Azia, he didn't have enough time to pull the trigger again.

Rashaud did a one-hundred-and-eighty-degree turn and popped Twin three times in the chest. *POP! POP! POP!* Twin's body hit the floor hard. His head scraped the wall on his way down. It looked like he was dead. That's not what Rashaud wanted. He'd already had it all planned out in his mind. He walked over to examine Twin and saw that he was hanging on to life by a string. His blood was staining the cement tiles on the basement floor. Rashaud leaned over to pick up the gun Twin dropped when he fell and looked at Keemah.

She was standing there with her mouth wide open. She looked from left to right—from Azia to Twin to Rashaud. She couldn't believe what had just occurred. She was frantic, paranoid, numb, and a whole bunch of other things. If someone had bumped into her at that moment, she would have fallen to the floor and shattered into a million pieces like an ice sculpture.

"Come over here," Rashaud directed. Keemah didn't move. "I said get over here." She flinched and shut her eyes tight. She was petrified. Rashaud moved in close enough to grip her arm and yank her to where Twin was laying on the floor. He shoved his gun into her hand. "Shoot that nigga."

So many thoughts raced through Keemah's mind. *This ain't happening. This has got to be a dream. This nigga is ill if he thinks I'm going to pull the trigger. He got to be crazy.* "I can't," she whispered softly, feeling short of breath.

Twin was tired of suffering. He stumbled over his words, "Just kill me and get it the fuck over with, bitch."

Rashaud walked over to where Azia's body had fallen and snatched her gun from her hand. He walked back over to Keemah and said, "Kill him or I'ma kill you. Take your pick."

Hearing Rashaud's demand sounded like deja vu to Azia, but she was more focused on the pain in her shoulder rather than what was happening around her. The burning sensation of the bullet wound was agonizing. She had never been shot before so she didn't know what to do. She started yelling out, "It burns! Get me some ice, get me something! The muthafucka shot me! It burns, it burns—"

Keemah's nerves were shot. She gripped the butt of the gun with her sweaty palms, closed her eyes as tightly as she could, and squeezed with her pointer finger. When the shot went off, the impact knocked her back a little. She opened her eyes to see what damage she had done. Twin twitched like a fish out of water for a few seconds. The bullet had landed between his nose and upper lip. It had cut through his mustache like a knife through cake. She watched him take his last breath before going completely still. Then she felt something warm running down her legs. She tried to stop the urine but couldn't.

Rashaud went to help Azia from the floor. "Keemah, help me."

She turned toward them, embarrassed for either of them to see that she had pissed on herself. The expression on Rashaud's face told her he was already aware of it.

"You're going to have to take her to the hospital while I get this cleaned up."

"But what are we gonna tell them?! They're gonna call the police—"

"Shut the hell up and just take me there!" Azia yelled.

"Don't worry about saying anything. Azia will handle it," Rashaud assured her.

Rashaud and Keemah helped Azia up the basement stairs. Keemah opened the front door and scanned the area from left to right. She didn't notice one of her neighbors standing at their screen door waiting to find out why the hell the music was so loud.

"Keemah!" the neighbor barked. Keemah almost jumped out of her skin. "I've been banging on your door for almost an hour! You better be glad I didn't call the police on your ass, playing music all loud like that! Turn that racket down!" The woman slammed her door shut and disappeared inside.

Keemah stood in her doorway holding her hand across her chest. She scanned the area one more time to make sure the coast was clear. There was no one else in sight. "Come on," she waved.

Rashaud helped Azia into Keemah's car and went back into the house to make a couple of calls to Biggs and his clean-up team.

"She needs a doctor!" cried Keemah, rushing through the emergency entrance of the University of Pennsylvania hospital with Azia's right arm draped around her neck. "She's been shot!"

A few nurses and a security guard rushed over. They took Azia to the back and took her vitals. Then they hurried her off to emergency surgery. A nearby police officer had seen Keemah and Azia entering the emergency area and made his way over to find out what was going on.

"What happened to your friend, ma'am? Who shot her?"

"I don't know! ... I don't know! ..." she cried out hysterically.

"Calm down," he said, trying to control the movements of her arms. "Where are you coming from?"

"I just want to make sure she's okay. I don't know what happened to her, but I can take a fucking guess if you need me to. Shit, she's bleeding to death. Go check on her." Her voice was so thin that her attitude didn't offend him.

"Sit here a minute," he advised, walking over to the nurse's station. When he turned to come back two minutes later, Keemah was gone. A track star couldn't have made it out of there any quicker. "Where'd she go?" he asked other waiting patients.

The few that heard him and knew who he was referring to pointed toward the exit. He ran outside to see if the car she'd pulled up in was still there, but it was gone and she was nowhere in sight.

Keemah cried all the way back to her house. She rushed through the door calling out Rashaud's name. He appeared from out of the basement. She ran over to him and broke down.

"What the hell is wrong wit' you, girl? Where's Azia?"

"I left her at the hospital."

He frowned. "You did what?"

"It was a cop!—He started asking me questions!—I was scared!—I didn't know what to do!—They took her to the back!—I'm sorry!—" Her words ran on like a run on sentence.

"You telling me there was a cop questioning you and you ran your black ass up out of there?! How the hell you get away wit' that?!" He walked over to the window and peeped out to see if she had been followed. He just knew there would be a swarm of Philadelphia's finest whipping around the corner at any second. "Are you slow?!"

"No! He went to talk to the nurse and I slipped out! I'm sorry! I ain't know what to say to him! He kept asking and asking—"

"A'ight, a'ight," Rashaud said. Both of their attentions zoomed in on the heavy footsteps coming up the basement stairs. "Go upstairs and clean yourself up," he ordered.

Keemah kept her eyes glued on the basement door. "Who's that down there?"

"Mind your business and go upstairs. I'll call you when everything down here is cleaned up."

Keemah walked slowly toward the stairs, waiting for the unknown person to present himself, but Biggs heard Rashaud order her upstairs so he stopped in his tracks and waited for Rashaud to return.

"Take ya ass upstairs and stop tryna be so damn nosy!" he shouted.

■ ■ ■

Azia was disoriented when she woke up after her surgery. The anesthesia the doctors had given her had her body on cloud number nine. She examined the room for several minutes. She thought she was dreaming until the plain-clothed detective asked her how she was feeling. Her eyes were fighting to stay open. Seconds later a nurse came in to check her vitals, gave her three pills inside a small cup and some water. She stared down at the medication. The pills were three different colors and three different sizes. "What is this I'm taking?" she asked.

"The white one is Motrin for the pain. The blue and green ones are antibiotics," she smiled. "How are you feeling?" She went to check the heart monitor for an update.

"I feel fine," she lied. "I want to go home."

Detective Joseph walked over to the side of the bed and made himself a part of the conversation. "You can do that. But first I need to know who did this to you."

"Who are you?" Azia asked. The detective wasn't wearing a uniform and he hadn't shown his badge. "How did I get here?" She knew damn well how she'd gotten there, but decided to play the amnesia role.

"I'm Detective Joseph," he said, pulling a card from his wallet. He placed it on the nightstand beside her. "I'll put it over here for now." He looked at the bloody gauze taped to her shoulder. "What happened to you?"

"All I remember is getting out of my car. Anything after that is a blur."

"Well, an officer tells me someone dropped you off here."

"That had to be my cousin. I was meeting up wit' her when it happened."

"Where is she now?"

"Your guess would be better than mine."

The detective thought something about their conversation was very strange. He listened attentively. "Why would she leave you here alone?"

"That's a question you would have to save for her."

"Where does she live?"

"Wherever her head lands at night."

"So she has no permanent place of residence?"

"Not that I'm aware of."

"Umph." He shifted positions and began to play with his beard. "Do you think she had something to do with it?"

"No! Why would my own flesh and blood do me like that?" Azia became tense. The beeping on the pressure machine picked up speed. "She wouldn't do me like that. I'm sure it was a case of mistaken identity, or a drive-by shooting, or something. Ain't nobody after me. There's no reason for them to be."

The nurse rushed in when she heard the accelerated beeping. "Alright, Detective. I'm sorry but I'm going to have to ask you to leave."

Detective Joseph looked at Azia. "You have my card. If you think of anything or catch up to your cousin, give me a call. Any time of the day, it doesn't matter."

Azia nodded her head and threw her hand over her face like she had the worse headache in the world. When he left, she begged the nurse to discharge her.

"I can't sweetie. You need to stay here and get some rest. The doctor is the only one that can give the order to let you go."

Azia thought back to her last hospital visit. "But you can't hold me against my will."

"That's true. But why would you want to put yourself at risk like that. They want to keep you for a few more hours, just to make sure the bleeding is under control." She placed a light snack on a tray and pushed it toward the bed. "Listen, why don't you nibble on this, get a little bit of rest, then we'll see how you feel?"

Azia thought for a moment. She was dead tired and really didn't feel like moving a muscle. "I can do that. But can you please do me a favor and pass me my cell phone."

The nurse twisted her lips. "Now you know you're not supposed to use those in here." She liked Azia. She didn't know what her situation was, but she reminded her of her own daughter. "I'm going to do it for you." She walked over to where all Azia's belongings were and grabbed the cell phone from her bag. She walked back over to the bed and placed it in her hand. "Don't be too long." She exited the room and closed the door behind her.

Azia placed several calls to both Rashaud and Keemah and got both their voicemails right away—no rings, no nothing. It was safe to assume they'd cut their phones off. *Why the fuck would they turn their phones off and I'm in here. Stinking muther—*. Her thoughts were distracted by an incoming call. Her heart skipped a beat when she read the name. "Hey, Mike," she answered in a baby-fied voice.

"It's good to hear your voice. How you been?"

Azia broke down in tears. Mike was caught off guard by the outburst. He wasn't expecting to get that in response to his question. He knew she had some issues she was dealing with, but he didn't know the extent of them. He gave her a minute to calm down.

"What's wrong?"

"I'm in the hospital," she sniffled.

"What happened to you?" She broke down again. "When are they releasing you?"

"I don't know."

"Is it serious enough for them to keep you?" Azia nodded her head like he could see through the phone. "Azia, is it that serious or what?"

"I don't know," she cried. "I got shot."

Mike thought he heard wrong. He turned the radio off completely in his car and repeated what he thought he heard. "You got shot?" She answered with silence. "What hospital are you at?"

"University of Penn."

"I'm on my way."

That was the last thing she heard before hearing dead air. She was happy Mike was coming to be by her side but nervous at the same time. She didn't know how to explain the bullet that had been removed from her shoulder. It would only make sense for him to ask what happened, but deep down inside she was praying he didn't. She knew she couldn't tell him the truth. What would he think of her if she did? She tried to come up with different explanations but none of them were convincing enough. He would be able to see straight through the lies. There was only one thing for her to do: either tell the truth and nothing but the truth, or tell nothing at all.

CHAPTER 19
Feeling Brand New Inside
"I can't let him take control any longer."
-Azia

It didn't take much for Mike to get Azia discharged from the hospital. He made a couple of phone calls and made it happen. Azia was fine. The bullet had been removed and they were able to stop the bleeding so she was in no danger.

"Thank you for coming to get me." She looked over at Mike who hadn't said two words to her since they got into his car.

He gave a long head nod to let her know he was listening.

She quit talking and took advantage of the silence, knowing it was just a matter of time before he began to interrogate her. She turned her body slightly toward the window and gazed out at nothing in particular.

Mike periodically turned his head to look at her. He didn't know why he jumped to go get her ass. He was not a knight in shining armor. The girl was in the hospital because of a gunshot wound. Stomachaches, headaches, colds, fevers, and things of that nature were the usual causes of hospital visits for normal women—not gunshot wounds. Azia was not the typical around-the-way girl. She had a lot of shit with her and Mike wanted to get down to the bottom of it.

"Where are you going?" he asked.

She took a minute to think. She wasn't ready for him to see her new home. That would do nothing but add on another fifty questions to the ones he already had lined up. "Do you mind if I stay wit' you?"

Mike pulled over to the side of the road and faced her in the passenger seat.

Here we go, thought Azia.

"No, I don't mind you staying wit' me. You can stay wit' me as long as you need to. I don't want to see anything bad happen to you, Azia. You're sitting in my car wit' a bullet hole inches away from your heart. And I'm afraid to ask why. I know you're much smarter than this. Whatever you got going on in your life is on you, but you're not going to bring all that extra baggage on me. I've survived these streets for several years without this kind of drama, and I'm not going to start now." Her eyes began to water. "I care about you a lot, probably more than I should, but you got some issues you need to deal wit' before you try to kick it wit' me. Stop running from your problems. Own up to them, sort them out, and get rid of them one by one. I don't believe you're a bad girl. I believe you got yourself caught up in a messy situation. I try not to pry into your personal life, but I feel as though you owe me an explanation."

Azia wanted to tell him everything so badly. It was on the tip of her tongue, but she couldn't say anything. Every time she parted her lips to speak, nothing but hot air came out.

"You can sit there all quiet if you want to, but I know you got something to say."

"I don't know where to begin."

He faced forward in his seat and gazed out of his windshield. "Well, when you figure it out, I'm here to listen. I'm tryna be as understanding as I can, but if you keep holding out on me, how do you expect me to ever trust you?"

"You can trust me," she cried.

He cut the wheel real hard and sped off, almost side-swiping another car in the outer lane. "That's what your mouth says."

Mike let Azia into his apartment, told her to make herself comfortable, and headed back out to give her some time alone. She undressed, went into the bathroom, and ran a bubble bath. The doctors told her not to get the wound too wet so she made sure she didn't fill the tub to the rim. She took a minute to look herself over in the mirror. The reflection wasn't the same girl from a couple years ago. This was someone totally new. She whispered to the mirror, *I lost myself.* Tears began to trickle down her cheeks so slowly a turtle could've won the race. *I can't continue to live like this.* She gave up. Not on life, but on death. She began to realize that if she kept living like she was there was a big possibility that she may not make it. *I got to do something. I can't let him control me any longer,* she said, referring to the devil.

She climbed in the bathtub, closed her eyes, and tried to relax her mind, but instead it ran wild. She envisioned everything exactly how it had happened from Mudda to Twin, missing nothing in between. Her eyes shot open. The whole place was silent. The only thing that could be heard was the soft sound of Ashanti's voice singing her hit song *Baby, Baby, Baby,* which wafted from the CD player that was mounted in the bathroom wall.

Against the doctor's orders, Azia slid her whole body down into the water. The only thing above the water was her head. She drifted into deep thought again. Moments later, she slid down further, letting her head join the rest of her body underneath the suds. Her count reached thirty-six before she couldn't take anymore. She came up for air just before the water took her last breath. She cried out hysterically. The drenched remains of what used to be a silky-soft perm covered her face. She used both hands to brush it toward the back of her head and lost herself again in deep thought. She was fed up. And when a woman's fed up, there ain't no telling what she might do.

■ ■ ■

The next three days flew by. Azia had heard nothing from Rashaud or Keemah since she was dropped off at the hospital. It was like they had vanished into thin air. She stopped by Keemah's house twice to see if she could catch her, but both times all the lights were off and the place looked empty. She had been too lazy to take a trip up to Rashaud's apartment. She figured that since they weren't answering their phones, then evidently they didn't want to be bothered. She felt abandoned and betrayed by the two people she loved the most.

Mike made sure he played his part. He still wasn't ready to take it to the next level, so he did the best he could as a friend. Azia decided to stay with him because she wasn't ready to go back to that big empty house and be lonesome. The silence alone would be enough to kill her. She needed his company, and as long as he offered it, she continued to take it.

Mike strolled into the house carrying a few bags of groceries and headed straight for the kitchen. Azia hopped up off the living room sofa and rushed to be by his side. Wings couldn't have gotten her there any quicker. She had been bored to death and couldn't wait for him to come home.

"I missed you," she greeted with a smile.

Mike grinned. He unpacked all the groceries and placed everything on the kitchen table. "Go ahead back in there and watch TV. I'm going to cook something special for you tonight."

Azia's face turned bright red. She couldn't control her blush. No man had ever cooked a meal for her before. She tilted her head to the side and asked, "Can you cook?"

"We about to find out ain't we?"

"Don't be in here burning down the spot," she chuckled.

Mike stood still and watched her disappear behind the wall. He was ready to prepare his very first dish. Taking the advice of his mother, chicken parmesan was the entrée for the night. She told him "Son, it's a lot of things you can mess up, but chicken parmesan ain't one of 'em. If you can't cook a piece of chicken until the inside ain't pink or boil a noodle until it gets soft, you don't need to live on your own." Thinking back to his mother's comment made him chuckle as he started to prepare the meal.

Azia sat in the living room watching Thelma and JJ on *Good Times* go at it every chance they got. She was so busy laughing her butt off, she never noticed Mike peeking in on her every so often. The aroma of freshly seasoned chicken brought her to her feet. She went to peek around the corner into the kitchen. Mike was setting the table for the two of them. He had just lit two tall candles and placed two plates opposite each other on the table when Azia stepped into the kitchen and asked, "Is all this for me?"

He turned back to look at her. "All of what? This ain't nothing big. I just want us to relax and get to know one another a little better. I have some questions I need to ask you."

What kind of questions? Her insides quivered. She didn't know what kind of questions he had, but she tried to mentally prepare herself for it. "I'ma go freshen up a little."

"Go ahead, I'll be here waiting."

When Azia came back, Mike had already taken his seat. He was sitting in the chair leaning forward on his elbows. He was covering his face with both hands. She walked over to him and started to massage his shoulders, neck, back, and around to his chest. "Are you okay?" she asked.

"Go sit down," he ordered, never answering her question.

She walked around the table to the empty seat. She leaned toward the plate to smell the sauce. "It smells good." She smiled to keep from looking frightened. She couldn't understand why her knees were shaking and her heart was racing. "Do you want to pray over the food or shall I?"

"You can do the honors."

Azia thanked the Lord for the food they were about to receive, then they both dug in. She was surprised. Everything was seasoned to perfection. "This is really good," she admitted, sticking a forkful of chicken into her mouth.

Their conversation through dinner was light and easygoing. That is until Mike asked her a question that could have made her choke to death on her food.

"I have something to ask you," he began. "I don't want you to lie to me either. I want you to be as honest as possible. You told me once before that you wanted me to trust you. I'm trying my hardest to do so. This just might be the night you earn that trust."

"What is it, Mike?" she asked even though she really didn't want to know. "I do want to prove to you that you can trust me, so whatever it is that I have to do, just tell me."

The sincerity in her eyes won her a couple of brownie points. "A friend of mine is missing. Actually two friends of mine are missing," he corrected. "I need to know what happened to them and how that bullet ended up in your shoulder."

Azia panicked. At that moment she wished she was Sabrina the witch. She wanted to brush a finger across her nose and magically disappear so badly. She bit down so hard on her fork that it scraped her teeth. The sound of the screeching metal made her cringe. Finally, she got her thoughts together. "Who are your friends?"

"We're not going to start this topic like this. Let me make it clear that I know you already know who my friends are. As a matter of fact, you knew one of them very well," he stated, referring to Mustafa. "You were the last person seen wit' him the night he disappeared."

He didn't give her any room to lie. "Yeah, I knew Mustafa. And you're not the first person to mention me being the last person to be seen wit' him either. But what I want to know is why is it that just because we rolled out together I got to be tied up in his disappearance."

"Are you telling me you had nothing to do wit' it?"

"I'm saying—"

He cut her off. "Before you answer that, I want you to know that you can be truthful wit' me. If what you are about to say is a lie, make sure you're ready to keep the lie going. Make sure you can back the lie when shit starts to unfold and your name is stuck in the middle. I can only help you if you're honest wit' me. Now take a minute to re-think whatever it is you were going to say."

The tear in Azia's right eye fought its way to the surface. She contemplated her next move for a moment. *What if he already knows? If I lie to him and he finds out, I'll never be able to gain his trust. What if he kills me for having something to do with it? He's calling these dudes his friends. You kill for your friends. I don't even care. Whatever he does to me I deserve. Whatever happens happens. I got to stand strong and start owning up to my faults. Ain't that what he told me to do?* She prepared for the worse best she could. "Mike," she whispered. Two tears turned into twenty in a matter of seconds. "I didn't mean for none of it to happen. I was scared. You don't know the things he used to do to me. He would have killed me if I said anything." She quickly put all the blame on Rashaud.

Mike's silence scared her. She didn't know what he was thinking and it was hard to read him. He dropped his fork and leaned back in his chair, crossing his arms. "So did you kill them?"

"No!" she yelled. "I promise I didn't! He did everything. He cut a guy's head off and brought it to me! He told me if I ever told anyone, he would do the same thing to me." Her cry began to weaken. On a scale of 1 to 10, her energy level dropped from 8 to 2. Everything became a big blur. "He made me do it. He made me do it, you don't understand. You don't know what he's capable of." That was the last sentence to roll off her tongue before everything went completely black.

The phone rang, jerking Azia out of her sleep. She assumed it was morning because she could hear birds chirping outside the window. She sat upright in bed and began to feel all over herself to make sure she was still in one piece. She was naked, but everything was still in tact. *Had it been a dream?* She climbed out of Mike's bed looking around for any signs of him. Because of the silence, she assumed he was gone. *Where the hell is he?* She walked to the living room to grab the phone. *Damn, was I dreaming or what? Shit, I can't remember.* Azia grabbed the phone and headed to the kitchen. She would be able to find the answer to her question there. When she saw the empty jars of Prego and the scrapings from the chicken parmesan, she knew it hadn't been a dream. *Well, he left me in his house. He didn't kill me. Maybe I got in his head enough for him to sympathize with me,* she thought while dialing his number. He answered on the first ring. "Good morning," she squeaked.

"Good morning," he replied nonchalantly.

"About last night—"

"There's no need for that, Azia. There's no need for you to worry. I told you, as long as you're honest wit' me I'll have your back. I could do a million different things to you right now—or I could have done them to you—but you opened up and kept things real wit' me. I wish you had done it from the beginning, but I understand the circumstances."

She exhaled heavily. Every word that skipped from his mouth to her ear sounded like an old Isley Brothers tune, soft and suitable.

"We still ain't done talking, but I want you to know you don't have to be afraid any longer. When you have someone like me on your team, there's no reason to be."

"I love you, Mike." The words rolled off her tongue before she could stop them.

He chuckled knowing that wasn't supposed to slip out and she laughed, too.

"That sounds kind of strange coming from you."

"I've been feeling it for quite some time. I was just waiting for the perfect opportunity to express the way I felt."

"That's a whole 'nother discussion. Maybe we can take another vacation to address and express any and everything on our minds."

"That sounds like a plan to me."

"Let me go. I got some business to tend to, and then I'll be home."

"Okay. If I'm not here, dial my cell. I need to run a few errands."

"Whatever you do, meet me back at the house by seven o'clock."

"Why? What's going on tonight?"

"It's a surprise. Just make sure you have something real fly laid out for tonight."

Azia became excited not knowing what to look for or expect. When the call ended, she danced around the place like a contestant on *Dancing With The Stars*. She was so happy to finally get rid of some of the heavy baggage weighing her down. Coming clean to Mike felt like how a pregnant woman feels the minute after she gives birth. Relieved! She threw on some music, showered, and dressed within the next hour, and headed out the door.

CHAPTER 20
You Ain't Saying Nothing
"Lay it on me thick. I got all the time in the world."
-Detective Joseph

The locks hadn't been changed on the apartment she and Rashaud used to share, so she let herself in, hoping that he was home so she could tell his ass off. Instead she was welcomed by clothes scattered all around the living room, some his, some hers; dirty dishes piled in the sink; and the worst smell she had ever come across. She didn't know what was in the trash can, but whatever it was smelled horrid. It smelled like bad Chinese food that had been sitting out for two weeks straight. She bypassed everything with her fingers covering her nose and went straight back to the bedroom. When she saw her closet gaping open she became furious. Someone had been picking through everything she'd left behind.

She walked over and pulled everything down from the hangers. *I can't believe he let some heffa go through all my stuff. He ain't worth two cents. I wouldn't piss on his head if his ass was on fire.* She stormed around the room grabbing anything she didn't want to leave behind. She put her hand back up to her nose and ran into the kitchen to get a trash bag. On her way back to the bedroom, she noticed a bunch of mail scattered all over the dining room table. She walked over to see if anything had come for her since she'd been gone. One piece in particular stood out to her, like it was begging to be read. She snatched it up from the table. It was a flight itinerary. Clear as day, at the top of the page, it read Virgin America Airlines. She immediately scanned down to see who the passenger(s) were. When she read the two names she could have passed out: Rashaud and Keemah. And their destination was Los Angeles, California.

This nigga must be ill, she thought. She continued to read, looking for the dates. The date of departure was the day after she got shot. *They hopped up and took a vacation when my ass was laid up with a bullet in me. How real is that? She's a phony mutherfucka.* She let the paper float to the floor like a leaf falling from a tree. She headed back to the room and tossed whatever she wanted into the bag. Then, out of nowhere, a thought hit her. Something in her gut told her to check the secret compartment she had found.

She used all her strength to push the dresser out of the way. For some odd reason, it seemed harder to do than last time. Then she remembered: the last time she had two arms instead of one. Once she created enough space to squeeze in and grab the piece of wood she stopped moving the dresser. She snatched the piece of wood out of the wall and jumped to her feet, then placed her hand over her mouth to muffle a scream. Her gut had pointed her in the right direction. The money that had once disappeared was back, only this time it looked like it had doubled. *It can't be real.* She took a handful and ran her hand over it. *Oh shit, it is real!* She tossed every last dollar of it into the trash bag on top of her belongings and got the hell up out of Dodge.

Azia's next stop was Gisele's house. She didn't like making unexpected visits, but she needed to explain her reason for being missing in action for the last few days. She made her way inside using the pass code she was given. Gisele was sitting in the parlor with the same Italian she had seen the last time she was there. They were sipping on what looked like hot tea from a distance. From the looks on their faces, they were having a warm conversation. When Azia appeared, they didn't look surprised to see her there.

The welcoming expression on Gisele's face eased the tension. "Azia, darling! Where have you been my angel?" She rose to her feet with open arms and they hugged.

Benny stood from his seat as well.

"I have been worried sick about you. It's not like you not to return phone calls. Now that I see you're okay, I'm offended."

"There's no need for that," she said, looking over at Beeny who was staring right through her. "If you knew what I'd been through in these last couple of days, I'm sure you'd change your mind."

"Well, let me introduce you to a very important part of our operation. Then you can tell me all about it."

The three of them walked out back to the patio. Azia and Benny shook hands and got more acquainted with one another while Gisele took a dip in the pool. They flirted a little, talked business a little, and politicked a little. He offered her the opportunity to move down to Florida to be the head of their operation down there, the same as Gisele was in Philly. Basically the same rules would apply as far as her cost of living. Her mortgage would be covered and she would be given a car on top of her profit. The only thing that would change was the five percent. If she accepted the offer, she would get fifty percent because she would have a lot more responsibility.

Azia contemplated for a moment. Running off to Florida to start a new life didn't sound like a bad idea. If Benny had caught her three weeks back, she would have been on the first plane smoking. But times had changed. She had enough money in her trunk at that moment to invest and take care of her for the rest of her life, as long as she flipped it right. She did pay attention to some of the things Abdul pulled her coat to. Then, on the other hand, she had Mike in her corner, the muscle of muscles. He was her King and she wanted to be his Queen. In her mind, they could be a modern-day Bonnie and Clyde, taking down whoever, whatever, and whenever.

Gisele climbed up the steps out of the pool and walked over to join the conversation. She dried herself off and took a seat. "So, did Benny lay it all out for you?"

"Yes, he did. But, Gisele, so much has changed since the last time we spoke." The perplexed look she gave troubled Azia. The last thing she wanted Gisele to think was that she was bailing out on her. "Before you say anything, I can show you better than I can tell you." She pulled her shirt over her head and tossed it beside her. The bullet wound was clearly visible; nothing was hiding it any longer. "I got shot the other night. Luckily it was here," she said, pointing to the exact spot the bullet entered, "instead of here," she pointed a few inches down to where her heart was. Gisele and Benny looked on in amazement. "I don't want you to think I don't appreciate everything you've done for me. You're paying on a house that I barely live in. How could I not appreciate that?"

"Let's take a walk," suggested Gisele.

Azia snatched up her shirt and followed Gisele back inside. Benny stayed outside to give them some privacy. They went into the room where they'd first met. It looked even whiter and brighter during the day. "Azia, I don't know what happened to you or how you ended up in the predicament you're in, but if you want me to know or need an ear, I'm here to listen. It seems like you really do have some issues that need to be addressed."

"I told you that once before."

Gisele was apauled. "I know you said it, but I didn't know they were this serious."

"I just need some time to get my life back on track. How can I work for you or even operate a business of yours in this state of mind?"

"Maybe you do need to move down to Florida. It'll be a fresh start for you."

Azia shook her head no. "I can't leave things here messed up the way they are. I have to settle the score. I can't keep running from my problems. Even if I do leave, this will always be home, so I know I'll be back sooner or later. And if that's the case, I don't want to come back to bullshit."

"I totally understand and I agree. My operation definitely doesn't need any problems, and neither do I," she smirked. "But, just because you're taking a break doesn't mean you're no longer an angel. Keep the house and car as long as you need to, they'll be taken care of. Go ahead and get your life situated. Benny and I will be here waiting on you when you return. I'm sure the same offer will be on the table. There isn't anyone else worthy enough to take your place."

"I'm glad to hear that."

They kissed and hugged and went their separate ways. When Azia got back to Mike's place, she felt like a second weight had been lifted off her shoulders. But she wasn't done. There was still something weighing heavily on her heart, somebody she had to take care of so that she could put the past behind her. The only question was how she was going to pull it off. She dug deep into her pocketbook and pulled out her wallet. She pulled out all the business cards she had stuffed in the side until she found the one she was looking for: the card Detective Joseph had given her at the hospital. She kissed it up to God, hoping it would turn out to be the answer to all her prayers.

■ ■ ■

Detective Joseph was frustrated, aggravated, agitated, annoyed, and upset with all the cases he had been given. He was pretty new to the whole homicide detective thing, but it couldn't be that hard to catch a leak. His luck couldn't get any worse. He had the captain up his ass waiting for leads and any new information, but there was nothing for him to report. That was until the phone call came through that gave him the break he'd been waiting for.

He and Azia met at a downtown coffee shop in Center City. She refused to meet at the precinct. The thought of being around that many policemen made her nauseous. He agreed to meet her at the Starbucks on 15th and Market Street, next to the Hysterical Clothespin. She was already there when he arrived, staring down at a daily newspaper. Every new story she read about going on around the world depressed her more and more: mothers were killing their own children, soldiers over in Iraq were losing their lives for no good reason. People were being shot up, robbed and killed, and terrorism was rampant. She was hoping to read something more positive but came across nothing that lifted her spirits. When she heard someone clear their throat over her head she looked up.

"Is it okay if I sit down?" Detective Joseph asked.

She held out her hand as a gesture for him to do so. Her heart was racing. She was starting to feel indecisive about being there. She had rehearsed, over and over again, what she wanted to say, but now that it was time, she'd forgotten half of it.

"How's your shoulder doing?" he grinned.

"It's doing better. It hurts like hell sometimes, but that ain't nothing some good ol' Percocet can't handle."

The detective smiled, and then pointed to the newspaper. "Anything good in the paper?"

"There never is," she said with a sigh. She rolled up the paper and tucked it away. "I know you're tryna make this conversation as comfortable for me as you can, but I didn't come here to beat around the bush and play games wit' you. I came to tell you something that I've been scared to tell for several months now. But before I say anything, I need to know that I am protected. I need to know that I won't be caught up in any kind of conspiracy theories or anything like that."

The clean-cut detective sat up as straight as he could. "I don't know what you're about to tell me so I can't promise you anything."

"Okay," she said, rising to her feet. "On that note, I need to be going. I can't afford to risk my life over something I was forced into."

"Alright, Alright," he said waving his hand for her to sit. "I'll see what I can do."

Azia sat back down. "What I'm about to tell you might blow your mind. I hope you have some time because it's not your average short story."

"What is this in regards to?"

Azia looked at him with hard eyes. "All the murders and disappearances that been taking place around the city."

Detective Joseph leaned forward in his chair. With his hands folded he leaned foreard stopping halfway across the table to read her eyes and said, "Lay it on me thick. I got all the time in the world."

CHAPTER 21
Watch Me Do Me
"Ain't nobody but God gonna be able to save you."
-Rashaud

The grand opening for Koka's Bar and Grill was off the chain. Everybody who was somebody came out to support Mike and his mother. The restaurant was filled and the wait was forty-five minutes to an hour. Originally, Mike had wanted to make the spot a nightclub, but he got to thinking and realized that all the hoorah and drama was not something he wanted to deal with. So his mother came up with the whole bar and grill idea, and it turned out to be a success.

Mike and Azia climbed out of his car at the same time, looking like a million dollars, compliments of Ralph Lauren's latest collection of Black and Purple label. The valet happily took the keys to Mike's BMW. He couldn't wait to see how smooth the ride would be. He gave dap, hugs, and shouted thank yous to all the people who had come out to support. Almost half an hour later, they made their way to the back where Ms. Koka was directing the staff like an orchestra conductor. The only thing she didn't have was the little baton to wave around in the air. She lit up when she saw Mike.

She looked right past Azia. "Baby, look at this turnout! I told you it was going to be off the chain!"

He nodded and spoke to a coule familiar more faces all at one time. "You did your thing wit' it. I owe you big-time." He moved forward a little to whisper in her ear. "I got someone I want you to meet."

Azia was expecting attitude but got the opposite. "Hello!" said Ms. Koka, greeting her with a hug. "You're a pretty little thing!" She took a step back to check Azia out from head to toe.

Please don't say nothing about these little-ass shorts I got on. Something told me to put on pants, she thought. *First impressions are lasting impressions. I should kick his ass for not telling me I would be meeting his mother.*

Ms. Koka continued. "I love the outfit. We gotta start hitting the stores together," she grinned.

Thank you, Jesus, she sighed. "It's beautiful in here. You really did a wonderful job of putting it together. Mike told me it was just a piece of land when you all first started." Azia looked around the room at the crowd of people who were tearing down on steak, lobster, shrimp, chicken, and all different kinds of sides. She found out later that all of the food in Koka's Bar and Grill was served sautéed and grilled or broiled: nothing fried. "Looking at all this food is making me hungry."

"I saved ya'll a table in the back." She directed them to follow her. "Mike, don't worry about a thing. I got everything in check. Momma gonna make you a wealthy man. Just sit back and watch." After they were seated, Ms. Koka swayed back across the room and disappeared behind a pair of swinging double doors that lead into the kitchen.

Azia tapped Mike in the chest with her menu. "Why you ain't tell me I was gonna meet your mom?"

"I didn't want you to be nervous. I wanted you to be yourself so she could have a chance to check out the real you."

Azia smiled. She had no idea about the restaurant until that night. She had seen flyers and posters advertising the date of the grand opening but never knew Mike was behind it. The place was stunning. "Did she decorate all by herself?"

"Even if she didn't she gonna take the credit for it." They laughed in unison. "I didn't tell you—you look beautiful tonight."

"No, you didn't but your momma did." She stuck out her tongue playfully. "When we get back to your place tonight, I want to sit down and tell you everything."

Mike stared into the sparkle in her eyes. "I'm wit' that. But right now, let's enjoy the night." He stood up from the table. "I see some folks I need to greet. I'll be back in a minute. Order whatever you want."

Azia watched her man glide across the floor like he had on Heelys roller shoes. She took a minute to close her eyes and say a small prayer. The Lord had blessed her in so many ways. Mike had forgiven her, she had escaped death by just inches, and her plan for Rashaud's downfall was in motion.

Before leaving Detective Joseph at the coffee shop, she had given him all the information he needed to tie his cases together. She pinned Rashaud to the murders of Mudda, Tonya, Busta, and Tommy, as well as the disappearance of the twins. She explained that she had no idea where the bodies were, but that they had been murdered for sure. She didn't mention Keemah's name. She would deal with her on a more personal level.

Detective Joseph was at a loss for words by the time Azia finished. He told her she would be given immunity only if she agreed to testify. He said that any involvement she had would be overlooked by the DA. Azia told him she would get back to him with an answer. She was banking, on Rashaud being taken down without her ever having to step foot in a courtroom, but giving her testimony would only make him sink deeper. So she was waiting for the night to be over so she could lay everything out to Mike. Everything! She knew he would be able to give her the best advice and stand in her corner, whichever way she decided to go with it.

The night ended quicker than she thought it would. They left the restaurant close to one o'clock in the morning. After they got to Mike's place, Azia watched him undress and toss his body back onto the bed. He welcomed her with his arms. She crawled up to him and put her head on his chest. He secured her in his grip. "So you ready to talk or what?"

"I'm ready. I'm tired of holding it inside." She looked up into his eyes. "Just promise me one thing. Promise me you won't let what I'm about to tell you affect this relationship we're building."

Mike took a deep breath. "I told you, as long as you're open and honest about everything, I'll be here to back you up. You're not perfect, you're human. Any mistakes you made in the past can't be unmade, but you live and you learn."

Azia spilled the beans, starting from Mudda and stopping at Detective Joseph. Mike found it all hard to believe. She couldn't be capable of doing such things. Her story reminded him of a book he'd read not that far back called *Down In The Dirty* by J.M. Benjamin. The things the females did in that story were unreal up until then. Azia didn't stutter. Just as he'd requested, she told him what the deal was from A to Z, and he promised to have her back. After she'd finished, she waited on his response. "Say something," she squealed, raising her body from his.

"What the hell can I say after a story like that?"

"Say something. Please, Mike. Say anything."

He pulled her back into his arms and she began to weep. "Don't cry." He wiped the tears from her eyes and took a moment to think things through. "Don't cry," he repeated.

Again, she picked her head up and looked him square in the eye. "Please tell me that you forgive me. Tell me that you trust me. I would never do anything to hurt you."

In his heart, he knew she wasn't lying. She was so broken up inside. Being with the wrong kind of man can do that to a woman. But now she was his woman and it was only right that he help put the pieces of her puzzle back together. Although she had no clue, he was in love for the first time. From then on out, he decided that it was up to him to keep her strong and focused. The whole Gisele thing blew his mind, but not more than hearing that she'd stolen over five hundred thousand dollars from Rashaud's place. He was ready to make her take it back because he didn't need it, and now that she would be a permanent part of his life, neither did she. But then it dawned on him that Rashaud was the reason he would no longer benefit from two of his most valued customers, Mustafa and Twin. So in a way he felt like that money was owed to him. If Rashaud wanted to come and battle for it, then he better come correct.

"What do you think I should do about the detective?"

"As much as I hate snitches, you have to follow your heart on that one, baby girl. I get the fact that he's fucking your cousin and that he put you through the pit of hell, but you're the one that's going to sit on that stand and give your testimony. Are you willing to sit in front of twelve jurors, a judge, a courtroom filled with people, and the devil himself?"

Azia went silent. The whole room began to spin around her as she tossed the question back and forth in her mind. Finally, she had an answer: "If that's what I have to do to make that nigga reap what he sowed, then so be it."

■ ■ ■

Two days later, Rashaud and Keemah returned home from their getaway. As soon as Rashaud entered the house, he sensed that something wasn't right. He pulled out his gun and held it close to his side with his finger on the trigger. The smell that was coming from the kitchen damn near knocked Keemah off her feet.

"What the hell is that smell?!" she cried out.

Rashaud heard nothing she said. He was in a zone. He was thinking about the unwelcoming presence in the apartment. He walked inside slowly, one-step at a time.

"What's wrong wit' you?"

He ignored Keemah's question. Room by room, he scoped one at a time, checking all corners and closets. When he got to the bedroom, he noticed that Azia's closet was almost empty. He put the gun back on his hip and walked over to it, thinking, *Damn, I wonder if she knows we went away together.* He walked back out to the living room to see if he and Keemah had left any signs and there it was, right where she'd left it on the floor.

"What is it, Rashaud? Keemah nagged. "What's wrong?"

He picked the itinerary up from the floor and scanned it. "You left the fucking itinerary on the table! She knows we went away together!"

Keemah snatched the paper from his hand. "How the hell she get in here?!"

"Wit' her fucking key! How you think she got in here?!"

"Well, that's your fault! You shoulda taken it back or got the locks changed when she left!" Keemah walked over to the sofa and flopped down with her face twisted. "Don't blame the shit on me."

Rashaud went to the kitchen to do something Azia had always done—clean up! As he turned, he caught a glimpse of the dresser in the bedroom. It wasn't pushed all the way up against the wall like he'd left it. Before leaving for L.A., he specifically made sure the dresser and the wall kissed tightly. Why wasn't it the way he'd left it? He felt his blood rush. *She couldn't have*, he thought storming toward the bedroom. He slid the dresser away from the wall like he was the Incredible Hulk. The wood was hanging slightly. He knocked it out of its place and fell to his knees. His blood boiled. "I'll kill her! I'll kill that bitch if she took my shit!" he yelled.

Keemah ran to the bedroom to find out what the ruckus was. She found Rashaud on his knees in the praying position. "What? What happened?"

Rashaud jumped to his feet, spun around like a professional break-dancer, and pushed her out of the way. He stopped at his phone, which was rested on the kitchen counter. He scrolled down to the number that was still listed as Wifey and pressed talk. Azia said nothing when she answered, but he could hear her breathing. "I know you on the phone! Where the fuck is my money?!"

"I don't know what you talking about."

"Don't play games wit' me, Azia! Where the fuck's my money?!"

"I don't owe you no fucking explanation! You owe me one! How was your trip?!"

"Girl, if you don't tell me where my shit is right now, I'm gonna find you and rip your fucking throat out! Ain't nobody but God gonna be able to save you!"

"How was she?" Azia asked, referring to Keemah. "She better than me?"

"You dirty bitch!" he yelled, startling Keemah who was a couple of feet away.

"I got your bitch alright! Tell her trick ass when I see her she better run!"

"You tell her your mutherfucking self! Tell me where my goddamn money is right now?!"

Azia chuckled. "It should be ringing your bell at any second."

Her answer confused him. "What?!"

She brought her tone up a notch and repeated, "I said, it should be ringing your doorbell any second now."

He turned to look at the door. There was silence. He didn't understand what Azia was talking about. Then the doorbell rang. He walked over to the door and looked through the peephole. "Who is it?" he ramped.

"It's the police!" Detective Joseph responded. "We have a warrant—Open up!"

Rashaud took five steps back away from the door. He snatched the phone away from his ear and stared down at it like it was poison. "You dirty mutherfucka."

BOOM! Azia heard something hit the door just before hearing what sounded like an army of soldiers bursting into the place. She and Detective Joseph had been working as a team. She'd advised him of Rashaud's return to the city, and he called her just before he went to pick Rashaud up. That's how she knew the doorbell was about to ring.

Mike was standing behind her taking everything in. Her latest scam along with the smirk on her face informed him of how sheisty she could be. She was enjoying every minute of it. From that day on, he promised himself to keep his guard up, even if she did sincerely have his back. With her, he figured, anything was possible. Out of fear of betrayal, like she had just done Rashaud, he would make sure to keep one eye open. He had love for her and he was willing to take a chance and build a life with her. But, there was too much at stake for him to get caught slipping.

Azia hung up the phone after hearing Detective Joseph and his team of officers drag Rashaud and Keemah out of the apartment. She pushed her silky hair away from her eyes, turned to face Mike and wrapped her arms around his neck. He lifted her from the floor and sat her on the countertop in the kitchen where they were standing. She stared him in the eyes without emotion for a split second then smiled, gave him a kiss on his lips and said,

"GAME OVER!"

ALLURE
ERICA KIMBERLY

Allure: to exert a very powerful and often dangerous attraction on somebody

Antonym: Dissuade

Kamryn Mackey is a beautiful and vibrant 19-year-old girl with a heart centered in the city of Los Angeles. She and her best friend, who is gay male, only source of income is through boosting from high-end department stores. But Kamryn soon has a change of heart about her illegal profession and decides to call it quits, so she thought. During a relapse and a lot of persuasion from her crime partner, Kamryn runs into a mysterious and overwhelmingly handsome brother who catches her eye.

When New York native Ricky Wade first visited Los Angeles at 17 years old, he only had ambition and a few hundred dollars. After a connecting with a heavy hitter in the LA drug world, Rick moves from The Big Apple to The City Of Angels and never looks back. Now at age 32, he has it all. With a focused hustle and a tiny circle of trustworthy partners, Rick has managed to evade law enforcement, while building a drug empire, which stretched across the Southwest region. These days, Ricky Wade is looking to expand his business. But first, he finds a love interest in Kamryn and decides to focus on pleasure.

Soon after meeting Rick, life Kamryn once knew changed right before her very eyes. She immediately recognizes the cons of his type of work, and proceeds with caution. From shopping sprees to exclusive vacations, Rick stops at nothing to win her over. Kamryn secretly adores his prolific lifestyle, one she could only dream of having. Within time, their whirlwind relationship takes off and Rick finds his place in Kamryn's heart. After being introduced to his finer way of living, Kamryn unexpectedly drops her guard and falls head over heels for Rick. After introducing her to his world, Kamryn soon becomes Rick's rider and ultimately the couple's relationship soar to new heights.

For Kamryn, things couldn't be better thanks to Rick. She begins to believe that together there is nowhere else to go but up... Until she finds herself in the terrifying center of a man's intrigue. With Rick's fate handed down to him, it'll be Kamryn fighting for her own freedom... And a price will have to be paid for it. The question is... Who will pay it? And how much?

(May 2011)

Memoirs Of An Accidental Hustler
J. M. BENJAMIN

Meet the Benson's…A young married couple, with four children living under the same roof in a nice neighborhood. On the outside looking in, one could easily mistake them for an average "Middle Class" family that had moved on up like "The Jefferson's"…But that's not the case. They are far from being in comparison to "The Huxtables" and life as they once knew it comes rapidly crashing down.

Eight year old Kamil, the next to the youngest of the Benson clan, shares how life was for he and his siblings, after being forced to adjust to the conditions of a "New Way" of living. He details what it was like after his mother made a bold and drastic decision to walk away from not only the "Finer Things" in life they had grown accustomed to, but his father as well.

A Brownstone in the Bed-Sty area of Brooklyn New York, traded in for a housing projects in a small town where his grandmother resided in Plainfield New Jersey, Kamil takes you on a journey of how he was exposed to another world and a different breed of people than he was used to in the city that became his home.

Bonded by the absences of their fathers, he and his brother befriend a group of boys from the neighborhood and form an un-breakable bond, vowing not to travel down the same road as their dads, making a pact to stay in school and out of the streets.

Kamil also takes you through his personal experience with the opposite sex, as a childhood crush develops into something much more.

As this story un-folds, walk with Kamil as he transitions from childhood to teen into young adulthood and struggles with the very things his mother walked away from and tried so hard to prevent he and his brother from embracing.

What starts out as a game and a means of survival…Ultimately ends up serious and addictive. This is the memoir of an Accidental Hustler…

Memoirs Of An Accidental Hustler
Glorious

Meet the Benson's...A young married couple, with four children living under the same roof in a nice neighborhood. On the outside looking in, one could easily mistake them for an average "Middle Class" family that had moved on up like "The Jefferson's"...But that's not the case. They are far from being in comparison to "The Huxtables" and life as they once knew it comes rapidly crashing down.

Eight year old Kamil, the next to the youngest of the Benson clan, shares how life was for he and his siblings, after being forced to adjust to the conditions of a "New Way" of living. He details what it was like after his mother made a bold and drastic decision to walk away from not only the "Finer Things" in life they had grown accustomed to, but his father as well.

A Brownstone in the Bed-Sty area of Brooklyn New York, traded in for a housing projects in a small town where his grandmother resided in Plainfield New Jersey, Kamil takes you on a journey of how he was exposed to another world and a different breed of people than he was used to in the city that became his home.

Bonded by the absences of their fathers, he and his brother befriend a group of boys from the neighborhood and form an un-breakable bond, vowing not to travel down the same road as their dads, making a pact to stay in school and out of the streets.

Kamil also takes you through his personal experience with the opposite sex, as a childhood crush develops into something much more.

As this story un-folds, walk with Kamil as he transitions from childhood to teen into young adulthood and struggles with the very things his mother walked away from and tried so hard to prevent he and his brother from embracing.

What starts out as a game and a means of survival...Ultimately ends up serious and addictive. This is the memoir of an Accidental Hustler...

Order Form

A New Quality Publishing

Down In The Dirty	$15.00
My Manz And 'Em	$15.00
Ride Or Die Chick	$15.00
Ride Or Die Chick 2	$15.00
Back Stabbers	$15.00
Have You Ever...?	$15.00
On The Run With Love	$15.00
From Incarceration 2 Incorporation	$15.00
	15.00
	5.00
	5.00
	5.00

Name

Reg (Appli

Address

City/State

Email

W

PURCHAS   .COM